THE
CHAOS
CURSE

KIRANMALA AND THE KINGDOM BEYOND

Book One

The Serpent's Secret

Book Two

Game of Stars

Book Three

The Chaos Curse

KIRANMALA AND THE KINGDOM BEYOND

THE
CHAOS
CURSE

BOOK THREE

SAYANTANI DASGUPTA

Illustrations by

VIVIENNE TO

SCHOLASTIC PRESS

New York

Library of Congress Cataloging-in-Publication Data Available

ISBN 978-1-338-35589-5

10 9 8 7 6 5 4 3 2 1   20 21 22 23 24

Printed in the U.S.A.   23
First edition, March 2020

Book design by Abby Dening

To my ancestors,

Parents, partner, children,

Writerly siblings

You who protect our stories

From extinction

You who weave words

And worlds

Into being

And to all the storytellers

At the margins

Memory keepers, path breakers,

Dream weavers all

You who honor our yesterdays,

Imagine our tomorrows,

You who sing, tell, speak

To keep alive

The beating heart

Of our storied lives

Table of Contents

1   I Saved Your Life (Now Say
    Thank You)   1

2   The Return of the King   16

3   Birds and Lizards and Pumpkins,
    Oh My!   30

4   A Tiger Named Bunty   43

5   A Tangle of Tales   52

6   My Mother, the Moon   64

7   Down the Rabbit and/or
    Wormhole   71

8   Rude Riddles   85

9   A Boy in a Tree   96

10 Colonized Beyond Repair   104

11 Bizarro Middle School   112

12 Rock-Star Scientist of the
    Multiverse   120

13 The Principal Is Not Your Pal   132

14 Middle School Monsters   143

15	Speak Friend and Enter	153
16	The Death of Difference	164
17	A Game of Wits	174
18	The Dirt-Biking Musketeers	184
19	Science, Sports, and Wedding Cards	196
20	Black Holes and Singularities	211
21	The Return of the (Other) King	233
22	Demonic Wedding Crashers	243
23	The Trojan Rakkhosh	258
24	The Power of Stories	278
25	Romeo and Demon-ette	291
26	The Gift Givers	302
27	The Choosing	319
28	A Council of Jazz Hands	337
29	The Big Musical Number at the End	352

THE
CHAOS
CURSE

CHAPTER 1

I Saved Your Life
(Now Say Thank You)

In most folk- and fairy tales, saving someone else's life is a super-big deal. Afterward, there's usually a royal wedding, a vault filled with gold, or some sort of kingdom-wide bouncy-castle party for the rescuer. So after I saved Prince Neelkamal from my evil biological father's underwater demon detention center, it's only natural I expected some sort of extra-special thanks, right?

It's not like I actually thought somebody would present me with my body weight in precious jewels or the keys to the Kingdom Beyond Seven Oceans and Thirteen Rivers or something. (And I didn't want a wedding. I'm only twelve, after all! I mean, gross!) But this wasn't the first time I'd saved my friend Neel's life, and this go-around, I'd traveled across the dimensions in a magic auto rikshaw, risked life and limb, solved impossible riddles, and fought monsters like a serious shero kick-butt daredevil. And what did I get for all my trouble? Bubkes. Seriously. Like, nada, zilch, zippo, nothing.

I'm not saying this to be greedy, but to explain why, when I saw the fancy royal party gathered on the shore of the Honey-Gold Ocean of Souls, I thought they were there for me. Particularly since Neel was Mr. Too-Cool-for-School-Princie-Pants and a bit slow with the thank-yous. I guess I figured he'd magically called ahead and set it all up for me. Which is a little embarrassing now that I actually think about it. Before we escaped my bio father Sesha's crumbling hotel-slash-casino-slash-underwater-detention-center, we were kind of busy. I mean, we were breaking Neel out of jail, fighting evil snakes, and stopping Sesha from killing me with two magical jewels turned neutron stars because he wanted to fulfill some prophecy, cheat death, and live forever. It's not like there was a ton of time for party planning. But I didn't think of all that until later.

"Oh my gosh! You shouldn't have!" I said in what I hoped was a surprised and yet humble voice as Neel, Naya, and I stumbled to our feet on the sandy beach. (The three of us having nonhuman parents was the only thing that made this swimming-up-from-the-bottom-of-the-ocean stuff remotely possible.)

"Oh dear!" squeaked Naya as she took in the scene. "We're not properly dressed for a formal state engagement!"

That was a serious understatement. Neel, Naya, and I were all soaked to the skin. But they, being respectively a half rakkhosh and full-blooded rakkhoshi demon, hardly looked tired. On the other hand, despite being part serpent princess and part moon child, I was not only bent over and gasping for air, but had my hair all plastered to my face, seaweed hanging off my clothes, and what felt like a live school of fish in my left sock.

I pushed my hair from my face in what I hoped was an elegant gesture, and took in all the people who'd obviously been waiting for us. There were a bunch of girls in pink saris—all a part of the resistance group known as the Pink-Sari Skateboarders, or PSS, which was headed up by my adopted cousin-sister, Mati. Half of the PSS girls were human, and the other half-rakkhoshi demons—an idea I was only just getting used to. But there were others too— two or three old bearded men who looked like the Raja's ministers, and a load of people who were a combination of nobles from the palace and royal servants. Everyone was dressed up and facing the water. Above their heads was a small gathering of bright blue butterflies, who seemed like they had been waiting for us too.

On one side of us, a singer with one hand on his ear and the other waving around in the air started warbling an up-and-down-the-scales classical tune while some musicians accompanied him—blowing on a shehnai, drumming on a tabla, and playing a stringed tanpura. Problem was, everybody seemed to be playing a slightly different song. To the side of the seated musicians were people carrying flower garlands and others with small lamps and incense holders.

"Aije, Princess Kiranmala!" yelled someone. It was one of the maids who had been assigned to take care of me when I was competing on the game show called *Who Wants to Be a Demon Slayer?* as the Kingdom Beyond's champion. I'd been so popular, with my face on billboards and posters and everything, that people had even taken to dressing like me. In fact, the maid waving wore an exact replica of my silver sparkly combat boots. I grinned drippily back at her, trying to give her a casual wave, like celebrities do when meeting fans.

"Thumbs-up on freeing Prince Neel! Shabash!" called another girl with a big green streak in her braid. She obviously hadn't gotten the memo that my hair had gone back to its normal black. I wondered if I should ask the Kingdom Beyond's teen fashion magazine, *Teen Taal*, to do an article on my hairstyle change.

"Too bad the game show turned out to be a big scam, and that the Serpent King wanted to kill you with the Chintamoni and Poroshmoni Stones so he could cheat death and live forever!" added a third girl, who was carrying, I noticed, a replica of my own bow and arrow. "We saw it all on the live broadcast! What a bummer!"

"Totally! Yeah! I mean, thanks!" I managed to call back. I guess you could classify my birth dad turning out to be an immortality-seeking homicidal maniac as a serious bummer. But I didn't let the smile fall from my face. This huge crowd was here to see me, or so I thought, and I didn't want to let them down. I wondered if I should offer to sign autographs or something.

That is, until I realized that no one was actually there to see me after all.

"Your Royal Majesty," squeaked someone in a ridiculously high voice.

I turned around graciously, trying to channel every royal princess I'd ever seen on television, only to realize that the man with the high voice wasn't talking to me at all. It was one of the bearded minister dudes, a tiny fellow with a purple turban on his head the shape of a state-fair-prizewinning turnip. And he was addressing Neel, holding out a little pillow to the prince. Wait a minute, none of this pomp was for me? I felt my face heat up like the sun.

Then I looked more carefully at the diamond-and-pearl-encrusted pillow in the minister's hand. On it, weirdly enough, was a cheap paper crown—the kind a little kid might get in a fast-food restaurant with a side of fries and a shake.

Neel, who had been a little more jumpy than usual since his imprisonment, kind of scooted back at the minister's offering. Like it was going to hurt him. "What's with the crown, Sir Gobbet? Am I just imagining it or is it made of construction paper?"

"We did the best we could, Majesty," said the little

minister named Gobbet. "We were in a rush, and a corona-tion isn't a coronation without a crown."

"Ooo! A coronation!" Naya clapped her hands like the goofy ray of sunshine she was.

"A coronation?" I mumbled, like the confused and dis-appointed girl from New Jersey I was.

"Coro-what-tion?" repeated Neel, looking both annoyed and confused.

"Your Majesty." With some difficulty, because of her one shorter leg, my cousin Mati now knelt before Prince Neelkamal in the sand. She then pressed her hands together in a respectful namaskar. Neel jumped back even more. He may have been the Raja's oldest son, while Mati was the daughter of the palace stable master, my uncle, but I'd never seen Mati get down on the ground before Neel like this. Apparently, Neel hadn't either.

"Don't do that! Stop!" Poor Neel tried to help Mati to her feet, his face horrified. "Get up, Mati! It's not like that with us! We're friends!"

"Sooo dreamy!" drawled the rakkhoshi Priya as she came over to stand next to me. Like the other Pink-Sari Skateboarder demonesses, Priya had been down in Sesha's undersea hotel when it started to crumble, but had been sucked out into the ocean a little before us. Yet somehow, her camo pants, tank, and the pink sari she wore around her neck like a cape were already dry.

By the look on her face, I thought at first Priya was talking about Mati being dreamy, but then she went on in a fake-girly voice, "Prince Neelkamal's just so darned dedicated to equality, you know? That kind of attitude is, like, really attractive in an absolute monarch filthy with inherited wealth and unearned power."

The fire demoness breathed stinky smoke out of her nose as she shot the sarcastic words out of her mouth. I was still feeling stupid for thinking that all these people were here for me, but at least I wasn't soaking anymore.

"Thanks for the blow-dry." I coughed, waving my hands in front of my face. "What's with the shave?"

"The revolution doesn't have time for hair products." Priya ran a long-taloned hand over her newly bald head. "But apparently, it does have time for fangirls. And boys."

Priya pointed, and I realized Neel was having an odd effect on the crowd. Not only was no one even looking in my direction, but a bunch of the younger servants, not to mention most of the palace ladies and more than a couple of the palace lords, were staring all googly-eyed at Neel. One courtly guy pretended to faint while a lady next to him fanned him with her hand.

"He's ba-ack!" I heard someone trill.

"And about time!" I heard someone else say all breathy and giggly.

Gross. I mean, seriously, people. Okay, maybe they were right about Neel being cute, but all this public swooning was really too much.

Meanwhile, even though his ears were a little darker than normal, Neel was acting all casual, like being an equal-opportunity heartthrob was his royal right. I rolled my eyes but stopped short of making throw-up noises, because I'm mature like that.

Priya's fangs glinted as she went on. "Don't be jealous. I know you have a thing for our half-demon prince."

"I do not!" A mixture of anger and some other emotion shot straight through my system. Where had Priya gotten that ridiculous idea? I really, really, *really* hoped Neel hadn't heard it too. "He and I are just friends! And not even that most of the time!"

Right then, the musicians stopped their songs, and as if on cue, the small crowd of people all knelt. The only one left standing in front of Neel was the turnip-headed minister, who waved his pillow, nearly dropping the paper crown.

"Your Majesty, you must be crowned!" the minister squeaked.

"Crowned! As what? Raja of french fries? Monarch of meat rolls?" Neel shot me a panicky look, then put his hands out straight, palms flat, as if to stop the paper crown from getting anywhere near his head. "Look, I just got out of a horrible detention center. Plus, I've lost my grandmother. I don't have time for sick jokes."

"What did you say? What happened to Ai-Ma?" Mati's voice was sharp. I felt my heart squeeze painfully at the mention of Neel's grandmother's name.

"It's true." Priya bowed her bald head, her sarcasm all

gone now before Mati's distress. "Ai-Ma sacrificed herself to save her daughter. And Princess Kiranmala."

The blue butterflies I'd seen before swarmed around me now, like they were mourning Neel's old demoness grandmother too. Ai-Ma had died saving Neel's mother, but she'd also saved me. If not for her jumping in, Sesha would have killed me, and I couldn't help but wonder if that made Neel blame me, even a little bit, for her death. I reached into my backpack and felt the warmth of the Poroshmoni and Chintamoni Stones, the two jewels that Sesha wanted to use to live forever. Instead, they had caused Ai-Ma's death. I pushed them deeper into my pack, promising myself I'd get rid of them the moment I found a safe place.

"I'm so sorry." Mati stood up with Neel's help now, grasping his hand. "I didn't know."

"It happened so fast . . ." Neel's voice cracked, and I felt my own eyes almost spill their tears. Naya was openly blubbering, and next to me, even Priya sniffed, loud and long.

I covered the serpent scar on my right upper arm with my other hand. I was so ashamed that my biological father was responsible for Ai-Ma's death. If I could cut the scar off my arm, I would.

"This terrible news is all the more reason to crown

Prince Neelkamal right away!" blustered Sir Gobbet. "Sesha grows in power every day! We must gather the forces of resistance, no matter how, er"—here the little man gave the PSS demonesses, then me, sideways glances—"unusual our alliances." He waved the pillow again in Neel's direction.

"No way." Neel backed up, swiping angrily at his eyes. "I'm not even the crown prince. My father made sure of that. Where is he anyway?"

I saw worried looks being exchanged among all the lords, ladies, servants, and musicians.

When no one answered, Neel asked again. "Why exactly are you trying to make me the Raja? Where is my father?" I reached out to touch his shoulder. Neel was looking way less confident than he ever had. Being in that detention center had really affected him.

"The Raja is all right, as far as we know," Mati said in a rush. "But he's gone into hiding. Had to flee the dimension with a few of his ministers in fear for his own life."

I started. I too had spent my life in a different dimension because I had been forced to go into hiding from the Kingdom Beyond.

"Gone into hiding? In fear for his life? Why?" Neel's voice got a little louder with every question. "How could you let this happen, Sir Gobbet?"

"It was shocking. A violent and unexpected takeover of the throne by the Kingdom of Serpents," began the tiny minister.

"A coup d'état!" It was the talking bird Tuntuni. He swam in a circle above our heads, then landed on Neel's shoulder, amending, "Or a coup d'snake, if you will."

"Tuni!" Neel gave our birdie friend a high five.

"Say, Princie! What did the ocean say to the shore?" squawked the bird. Next to complaining, telling bad jokes was one of his favorite hobbies.

"This is really not the time," I began, but Naya interrupted me. "What did the ocean say to the shore? Nothing! It waved!"

"Yes!" The bird collapsed in laughter while the rest of us rolled our eyes. "Oh, I've got another good one! Why did the fish blush?"

"Dude, my dad's gone into hiding in another dimension. I'd like to hear how that happened," said Neel.

"Why did the fish blush?" Naya crinkled her nose. "Because it was gill-ty?"

"No!" shrieked Tuntuni. "Because the sea weed! Get it? The sea wee-ed?"

I had to laugh at that one. Tuni and Naya were practically in stitches, and I even caught Neel and Mati cracking little smiles.

"Sire, let me tell you about the coup d'snake," sputtered little Sir Gobbet. "And why it really wasn't, most absolutely, my fault."

This brought all our attentions back to the matter at hand. "How could this happen? Sesha was just with us in the undersea hotel," Neel said.

"Not true." Naya showed us the time on her miraculously-still-working cell phone. "It took us a while to swim to the surface."

"And he did disappear into that puff of green smoke," I added. "He could have magically teleported to the palace!"

"It all happened so fast, Your Majesty!" Sir Gobbet was in tears now, and they dripped fatly from his tiny eyes all the way down into his long white beard. "One minute, the Raja was on his throne, and the next, he'd lost control of the kingdom!"

"That imposter, that fiend who took my job was in on it!" shrieked Tuni, flapping his yellow wings in agitation. "That bane of my existence, that worm-eater of a minister, Gupshup! He handed the kingdom right over to Sesha! That shutki-fish-eating stinker!"

I was about to tell Tuntuni to chill, but I didn't. Because just then, there came from the ocean behind us a tremendous splashing. Tuntuni squawked and spit, and we all whirled around. When I saw what was rising out of the water, I felt anything but calm. I fumbled with my bow and arrow, fear shooting through my body.

"Rakkhosh!" I shouted. "It's an attack!"

CHAPTER 2

The Return of the King

The crowd of demons rose out of the Honey-Gold Ocean of Souls. There were air rakkhosh with their wings unfurled, fire demons shooting flames out of their noses, water demons with webbed fingers and toes, and land demons who looked every-which-way weird, with horns sticking out of their foreheads and teeth for hair. Plus, all the rakkhosh looked bruised and battered, with banged-up noses and broken wing joints, like they'd just come from a fight. It was a surprise attack!

"Rakkhosh!" I shouted again. I looked over my shoulder and realized that while the ministers and other human courtiers from the palace looked nervous, and Tuntuni was flitting around in panic, no one had pulled out a weapon or anything. Naya looked seriously hurt, and the Pink-Sari

Skateboarder girls—demonic and human—all seemed to be laughing at me.

"No kidding they're rakkhosh!" Priya shot little flames out of her mouth with the words. "So are half of us. Or have you forgotten, Princess? And if I'm not wrong, you yourself freed these sad saps from the detention center when you destroyed dear old daddy's underwater hotel."

"I wasn't the only rakkhosh in that detention center," Neel reminded me. "There were a lot of others kept captive too."

"But they're not like you, Princie!" Tuni squawked. "You're one of the good ones!"

"Stop being such an anti-demon bigot!" Mati scolded. Her words were aimed at the little yellow bird, but I could tell she meant them for me and the other frightened humans too. "I would think you would know by now that no one type of creature has the market on monstrosity. Rakkhosh can be good or bad, based on their choices—just like human beings!"

I felt a twinge of shame at my cousin's words, but getting over my fear of rakkhosh was easier said than done. Based on my previous experiences with some of them, as well as all the monstrous stories I'd heard since I was a kid, it was hard to stop thinking of all rakkhosh as bad. But even as I relaxed my guard, the rakkhosh who had come up out of the waves made a tight circle around me. I gave a little yell and whirled, not sure where to aim my bow and arrow. "Some help, please!" I shouted.

But what the rakkhosh did next shocked me into lowering my weapon. Some knelt, some gave me a respectful namaskar, some salaamed, and some even touched my feet with their warty hands.

"From demonic detention you did us free," rhymed one green-skinned and boil-covered fellow. "We are yours, if ever you need."

"We won't discriminate against your blood," said another creature with crooked and bitten-up bat wings. "You may be half snake, but we know you're good."

That statement stopped me cold. *They* wouldn't discriminate against *me*? My sweet rakkhoshi friend Naya gave me a little grin, but Priya gave a knowing laugh, like she could tell what I was thinking.

"My friends, all, please rise up. The resistance is happy to have your support," said Mati. "We have much work to do to get the kingdom back from Sesha's rule."

"Our arms and wings and flames are yours," said a water rakkhoshi with shells for hair. "Even those of us who walk on all fours!"

The courtiers and palace servants moved away a little as the rakkhosh joined them. Naya linked her arm through mine and said in a low whisper. "Isn't it wonderful, Your Princess-ship, how our people are working together?"

I looked into her trusting face and felt my doubts about the rakkhosh easing away, at least a little. "Yeah, wonderful!"

"Everything is upside down! Monsters are good and humans are monstrous!" sobbed Sir Gobbet.

"No one said change was easy. And changing our ideas is sometimes the hardest thing of all." Mati patted his turban as the little man kept blubbering. I noticed her and Priya exchange amused smiles.

"The people of the kingdom need a new Raja to rally behind!" Gobbet snorted, wiping his nose and eyes with a lacy handkerchief. "With your brother Lalkamal vanished, the kingdom needs you, Your Majesty, Prince Neelkamal! Your people need you!"

"Not necessarily. I mean, there's something to be said for a parliamentary system, you know," said Neel, chewing on a fingernail. "Or participatory democracy! I mean, monarchies are so last century, amirite?"

"Neel!" Mati and I shouted at the same time, as Naya sputtered, "Your Royalness!"

Priya, on the other hand, gave an approving snort.

Gobbet rounded on him with the fancy pillow and paper crown. "Come on, Your Majesty, just put it on. It won't hurt a bit."

"Stop calling me that! *Majesty!* That's not me! I don't want to be king!" Neel looked seriously freaked out. I knew his father had once convinced Neel he wasn't good enough to rule, just because he was half rakkhosh. In fact, the Raja had stripped Neelkamal of the title of crown prince, even though he was the eldest, and given it to his younger brother Lalkamal. But I wondered if Neel was feeling nervous because of that, or because his confidence had been shattered from all those weeks in demon detention?

"You're the only one who can do it. It's not like your brothers Buddhu or Bhootoom are up for the job." Mati was right on this score. Neel and Lal's monkey and owl brothers were seriously on the silly side. "It doesn't matter if you're not crown prince, because we don't even know where Lal is." Mati's voice tensed a little as she said these last words, so I jumped in quickly to fill her in on her childhood best friend being captured by a ghost, something Neel, Naya, and I had only just learned.

I opened my still-sodden backpack and held up my Lola Morgana thermos. "We've got him in here."

"You shoved Prince Lalkamal into that cheap merch from the *Star Travels* TV show?" squawked Tuntuni.

"Not Lal!" I said. "The ghost who took over Lal's identity after jamming the real Lal in a tree trunk!" I handed the thermos off to Mati, who looked at it wonderingly.

"Her Royalosity Princess Kiranmala tricked that nasty bhoot into entering the Lola Morgana thermos all on his own!" said Naya in her usual enthusiastic way.

My new rakkhosh fans sent up a little cheer.

"No wonder he was acting so weird all those weeks—so power-hungry, so unlike his normal self. I can't believe I never realized that wasn't the real Lal." Mati's eyes were a little glassy as she turned the thermos around and around in her hands. "Where is he? The real Lal, I mean."

Instead of answering directly, I repeated the rhyme the captured bhoot had told us. "A peanut where my garden grows. A pike all the way from my toes to my nose!"

Everyone was quiet for a second, until Tuni announced, in a game show contestant kind of way, "OOO! I know! I know the answer! It's Ne-e-ew Joi-sey!" The bird did a loop-da-loop swirling dive in the air. "It's shaped like a peanut, called the Garden State, and covered north to south by the New Jersey Turnpike! The real Prince Lalkamal's in New Jersey!"

"Exactly! So, we'll go across the dimensions, then go home to my parents in Parsippany! It'll be squishy, and maybe we'll have to borrow some sleeping bags from Zuzu's family, but it'll be so cool to have you all there!" My bestie, Zuzu, had a lot of brothers and sisters, and so always had extras of everything. I thought of my own babyish pink Princess Pretty Pants™ sleeping bag and hoped Neel wouldn't laugh at it.

"What?" I was just noticing everybody's frowning faces. "Okay, so we can start out for Parsippany right after Neel gets crowned or whatever."

I expected Mati to be even more enthusiastic about freeing Lal than I was, so I was kind of surprised when she hesitated. She handed the Lola Morgana thermos off to Priya, before replying, "No, Kiran, you're going to have to go back to New Jersey on your own."

"Are you kidding me?" My eyes met Neel's. He looked as confused as I felt.

"Seriously, why can't we all go get Lal?" Neel asked. "And, like, get some baklava at Kiran's friend's diner while we're at it?"

The mention of Zuzu's family's baklava made my stomach growl. Man, all that swimming from the bottom of the ocean had given me an appetite. I grinned at Neel. I wouldn't mind a nice high-carb visit to the Mount Olympus Diner either.

"Bakla-vah? Bakla-na! Shame, my prince! We can't let the Kingdom Beyond Seven Oceans and Thirteen Rivers become a part of the Kingdom of Serpents!" sputtered Sir Gobbet. "That is why we are here. Not just to crown you and make you the Raja, sire, but then to urge the people of the kingdom to rise up behind you! Your people need a symbol to rally around, and that symbol is you!"

"Why can't I be a symbol after I rescue my brother? Maybe eat something? Have a shower?" Neel asked. "And, like, a nap?"

"No, we can't get distracted." Mati tucked the end of her pink sari firmly into her waist. "We can't let our personal feelings come before the needs of the kingdom. Including hunger!" Although she did make a little motion, and another one of the PSS girls brought Neel, Naya, and me small silver tiffin boxes.

"Can't let personal feelings get in the way?" I sputtered, more than a little surprised at my cousin's attitude. I dug into some of the delicious biriyani in the tiffin box, chewed, and swallowed before adding, "But Lal's your best friend! Don't you want to rescue him? Who knows how long the ghost has had him in that tree trunk!"

Priya shot her a look, and Mati seemed pained. Then she shook her head. "He's my best friend, yes, but he is going to have no home to return to if we don't protect it. We've got to go on a campaign—show Neel around the kingdom, get support from the common people to overthrow the Serpent King. We've also gotten several disturbing reports that Sesha may be planning some kind of an alliance with . . . well . . ." Mati's voice trailed off.

"Who?" Neel insisted.

When Mati said nothing, Priya drawled, "Your mommy dearest, my prince!"

"My mother?" Neel repeated in a stunned voice. "You think Kiran's birth dad is planning an alliance with my mom? That's ridiculous!"

"That's the report that's reached us," confirmed Mati. "The people of the Kingdom Beyond are terrified, ready to hand over control to Sesha just at the thought."

"But that's garbage!" I snorted. "Sesha and Pinki allies? They *hate* each other! Last we saw them, Sesha was trying to kill Neel's mom and use her powers to change these jewels into neutron stars!" I held up the Thought and Touch Stones from my backpack for Mati to see before carefully putting them away again. "And then, after Ai-Ma . . . um . . . sacrificed herself saving us, Neel's mom went chasing after Sesha to murder him and get revenge! No way they would ever become allies! They're worst enemies!"

"And Sesha's entire stance has always been very anti-rakkhosh. I can't believe the alliance is real either," Mati admitted. "But having Neel crowned is a sure way to squash the rumors. The people will be confident the Demon Queen's not going to turn against the kingdom if her son is Raja."

"It is what she always wanted for you, anyway," I murmured to Neel.

"No way, though, she's teaming up with Sesha," he said. "This is just false propaganda, like that stuff about you and Lal when you were competing in *Who Wants to Be a Demon Slayer?*"

I squirmed a little at his words. So Neel knew about those stories linking me up with his brother? They'd obviously been totally fake news, but it was still embarrassing to think Neel had heard the gossip.

"So what do you say, sire?" sputtered Sir Gobbet, waving his pillow. "Ready to become Raja?"

"But . . ." Neel threw me another desperate look.

I could see how unsure he was. With a heavy heart, I realized that things weren't going to go as I'd imagined, yet again. There wasn't going to be a sleeping-bag slumber party at my parents' house, or late-night giggly stories or all-kingdom pillow fights. Neel and I weren't going to go on this adventure together, and I wasn't going to get to show him around my hometown of Parsippany or introduce him to my bestie, Zuzu. But I shoved my disappointment aside. There were bigger things at stake now.

"Mati's right, Neel," I said finally. "We can't let Sesha take over the Kingdom Beyond. I don't know what his plan is, but it can't be good. And if it gives the people confidence to see you as Raja, you've got to accept the crown."

"I don't know . . ." Neel muttered. Then he took a look around the beach. At all the people who were looking to him to solve this crisis. He whispered in a voice so low only I could hear it, "What if I can't do it?"

I thought for a minute about saying something nice and supportive, like how of course he could or how I believed in him. But I knew Neel well enough not to go down that route. Instead, I looked into his dark eyes and drawled, "Don't act like such a 2-D! What are you, scared or something?"

Neel held my gaze for a second longer than he had to, his lips twitching a little like he was trying not to smile. Then he made a snorting noise. He obviously knew I was teasing him, calling him by the insulting name he'd once given me—because I was from a dimension where everyone expected everything to be uncomplicated and easy, for the mysteries of the universe to have simple answers. He sighed, shutting his eyes tightly, like he was being forced to drink some bad-tasting medicine. "All right, I'll do it," he finally gritted out.

Everyone seemed to hold their breath as Sir Gobbet placed the paper crown on Neel's head. As soon as he did, the crowd went wild.

But as everyone else was cheering and clapping, the strangest thing happened. One of those blue butterflies flew over to Neel and landed right on his shoulder. For a split second, he looked seriously different. Not just different; like someone else entirely. Neel's skin got paler, his hair grew lighter, and his face got way older. He gave me a strange look, and I could have sworn he said something like, "Are you the elf maiden? Or a hobbit?"

"Who you calling a hobbit?" I snapped. But with those words, Neel shook his head and seemed to come back to himself again. The butterfly lifted off his shoulder and flew airily back into the sky.

What had just happened? It was like, for that half a second, the two of us had fallen into the wrong story. He was the wrong king, and this was not our world, but a world of elves and wizards, hobbits and kings. No one else seemed to have noticed, because they were so busy cheering for their new Raja. The girls with the flower garlands draped a few of them over Neel's neck, and then some garlands over my neck, Mati's, Naya's, and even Gobbet's too. The tickly smell made me sneeze, so I handed mine to Priya. Tuntuni flew around, dropping fragrant petals over everyone's heads, and the musicians started their different, clashing songs again. A few people took up the tongue-waggling ulu-ulu call to mark the special occasion. Everyone looked really happy, except Neel. I took a step to go over to him, wanting to ask him if he'd experienced the same slipping into another story that I had, but Naya grabbed my arm.

"Even if His Rajaness Neel cannot go, I will go with Her Princess-ship back to New Jersey to rescue Prince Lalkamal!" the girl announced.

"No, Naya." Mati shook her head. "We need all the rakkhosh who are on our side here right now. Especially you air clans. Tuntuni can go with Kiran."

"But I'm needed here!" The yellow bird squawked, spitting a few remaining flower petals out of his beak. "To help rally the country with my eloquence! To lighten the mood with my humor! To kick that Minister Gupshup's tuchus and get him out of the palace!"

"Dear birdie, we all must go where we're needed," Naya said.

The three of them were so busy arguing, and so firmly in this world, I was sure I must have imagined Neel's temporary transformation into that other king from that other story. I must be tired, or underoxygenated, or suffering some kind of post-snake-fighting trauma. That was it. That must be it.

"Tuni, you'll go with Kiran," Mati said again. "She'll need help. And we can't afford anyone el . . . ah, I mean, you're the right bird for the job."

"You'll be all right, Kiran?" I wasn't sure, but it seemed like Neel's eyes were scanning my face, like he was looking for something. But maybe I was imagining that too.

"I'll be fine. Totally!" I pasted on a fake smile, acting all cheery even though I felt anything but. "We've all got to do our part for the resistance!"

CHAPTER 3

Birds and Lizards and Pumpkins, Oh My!

Tuni and I had been at it for hours. Driving around in our auto rikshaw, calling ourselves hoarse. It was early evening, and the moon would soon make her appearance in the sky. The plan, which had been to get my moon mother's attention before she rose for the night, wasn't going exactly perfectly.

The others had left us long ago. As soon as Neel was crowned, everyone was in a hurry to get off the beach and on their way. The crowd had rushed around, packing up instruments, mounting skateboards, and the few chariots and horses they had with them.

"So how am I getting to New Jersey to rescue Lal? Will Bangoma and Bangomee help?" I'd asked. The giant, human-faced birds had once created a wormhole from New

Jersey to the Kingdom Beyond just by flying faster and faster in circles. If they could do that for me again, then Tuni and I would be back in Parsippany in no time.

The only problem was, the giant birds made the wormhole last time not out of the goodness of their hearts, but because they were paid by Neel's mom, the Rakkhoshi Queen. And the PSS didn't have near enough money to hire them for as big a job as intergalactic wormhole creation.

"I don't blame Bangoma and Bangomee. They have a lot of expenses, what with all those giant baby birds to feed," Mati said.

I was disappointed. I'd liked the strange-looking magical birds. But more importantly, how was I going to travel to New Jersey without them?

"Please don't tell me that I have to cross back through the transit corridor, then!" The transit corridor wasn't an easy place for those without official papers, as I'd discovered on my first visit to the Kingdom Beyond. I'd had to face a riddling monster of a transit officer, who had almost eaten me rather than let me pass through.

"No, we can't go through the transit corridor because Sesha's obviously got that under watch, that snaky-pooper!" chirped Tuntuni from the handlebars of the auto rikshaw. The half-car–half-taxi–half-motorcycle–half-spaceship thing

I'd driven here from New Jersey had some sort of magical spell on it that allowed it to travel safely in outer space, but it couldn't make a wormhole from scratch.

"We don't want to risk the Serpent King getting his hands on you again," added Sir Gobbet.

"So what are we supposed to do?" I asked.

"Find your moon mother," Neel suggested, looking a bit silly in his paper crown. He'd pushed it to the side to make it look cooler, but there's not that much swagger anyone can pull off in a burger-joint-type crown. "She's way powerful—she defeated Sesha once. Your birth mom connected us and let us talk when I was in the detention center. She should be able to help get you to New Jersey now."

I bit my lip. I wasn't that sure. My biological mother had helped us, it was true. But being a celestial body, she wasn't like other mothers. Certainly nothing like my own warm Ma, who had adopted and then raised me on food and hugs and loving scoldings. My moon mother was the opposite: kind of aloof, cold, remote. As evil and involved as Sesha was in my life, the moon always seemed to hover above me, kind enough, but still always out of reach.

"What if I can't find her?" I asked. "Or if she can't help?"

"Don't worry. Just let us know, Your Princess-ship,

and we'll come up with a new plan," said Naya. "Send a gecko-gram."

"A what?"

"It's something I've been working on!" explained Naya, pulling out a notebook with a lot of hand-drawn diagrams in it. "Lizard-based communication! You see, their nervous systems are very primitive. But with this immunologic boost I've developed to their limbic system, and something I'm calling lizard-to-lizard twinning, they can recognize a limited number of sounds and relay them to each other."

I stared at Naya's notes, my mouth open. I couldn't understand anything I was looking at, besides not really being able to follow what she was talking about. "You've invented lizard-powered cell phones?"

"Well, not exactly, but interestingly enough, some of the principles are similar," Naya said. "I've also been developing an intergalactic communication device I'm calling chaa-chat. It uses the tannins in tea as a medium, and then translates sound waves through the saucer, but it's not exactly functional quite yet. Still burning people's mouths . . ."

I couldn't help but be amazed. "I didn't realize you were so into inventing stuff!"

I'd only just learned my fellow Parsippany sixth grader

was from the Kingdom Beyond Seven Oceans and Thirteen Rivers, and also a rakkhoshi. But somehow, the idea that she was so into science seemed just as surprising. I'd always thought of Naya as good-hearted but kind of ding-batty. I mean, she was addicted to her cell phone, was always posting pictures on social media, and had even been a part of the flying fangirls group that crushed on Neel and called themselves the Neelkamalas.

"Why did you think I was so into cell phones?" Naya fixed one of the many ponytails on her head, adding, "Just because someone likes glitter lip gloss and selfie filters doesn't mean they're not scientifically minded."

"Now that you've cleared all that up," Mati interrupted, handing me a tiny lizard with a slithery tongue, "meet Tiktiki One."

I tried not to shudder as the clammy animal scampered onto my hand, fixing its swively eyes on me. "Tiktiki? Isn't that just the Bengali word for 'gecko'? Doesn't it have an actual name?"

Mati and Naya both gave me weird looks. Finally, Naya lowered her voice, like she didn't want to hurt the animal's feelings. "Your Highnosity, this is a lizard. Lizards don't actually have *names*."

I rolled my eyes, trying really hard not to freak out at

the slimy feeling of Tiktiki One now walking up my arm. "All right, so how does this work?"

"Easy," Naya said. "Just whisper to Tiktiki One any message you want to send, and then pull off its tail. It'll scamper off probably for some peace while it transmits, but eventually, we'll get the message through one of the geckos we'll have with us."

"Pull off its tail!" I exclaimed, staring at the slimy thing with its greenish skin, buggy eyes, and rubbery tail. "You've got to be kidding!"

"Every cellular communication device needs a send button!" Naya explained, as if pulling off a gecko's tail was no big deal. "And these are special tiktikis! Their tails grow right back! Oh, and don't worry if it takes a while for it to return; these geckos sometimes like to go on walkabout."

The lizard on my arm gave me a doubtful look, then it flicked out its tongue and slithered from my arm down to the back of the auto rikshaw driver's bench. Great. Not only did my parents refuse to get me a real cell phone, now I'd have to use a slithery lizard with a fast-regrowing tail. This was way worse than even a flip phone.

"Good luck, Kiran." Ignoring everyone around us, Neel grabbed my hand. "Come back with my brother as soon as you can. Don't leave me stuck as the Raja for too long."

"I'll try," I promised, super self-conscious of my hot and kinda sweaty hand in his. I was also really embarrassed about all the eyes on us. But still, it felt good to have this small moment of connection.

Naya and Mati each gave me a hug, and then Naya, snifflingly, insisted we all take a selfie together. Neel, Mati, Naya, Tuni, and I posed, and Naya chose a silly special effect that made us all look like we were unicorns with rainbows coming out of our noses and eyeballs.

"That is not cute!" I'd said, even though I was laughing.

"Yeah it is," Neel had replied, his eyes locking with mine. I felt something melt in my chest even as somewhere

to the side of me, Priya started making way-too-obvious coughing noises. Mati and Naya exchanged a silly look and I tried to ignore all of them. My cheeks felt hot, but I couldn't help grinning a little too.

Neel gave me one last searching glance. "Hey, thanks for saving my life back there in the detention center. I owe you one."

Finally! The words I'd been wanting to hear for so long. My stomach was doing flip-flops of joy. Neel hadn't forgotten what I'd done for him after all. And somehow, that recognition felt so much more powerful a reward than any party or magical weapon or castle full of jewels.

I felt a smile spreading slowly over my face. "You know you do!"

"Good luck, Moon Girl," Neel said in a voice meant only for me.

I gave Neel an awkward grin. "Thanks, Demon Prince. Have fun storming the palace!"

And then the PSS helped Neel climb on the back of an elephant with a regal howdah on his back. Neel had sat on the fancy throne, waving and giving me thumbs-up signs. Naya had blown kisses upon kisses. Finally, the elephant gave a long trumpet, and they were all gone, leaving Tuni and me to find my moon mother alone.

In the beginning of our search, I'd started out hopeful. "Um, Mother?" I'd called, keeping an eye on the sky. "It's Kiranmala. Can you hear me?"

Tuni, for his part, flapped around and sang a song I'd heard Ma sing. "O, aaa-maar chander alo!" he called. "Oh, my moonlight!"

Soon, when it was obvious my moon mother wasn't answering anytime soon, I started to get pretty annoyed. Why was my birth mother ignoring me when I needed her? Why couldn't she be around, trying to feed me and asking me nosy questions, like a normal mom?

I drove the auto rikshaw super slowly, trying not to freak out at the tiktiki sleeping right by my shoulder. We were far from the beach, and I was just driving through a patch of forest outside a village, when I saw something strange out of the corner of my eye. I thought for a minute it was a big orange moon heading right for us. Only, it wasn't actually a moon. Oh no! I swerved, but it was a little too late. The giant rolling gourd kept bouncing along the forest path, picking up speed as it did, on a direct collision course with the auto rikshaw!

I tried to reverse but instead bounced over a gnarled root in the road. "Ahhh!" I yelled, sure we were done for. My head slammed into the top of the auto as we went full-on airborne.

"We're gonna be baked into a Halloween pie!" Tuntuni shrieked.

"Watch out!" I yelled, trying to control us as we headed directly for Cinderella's pumpkin.

"Every bird for himself!" Tuni flew up out of the rikshaw at the last minute.

Tiktiki One, for its part, woke up, made a weird little clickety-clack noise, and then jumped with its clammy feet onto my head! Ewww!

The auto rikshaw hit the giant pumpkin at an angle, and as soon as we made contact, the gourd exploded, shell cracking in a zillion pieces and orange goo flying out. The windshield was covered in orange slime, and I could see nothing. I slammed on the brakes, and the machine stalled with a dramatic shudder. "Suffering succotash!" I yelled for who knows what reason, before grabbing Tiktiki One from my head and yanking the animal off.

Once I turned on the windshield wipers to clear a little of the windshield, I was shocked to realize that other than the orange stringy insides of the vegetable, something else had flown out of the gourd too. Or rather, someone. On the road in front of me, just inches from the auto rikshaw's wheels, had fallen an ancient woman as wrinkled as an old leather shoe.

"Oh, no, no, no! The tiger will for sure get me now!" wheezed the old lady, clutching the end of her white sari around her head.

I rushed out to help the woman. "Are you all right, Grandmother?" I helped her get unsteadily to her feet. She was tiny, and frail, with skin like paper and bony hands that I was afraid to squeeze too hard for fear of hurting them. I peered at her, wondering if she was my moon mother in disguise or something, but the next thing she said made me think that couldn't be true.

"One month ago, I was heading to my daughter's house, all skin and bones, when a vicious tiger threatened to eat me," the woman said. Her glasses were covered with pumpkin goo, and she lisped a little, because she didn't have all her teeth. "I convinced him to wait until I had eaten well and gotten all fattened up, but he promised to be waiting for me on the trail home."

"So to hide you from him, your daughter put you in a hollowed-out gourd and sent you tumbling!" I said, the pieces clicking in my brain. "I know this story!"

My baba had told me it a million times, like he did all

his stories from the Kingdom Beyond. This wasn't my moon mother at all, then, but an old woman from a well-loved folktale!

Just as I thought this, though, something even stranger happened. Something stranger than finding an old woman rolling home in a pumpkin gourd. Like what had happened with Neel before, a bright blue butterfly landed on the granny—this time on her nose. And in the next second, the grandmother's image flickered like she was on a faulty television screen. When my vision corrected, no longer was she an old gray-haired woman afraid of a tiger, but the tiger itself!

The animal gave a rumbling roar, showing a glimpse of its shining teeth. I jumped about a foot in the air in my scramble to get away from it.

"Oh, my rotten tail feathers! If that's the tiger, then we're the old woman about to get eaten!" Tuntuni shrieked, flying quickly back into the auto. "Get in, Princess! Start the engine now!"

I stumbled into the driver's seat, pressing down on the start with a panicky finger. Even though the engine turned over and over with a screeching noise, it didn't catch.

The tiger was huge, sleekly muscled, with stringy pumpkin innards mixing into its orange-and-black-striped fur, and bits of rind trapped in its whiskers and wide jaw. It studied us with its dark, hungry eyes. Then it gave an ear-splitting roar.

"We're gonna die!" wailed Tuntuni, throwing his yellow wings around my neck. This time, I didn't actually think he was wrong. "I'm too pretty to croak in a tiger's digestive tract!"

CHAPTER 4

A Tiger Named Bunty

Hurry up!" yelled Tuni, jumping with all his weight on the start button. "Unless you want your baba to tell the story about a princess and a bird who got eaten by a pumpkin-spiced tiger!"

When Tiktiki One click-clacked its tongue, Tuni added, "Okay, fine, a princess, bird, and lizard eaten by a pumpkin-spiced tiger!"

"Stop that! You're not helping!" My hands were shaking as I tried to get the little bird to stop pressing on the starter. "I think you flooded the engine!"

Tuntuni kept shouting useless instructions, though, and the lizard kept clickety-clacking. That is, until the tiger roared again.

"Stop your superfluous shrieking!" shouted the tiger, white teeth flashing in the sun.

At that, Tuntuni and I shrieked at the top of our lungs, and even Tiktiki One clattered so loud it was clear the little lizard was terrified. Both animals hid behind my back as I now began pushing on the start button with frantic fingers.

"You're undoubtedly flooding your fuel injector!" roared the tiger.

"Leave us alone!" I yelled in a total panic. "I swear we won't taste very good!"

"I'm such a little bird, just feathers and bones, really!" shouted Tuni from behind me. "Hardly any meat! But the lizard here, he's delicious on a skewer I bet! With a little lime and salt! And the princess—just look at all that juicy muscle! She'd be great breaded and fried probably! Or maybe with a little jhinge posto!"

I turned around in the seat to stare at the bird, and saw that Tiktiki One's buggy eyes were swiveled around in outrage too. "You traitor!" I shrieked, moving both animals back onto the auto rikshaw handlebars. "Stop suggesting recipes to eat us with!"

"Every bird for himself!" Tuni said sheepishly.

The tiger, meanwhile, did something totally unexpected.

As if we were the funniest thing it had ever seen, the huge animal flopped down on the ground, grabbed its belly, and began to laugh.

"Don't laugh at us!" I yelled, which only made the tiger laugh harder.

"It's just an act, Princess!" shouted Tuntuni above the tiger's guffaws. "What did you do with the old granny, you deranged feline?"

"I did nothing with her!" The tiger's nostrils flared and muscles rippled as it kept laughing. "Such an accusation is highly unjust!"

Tuni gave me a little peck with his beak, and I knew he wanted me to back him up. "Then where is she?" I managed to ask, my voice quavering only a little. "The old woman from the story? In the original folktale, you're not supposed to be in the pumpkin—she is!"

"I am not precisely sure," the tiger admitted, wiping tears of laugher from its giant eyes.

"Then tell us how you ended up in that pumpkin, you dirty rat . . . er, cat?" said Tuni like he was an old-timey private investigator.

"I am ashamed to say that I did indeed threaten the old woman a little," said the tiger. "But it was primarily to keep my jungle credibility up—it's remarkably hard with my level of education and eloquence to maintain my status as a fierce carnivorous predator. 'Bunty has lost their edge.' I've heard several animals say so only recently at the local watering hole."

"Bunty?" I interrupted, wrinkling my nose. "Your name is Bunty?"

"The one and only." The tiger gave a bow of its giant orange head. "If speaking English, you may use *they* or *them* pronouns when you refer to me."

"Okay," I said, thinking of my friend Vic back home who didn't use *he* or *she* pronouns either. Conveniently, in Bengali, there was no *he* or *she*, and everyone used the same pronoun, *o*.

"In the words of that great philosopher J. Tumblerpond," Bunty continued, "'I don't wanna be a fool for you. Genders split in two. It may sound performative, but it ain't no lie. Binaries, baby! Bye! Bye! Bye!'" As they said this, Bunty had padded over to the auto rikshaw and started helping me clean the windshield, licking it free of all the pumpkiny innards.

"Thanks." I was feeling less and less nervous of the tiger by the second, even though I'd never heard of this J. Tumblerpond person.

"My pleasure," purred the big cat, before crunching on a few stray pumpkin seeds.

"Wait a minute, Princess, don't get so friendly so quick," Tuni squawked. "Don't you want to find out what this tiger did with the old buri?" The bird stuck out a wing in accusation. "Fess up, Professor Bunty, did you chomp her down like a bowl of kitty kibble?"

"Chomp the old woman? How erroneous!" Bunty protested. "You are quite convinced I am carnivorous, aren't you? So prepared to prejudge! So ready to reduce me to a stereotype! From where does this tremendous terror against tigers come if not from imposed colonial constructs?"

I was starting to trust Bunty more, but was still confused. "If you didn't eat her, where is she? What did you do with her?"

"Veritably, I've done nothing with her!" the tiger said. "I was just telling you that, yes, I had threatened her a bit, to keep up the pretense of my vicious reputation. And then, this morning, a few moments after I saw her daughter sneaking her into the pumpkin, voilà! I suddenly found myself vaulted with great velocity into that selfsame vegetable!"

"That doesn't make any sense!" snapped Tuni. "One person can't just swap out for another!"

"You would think not," I muttered, remembering Neel falling into the other king's story.

Tiktiki One click-clacked its tongue like it was agreeing with me, and Tuntuni bellowed, "People—or animals—can't just substitute for each other in their own stories!" In his agitation, Tuni jumped on Tiktiki One's back, making the little lizard click-clack even louder. "A villain can't just take over the role of the victim!"

But even as the talking bird said this, I remembered something Mati had said on the beach. She'd said that heroes and monsters weren't always so easy to label. It wasn't what you looked like, who your family was, or where you came from that made someone bad or good, but the things you did each and every day. But still, what did all that have to do with stories smushing into one another?

My face must have shown my confusion, because Bunty asked, "You have noticed it, haven't you, the shrinking of multiplicity? The shifting of narratives?"

"Um, no. I mean, yes," I hedged. "I mean, uh, what's a narrative again?"

"Narratives are stories," explained the tiger. "Haven't you noticed some story slippage?"

And then Bunty's image flickered again. I saw, in a flash,

the old woman's face, then the tiger's, the old woman's, the tiger's.

"Oh, geez. What is going on here?" I whispered, mostly to myself.

"Why can't a tiger become a vegetarian?" squawked Tuni, obviously impatient with the turn the conversation had taken.

"Not now, Tuni—" I began, but the yellow bird cut me off.

"Because they can't change their stripes!" The bird flew nervously around my head. "Let's get out of here, Princess, before this beast decides we'd be a purr-fect meal!"

Bunty sniffed. "It's really ridiculously rude to discuss someone in their presence. You're worse than the Anti-Chaos Committee."

I wasn't sure what an Anti-Chaos Committee was, but had something more important to ask about. "Okay, let's say, just for argument's sake, I had noticed something. This swapping-of-stories thing. Do you know why it's happening?"

"I don't know why the stories are getting mixed up." Bunty looked thoughtful. "All I know is there have been several brazen breaches in nature's normative narrative threads. There seems to be a conscious collapsing of complexity, a dumbing-down of diversity, a melding of multiplicity." As Bunty said these long words, I was distracted by another one of those blue butterflies, wafting slowly by.

"I don't understand what any of that means," I finally admitted.

"Don't ask that granny-eater any more questions!" Tuntuni yelled. "We've got to go find your moon mother before she rises in the sky!"

My old friend Tuntuni was right. We'd already delayed too long. It was time to go. But when I got back into the auto rikshaw, the tiger got up and padded over in our direction, as if they wanted to come with us. Tuni put up a wing. "Oh, no, Professor Tiger, you're not invited."

"But I can unquestioningly help you on your quixotic quest!" roared the beast. "To find your matrilineal ancestress, the moon!"

"Princess!" squawked Tuntuni in my ear. "Be reasonable! If they look like a killer and sound like a killer, what's to say they aren't a killer? What if the tiger only wants to help because they want to eat your moon mother or, worse still, us?"

I knew that what Tuni was saying was the sensible thing, but it still felt bad to be stereotyping Bunty in this way just because they were a tiger.

"No offense, Bunty," I said finally, "I think it's better if we part ways. You find your way into your right story, and we'll find our way back to ours." Then, thankfully, the auto rikshaw started. I gunned the engine and drove away.

I couldn't help but feel guilty, though, as Tuntuni, Tiktiki One, and I left the tiger shaking their head in our rearview.

CHAPTER 5

A Tangle of Tales

Almost right away, I regretted leaving Bunty behind. Because the scenery passing by was so weird, I knew that the story-smushing thing was happening again, and I wished the smart tiger was with us to help me understand what was going on.

Within minutes of leaving Bunty, I saw, jogging along the side of the road, a wedding party. There were four dragonflies bearing the sticks of a house-like palanquin on their shoulders. Inside the palki was a little doll dressed as a bride, sandalwood decorating her face and her red silk sari pulled modestly over her head, under a shola pith tiara. Next to her palanquin, riding on a rocking horse, was a little groom doll dressed in white dhoti panjabi with a pointy bridegroom's topor on his head. Bringing up the rear of the wedding party was a motley dancing crew: some frogs with mushroom umbrellas over their heads, some giant ants, and an elephant and a horse prancing around on their rear legs.

I was reminded of a bunch of Bengali nursery rhymes I'd heard from Baba, like one about an elephant and horse dancing at a wedding, but before I could ask Tuntuni about it, I saw who else was dancing in the wedding party. A plump stuffed bear with a tub labeled *Hunny* and a sweet little piglet in a striped shirt.

"Well, that doesn't seem right," I muttered. The bear and piglet were definitely characters from a totally different set of cultural stories.

"Don't be so judgy about grammar," sniffed Tuntuni. "So what if the bear doesn't have a great sense of spelling? He's a *bear* after all."

I drove on, not bothering to explain to my bird companion that it wasn't the bear's spelling of the word *honey* that was bothering me. Why were so many stories from different cultures mashing up like this?

We hadn't gone but half an hour when something else weird happened. It was almost sunset, and I was getting more and more worried about ever getting my moon mother's attention before she rose in the sky. Tuni and I were calling and calling to her, our heads turned upward, which is why I didn't notice—until it was too late—the sticky white strands covering the road like a huge spider-web. I swerved the auto rikshaw hard and ended up driving us into a ditch.

"Hang on!" I yelled.

"Second accident in a day! There go your rikshaw insurance raaaaaaaaates!" shrieked Tuni as we crashed, the auto landing with a metallic screech down in the ditch.

"You okay?" I rubbed my head where I'd slammed it into the side of the vehicle. The front of the auto rikshaw was all crumpled, and there was a big metal piece sticking out of the bottom. (An axle? That's a car thing, right?)

"Oh, my wing! My beak! My poor handsome head!" groaned Tuni. "Princess, if you had a driver's license, I would tell them to revoke it!"

The gecko just sat there, blinking at the both of us.

I managed to get myself out of the beat-up, sideways auto and then limped off to look at the stuff blocking the road. The path in front of us was covered in white stringy goo. It looked like we were at summer camp and someone had decided to pull a prank by decorating our cabin with crisscrossing string. The string wasn't just across our path in the road, but threaded through the groves of thorny trees on either side of it. There was something about this that felt like a setup. Immediately, I took out my bow and arrow and looked this way and that.

"Keep your eyes peeled for trouble," Tuni hissed, again sounding like he'd escaped from some old-timey movie about a hard-boiled detective.

I made a motion like he shouldn't talk. Then I used two fingers to point to my eyes, before scanning my fingers out over the landscape around us.

"What is that? Do you think we're in some kind of police show or something?" Tuni scoffed, totally not bothering to keep his voice down.

I rolled my eyes. My birdbrained friend was so annoying. Ignoring Tuni, I continued to scan the roadside, my weapon at the ready. It didn't take us long to see where the string was coming from. A few yards away from where I'd crashed the rikshaw, a woman sat by the edge of the road. She was spinning the threads, which flew off her spindle as if by magic, coating everything in sight. She lifted her head as we approached, but she didn't exactly look like she was about to attack us or anything. On the other hand, there was something odd about her. I mean, what were the chances of bumping into yet *another* old woman so soon on our journey?

I put down my weapon. "All right, Bunty!" I laughed, striding toward the spinning granny. "I know it's you!"

"Take off that wig already!" Tuni added, dive-bombing the old woman's gray hair and trying to pull it off with his beak.

The only problem was, the old woman's hair didn't come off. "Stop that! Who are you and why do you hurt a helpless old woman?" she shrieked, almost knocking over her magic spinning wheel.

"Wait, Tuni . . ." I was starting to get a bad feeling about this.

"Who are you?" The old woman moved her head in my direction, and I realized she probably couldn't see me, as her eyes were coated in a white film.

"You can't fool us, tiger!" Tuntuni yelled, dive-bombing her hair again. This time, even Tiktiki One got in on the act, climbing up to the old woman's white-sari-clad shoulder, then flicking its tongue at the woman's wrinkled face.

"Stop! Stop! Why do you hurt me so?" the pathetic old lady cried, sounding so real that my stomach dropped about a thousand feet.

"Tuni! Tiktiki One! Hold on! Halt!" I went to pull the bird and lizard off the granny. "That's not Bunty!"

"Let me go!" Tuntuni squirmed in my hands, his claws

aiming at the old woman's face. "I'll rip that cheap mask off! I know it's the tiger under there!"

"What do you demented dilettantes think you're doing?" The voice coming from behind us was way too familiar. I turned around to see Bunty the tiger bounding toward us from the direction we'd left them. "Stop assaulting that spinner! Stop mauling that matriarch!"

Tuni did that cartoon thing where you look at one person, then the other, then back at the first. His little yellow head swiveled from Bunty to the old woman to Bunty again. And then he retracted his claws with a horrified expression.

"I'm so sorry, you sweet old, darling, dearie grammy," he burbled, flying around her head and trying to smooth down her hair with his wings. "You just keep on spinning and forget this ever happened."

As Tuni said the word *spinning*, however, the old woman's spinning wheel suddenly flickered. It transformed from a wooden wheel spinning the sticky white threads, to a spinning toy top, to a giant salad spinner spitting out glistening strings like they were a bed of leafy greens.

"Oh!" the old woman shrieked. Then she rose from her seat, and suddenly, she flickered too. Her white sari transformed into some dirty patchwork robes and her gray hair

into a crooked jet-black bun on the side of her head. Her neck was loaded down with shell and bead necklaces, and her bare feet were thick with dust. In one hand, she held a one-stringed ektara, and with her other hand, she played a small drum that was strapped over her shoulder.

"I am no grandmother!" the woman shouted. "I'm a Baul khepi, a crazy one, a mystic minstrel whose life is dedicated to that which is more powerful than us all!"

I knew Bauls were wandering singers who made music and lived on donations, not bothering with the normal social rules like living in one place or having a job. I thought about the khepi's words and figured they must be some kind of a riddle, like so much in the Kingdom Beyond Seven Oceans and Thirteen Rivers.

"Your life is dedicated to that which is more powerful than us all," I murmured. "Is it love?"

"No, no, I know this one!" said Tuni, waving a wing in the air like he was in a classroom. "It's snacks!"

"No, the answer is obviously death!" volunteered Bunty, gnashing their teeth.

Tiktiki One just blinked, flicking out its rubbery tongue to eat some mosquitos. I guess its answer was hunger.

"Silence!" the khepi shrieked, lifting her small one-stringed instrument in the air. The dried-gourd base of the ektara glowed as if reflecting her own emotions. "I wasn't asking for answers! It was a metaphor, you doofuses!"

"Well, you could have told us that before we started guessing," said Tuntuni, but the bird's words got quieter by the end of the sentence. The woman raised her glowing ektara even higher in the air. As she strummed the one string with her finger, the instrument not only made its twangy sound but seemed to generate some sort of energy force field around it that made the Baul khepi glow like a meteor. "I may enjoy sitting in forests and spinning stories in my spare time, but I can still smite you for your insults!"

"No, no, no need for smiting!" I assured the furious woman, trying to back away as quickly as I could. "We've already been smote this week. I mean, smitted. Smook?"

"Definitely!" added Tuni, flying backward even more quickly. "We've totally fulfilled our smitings quota! We're all set! No need to put yourself out!"

Tiktiki One just click-clacked its tongue, which could have meant anything, and Bunty the tiger gave a little shrug. "Regardless, I was not with these ignoramuses, Your Baulness! Indeed, I am hardly acquainted with them! Never even seen them before!"

The spinner-slash-mystic-minstrel ignored all this and squinted at me, halting her playing as she did. "Wait a minute, I recognize you. You're that Moon Girl, aren't you?"

"I'm Kiranmala—the daughter of the moon," I said hesitantly.

"She's an old friend of mine, your mother," said the khepi. "She too is a wanderer, never the same, not attached to the illusions of this earthly life."

Wasn't that the truth, I thought. I just wished my moon mother could be a little more attached to at least one thing in this earthly life—me. But still, she was the only one who could help me right now, and maybe this mystic could help me find her. "Do you think you might be able to help us get my mother's attention?"

The Baul woman thought for a minute, her eyes now clear and shrewd. "Why?"

"It's a bit of an emergency," I said, noting how low the sun was now in the sky. "I have to get to New Jersey, rescue my friend Lal, and then make it back here to help stop Sesha from taking over the Kingdom Beyond."

"Fine, fine." The singer nodded. "All very noble and worthy of you. There will be a price, though."

"Oh, all right, take the tiger!" Tuni indicated Bunty with his two wings. "You drive a hard bargain, Ms. Khepi, but if you must have your price, there it is!"

"Not remotely amusing," said Bunty, snapping their teeth in Tuni's direction.

"Well, you can't blame a bird for trying," Tuntuni sniffed.

"I don't need a tiger! I just want you to gather up my lost story threads, you fools!" the woman roared. The salad spinner was, I noticed, still spitting out strings of sticky white thread even without the khepi operating it. "Or I will smite you such a smiting as you have never been smote before!"

"Very well, then, as I'm apparently superfluous in this situation, I will skedaddle. Most delightful to meet you all. Best of luck with the story strings and all that," said Bunty, backing slowly away.

"All of you must help!" shrieked the minstrel. She pointed her ektara at the animal, making streaks of fire leap from the instrument's strings.

"I say, really, that seems hardly necessary . . ." began Bunty.

"You dare defy me?" the Baul woman shrieked. In response, her ektara sent out sparks at Bunty's feet, and the tiger had to jump to get out of their way. Then she clashed her small finger cymbals together, and the waves of sound reached out to slap at the poor animal's ears. Bunty yelped and jumped, rubbing at their singed fur and sore ears.

"I'd be delighted to help!" Bunty yelled. "I was just saying to Princess Kiranmala—I mean, this young person I've never met before, how much I enjoy gathering up slippery threads of whatever that is scattered stickily all over the sylvan forest scene."

Now that I knew we'd be gathering them, I cautiously eyed the endless threads wound all over the forest. "What did you say these were? Story threads? Why are they tangled like that?"

"Do you want to waste time asking me questions, or find your mother?" the Baul woman responded, and so I busied myself, along with Tuni, Tiktiki, and Bunty, in gathering the glowing white threads from the thorny trees.

It wasn't easy, let me tell you. The strings were sticky and slippery, and near impossible to get a hold of. It grew dark—though with no illuminating moon yet in the sky—as we gathered the woman's lost story threads, and my hands were raw and bleeding from getting cut on the thorn trees.

Finally, we were done. It wasn't pretty, but the glowing, sticky threads were disentangled from the trees and in a big pile in front of the patchwork-wearing khepi. She sighed when she saw them and played a little tune on her ektara:

The story threads are twisted, torn
And no new stories can be born
Smooshed together stories same
Uniqueness gone, in chaos's name

Before I could ask the Baul woman what the song meant, or more importantly, how she was going to get my mother's attention, her face began to shimmer and transform yet again.

CHAPTER 6

My Mother, the Moon

The Baul woman swirled around and around, dancing like a spinning top herself. The colors on her multicolor coat melted into one, growing brighter and brighter until they were just a pure silver light that lit up the night. I watched, mesmerized, as the body of the Baul woman disappeared into the growing brightness. Bunty, Tuni, and even Tiktiki One dived for the ground, bowing low. Only I stayed standing.

"Hello, daughter." My moon mother's voice was like bells on the wind. Her light illuminated the dark forest so that it looked like day. Her presence had made the animals freeze in place and time. Even the trees seemed to hold their breath before her.

My mother was dressed a bit like the Baul minstrel had

been—but in a white sari shot through with beautiful silver threads, her dark hair on the side of her head in a bun bound with jasmine flowers. The minstrel's ektara was in her hand too—and I couldn't be sure if the Baul had always been my mother or if this was one of those story-smushing situations again.

"Mother!" I reached out my hand, but my flesh touched only her transparent energy. Where we made contact, I felt filled with energy and power. Even though I'd been frustrated with her before, now I felt myself glowing in her presence, as if from the inside out.

"Mother, I don't know what's going on with all these story threads getting tangled." I pointed to the pile of glowing threads still at her feet, and the salad spinner still spitting out glowing string. "But I've come to ask you about something else—if you could make me a wormhole through the fabric of space-time to the other dimension."

"Oh, is that all?" My moon mother's laugh was tinkly and sweet. "Most daughters just ask for an after-school snack or a little allowance."

"Or a cell phone," I added, wondering for a second if Ma and Baba would finally let me have one if my moon mother gave it to me. "I know. But for now, the wormhole would be awesome."

"But you have destroyed the magic auto rikshaw." My moon mother pointed to the now-smashed-up vehicle. Then she looked thoughtfully at my frozen companions. "You'll have to travel through the wormhole by tiger, I suppose."

"By tiger?" I repeated.

"Well, you can't well ride that tiny bird or lizard," she said in an "isn't that obvious?" sort of way.

I nodded, pretending I had the first idea of how I was going to convince Bunty to be my interdimensional ride. But I pressed on. There was something else I'd been worried about, and I hoped she had an answer.

"Mother, how do I find Lal? How do I figure out where the tree is in New Jersey that he's hidden inside?"

My moon mother closed her eyes, intoning,

Your enemy's enemy
Is your friend
Find your prince
Where the road bends
A tree between worlds
A serpent's friend
Hate not love
Makes difference end

I dived into my backpack to grab a pen, then scribbled my moon mother's rhyme on the inside of my arm. I knew from experience I'd probably need it later, and didn't trust myself to remember it right.

As I did so, I noticed my mother peeking into my open pack. Her face suddenly changed, taking on the look of someone else entirely. I knew she was looking at the Chintamoni and Poroshmoni Stones at the bottom of my bag when she whispered, in a hoarse, old-man-type voice, "Are those the star stones? You must keep them secret! Keep them safe!"

I put the pen in my pack and shut it again. "Why? Are they dangerous?

"Dangerous, yes," said my mother, looking more like herself again. "But also perhaps very useful." She touched her finger to the side of her nose in a secretive gesture.

I nodded, tapping the side of my nose too. "I'll remember."

I took a look at the poem I'd scribbled on my arm. I was stuck on the first lines. My enemy's enemy, and then that part about the tree where the road bends . . . wait a minute.

"Lal's in the tree in front of Jovi's house?" I asked, not wanting to believe it. My middle school frenemy Jovi Berger had the house next to mine, where our road bent. And she did have a great big tree in her yard. Could it be possible? Could Lal really be in it? Or was this another story swap?

"Mother, what's happening with all the stories? Why do they keep getting mixed up?"

"Such a strange kitchen appliance." My moon mother looked at the wildly spinning salad spinner. "Usually that's a spinning wheel spinning out story threads . . ." she murmured, becoming all vague and distant again.

"Mother!" I demanded, feeling my old frustration returning. I thought back to her poem. "What's going on, with these stories, with the chaos and the serpents?"

As usual, she didn't answer me directly. "Sesha's Anti-Chaos Committee is growing more powerful, but I never thought they would resort to g-force-generating kitchen gadgets. This is, perhaps, worse than I thought." Her light started to flicker. "Thank goodness I am no longer married to your father, so he cannot tap into my power. The multiverse help any woman who chooses to marry that scoundrel."

With every word, she grew more transparent, like she was fading away.

"Sesha's Anti-Chaos Committee?" That glowy, delirious feeling when I'd first come into my moon mother's presence was almost entirely gone now. I wanted to scream, shake her, demand she be more real. Why did she always disappear, right when we had just connected? She was like vapor, so hard to hold on to. "How do we stop whatever they're doing?"

My moon mother didn't answer but raised her head, as if hearing something from the sky. "It is almost time for me to rise," she said, her body growing even fainter as she said this. I could see right through her now.

"Wait! How do I make a wormhole and get home to New Jersey? How do I figure out what Sesha's up to and stop him? Please, Mother, can't you help me? Please, stay, for once!" I grasped on to the end of her silky sari, as if I could keep her with me by force.

And then, to my surprise, my moon mother didn't just fade but her face started to change too, like Neel's had. A stream of blue butterflies shot out from the folds of her sari. Her skin grew lighter, her hair changing from black to red-blond, her sari into a big fairy-tale-type dress with a hoopskirt.

"Mother! Wait!" I watched in horror as she became swallowed by a big bubble. We were getting smooshed into the wrong story again! This time the one about that girl who goes to another world through a tornado. "Mother! How am I going to get home? And what's with this

Anti-Chaos thing? Is it why Sesha's taken over the Kingdom Beyond?"

But my moon-slash-good-witch of a mother was already rising into the air, rising out of my story and into another. She held a long fairy-godmother wand in her hand, and a giant pink crown was perched on her now-light hair. The blue butterflies fluttered around her skirts. But her face was twisted, as if she was desperately trying to stay in this reality.

"No! I am myself! My tale stands on its own! I will not have my story forgotten!" she shouted.

Even though my moon mother's skin and clothes turned back to what they had been, the bubble she was in continued to rise higher and higher into the air, and the butterflies seemed to multiply in number. "Here! Daughter! Take these!" she called.

I looked, startled, at what my mother had dropped at my feet. "What do I do with them?"

"Click them together three times!" she said, her voice faint as she rose higher and higher into the night. She was already up in her moon form in the sky when I heard her last instructions. "And, darling moonbeam girl, don't forget the magic words!"

CHAPTER 7

Down the Rabbit and/or Wormhole

"Ruby-red slippers, huh?" Tuni said, eyeing my moon mother's parting gift. As soon as she had risen in the sky, my animal companions had unfrozen.

"Close enough. Ruby-red combat boots," I said, lacing up the second one.

"You realize they were silver shoes in the original text, don't you?" said Bunty. "I am a great aficionado of all tales 2-D. The change to ruby-red slippers was purely a cinematic embellishment."

"Sure, okay, whatever." I'd taken off the sparkly silver boots I'd been presented recently as the Kingdom Beyond's champion on *Who Wants to Be a Demon Slayer?* But when I tried to tie the silver boots together and take them with me, something very strange happened. The boots melted—well, not melted exactly—but kind of slowly evap-orated out of my sight! And in their place a swarm of blue butterflies seemed to explode, straight out of my hands and into the sky!

"What the what was that?" I shouted, but Tuni, Bunty, and Tiktiki One just looked at me in surprise.

"What are you expostulating about, Princess?" Bunty lifted their giant head toward me.

"Don't tell me you didn't see it!" I sputtered, waving my hands in the air, toward where the butterflies had just been.

"See what?" Tuni put a yellow wing to my forehead as if testing for a fever. "Are you feeling all right?"

"But my shoes . . ." I began, pointing to my new red boots.

"Are on your feet?" Tuni said, then added, "Hey, I've got a good one! Knock knock!"

"But . . ." How could the animals have forgotten that I'd been wearing different shoes only seconds ago?

"Who's there?" answered Bunty.

"Listen, my shoes disappeared . . ." I tried again.

"Wooden shoe!" chirped Tuni.

"Wooden shoe who?" asked Bunty.

"Hey, come on!" I protested.

"Wooden shoe like to know?" Tuntuni giggled as he

flew in a circle above our heads. Bunty rolled onto their back, paws in the air, roaring with laughter, and even Tiktiki One blinked its eyes as if giggling, before going back to eating gnats and mosquitos out of the air.

I sighed. Obviously, I'd have to let the disappearing boots go. No one but me even seemed to remember them.

"So how do I do this? Make the wormhole, I mean?" I asked Tuni.

"How am I supposed to know?" the bird squawked. "I was frozen the whole time you were taking to your moon mommy. It's not like I heard anything she said." Tiktiki One slithered out its tongue and swiveled its eyes in agreement.

"She said I should click them together three times," I mumbled, feeling totally foolish as I did so. I felt even more foolish when, after the third click of my heels, absolutely nothing happened.

"That was undoubtedly, unquestioningly, indubitably . . . underwhelming," drawled Bunty, lazily picking their teeth with a long claw. "If this was a professional plenary session, I would definitely recommend they not invite you back."

I wished I had my silver boots so I could chuck them at the know-it-all tiger's head.

"Do these shoes have a button or a hidden compartment or something?" clucked Tuntuni, flying around my feet.

"Ouch!" I kicked out as he pecked at my ankle by mistake with his sharp beak.

"When in scholarly doubt, go back to the original text," said Bunty.

"The original text?" I repeated, not understanding what the tiger could mean.

That's when my up-till-now-useless gecko totally came through for me. It made a clickety-clackety noise with its mouth, but as it did, I could swear it said, "Noplacelikehome!"

"Of course!" It was so silly of me not to realize! "Tiktiki One, you're a genius!"

The lizard blinked rapidly, then hit itself in the eyeball with its long, rubbery tongue.

My moon mother had said I had to remember the magic words. And as it was in that tornado story, so too was *home* a magical word for me. Unlike my moon mother and Sesha, my adoptive parents, Ma and Baba, were completely ordinary and human. Yet they had a magic that came from always being there for me. They weren't royal, or mystical, or special in any way—except in all the ways that counted. They, not my biological parents, were the ones who raised me, fed me, washed my clothes, made sure I studied, cared for me when I was sick, and tucked me in at night. And there was no place like the home they created for me with their support and love. I just had to get home to them, and they would help me figure out everything. They would help me rescue Lal. They would help me stop Sesha. Suddenly, I wanted to see them, to be with them, so desperately, it made my whole body ache. So this time, when I clicked my heels together, with each click, I said the magic phrase, believing every word.

Click. "There's no place like home."

Click. "There's no place like home."

Click. "There's no place like home."

And with that, everything got misty and wild, and there appeared in front of us the magical shape of . . .

"A clothes dryer?" shrieked Tuntuni, doubling over with laughter. "You sure you weren't actually saying 'There's no place like a laundromat'?"

"'There's no place like a clothes hamper'?" chuckled Bunty, and then actually high-fived Tuni. Only Tiktiki One didn't laugh, bless his buggy-eyed clueless lizard heart.

"I don't understand." Had I made this home appliance appear simply by thinking about my parents washing my clothes? What was going on here? I was totally confused until I decided to open the industrial-sized dryer's giant door.

"Whoa! Check it!" I stared in amazement.

Instead of mismatched socks or white T-shirts dyed pink by a leaky red blouse, a whole universe of colors and shapes swirled inside the machine. Some multicolor galaxies tumbled by at top speed, as did some stars and planets. There were squeaking clouds and shapes, as well as giant forks, spoons, and knives that seemed to be making weird musical noises. I was pretty sure I saw a couple dinosaurs swim by, but they weren't made of flesh, or even bones, but blocks and flowers and what seemed like origami paper too. Then a worried-looking rabbit ran by, scowling at his pocket watch, and also a little terrier barking at a green-faced witch. A giant polar bear dressed in armor gnashed his teeth at us, before transforming into an exploding bouquet of blue butterflies. There were flying keys and a pen that looked like a sword, and a mouse sailing by in a teapot. This wormhole looked like someone's dreams after they'd fallen asleep in a library, all different stories jumbled up in their head. Was this because of that story-tangling stuff? And again with those darned blue butterflies! But I couldn't worry about all that right now; I had to rescue Lal and get him home to his brother. Then, with the help of all my friends, we'd take on my bio dad and whatever evil plans he had cooking.

I gave Bunty a doubtful look. "So this is the part where we get on your back and go through the wormhole, I guess," I said.

"Pray do so," said the tiger, pleasantly enough.

And so, Tuntuni and Tiktiki One climbed onto my shoulders as I got on Bunty's back. The tiger didn't have a collar or anything on, but a big thick chunk of striped skin at their neck. I held on to this a little tentatively at first, but then harder as, without warning, Bunty jumped from this dimension and into the neon colors of the magical clothes dryer.

At first, it was like being inside a box of rainbow sprinkles. Everything was shining and dizzying and bright. Also, super out of control and out of balance—like the Jersey Shore roller coasters I hated so much. "Whoa!" I yelled, feeling my recently eaten biriyani rise in my throat.

We were running upside down through what looked like some sort of a spaceship, with computer screens and controls everywhere. And then, as Bunty leaped out a hatch, we were in a house that looked remarkably like my own split-level in New Jersey, only with shag carpeting made of grass and a ceiling that hung heavy with stalactites. I held on to Bunty's neck as the tiger ran out the side door of the house and into what looked like a giant wardrobe. The back of the wardrobe swung open onto a shimmering forest whose trees hung with picture frames, cameras, and old-model cell phones instead of leaves. I almost asked the tiger to slow down so I could pluck one. But before I could tell Bunty anything, the scene changed again and we were surfing on some waves that weren't made of water but, I guessed, the very fabric of space-time.

"They're gravitational waves!" Tuntuni trilled, looking terrified. As for me, I felt shiny with excitement.

I smiled at some tiny fellow surfers with itty-bitty surfboards who looked like the workers from that story about the secret chocolate factory. One of the little surfers gave me a whooping hang-ten back. I thought for a moment of Buddhu, Neel's preposterously laid-back half-monkey brother, and wondered where he and their half-owl brother Bhootoom were.

The scene changed again. Now we were standing at the top edge of an old-fashioned, if unnaturally giant, typewriter. There was a sinister, swirling darkness in between each key that bubbled with something that smelled poisonous. This magical ruby-red-boot-created wormhole was weirder than any other interdimensional traveling experience I'd had so far. But if it was following standard story threads, I knew what facing a giant typewriter meant.

"If this is like other stories I've read, we must have to jump from key to key," I said to Bunty.

"I'm trying, but I can't!" As the tiger tried to jump to the first row of keys, there seemed to be some sort of invisible force field stopping the beast from making it across the machine. The tiger reached for the *T*, the *Y*, and the *E*, but couldn't seem to get beyond whatever magic was holding them back. Bunty roared in frustration.

Tiktiki One click-clacked its tongue and rolled its eyes almost 360 degrees around, as if trying to give helpful input, but none of us could understand what it was trying to say.

"I bet we have to spell something—like a magic phrase or word," I said, vaguely remembering a scene from a story in which people had to do that.

"I know!" yelled Tuntuni. "Something like 'jadu-kar' or 'chi-ching-phak' or 'jhuri-jhuri-alu-bhaja'!"

The first two phrases Tuni said meant "magic" and "abracadabra," but I was pretty sure that last phrase was just describing crunchy french fries. "What about where we're going?" I said. "Like 'Parsippany' or 'New Jersey'?"

"Indeed, that makes infinitely more sense than jhuri-jhuri-alu-bhaja!" said Bunty, which made Tuntuni sniff in offense.

"I happen to be a little hungry," said the bird. "Crunchy fried potato strings sound pretty good right now."

My stomach growled at the thought. Crunchy alu bhaja sounded pretty good to me too.

I was super hopeful about the location suggestions I'd made, but when Bunty tried to jump toward the *P* or even way down toward the *N*, nothing seemed to happen. After that, he tried Tuntuni's words, but those didn't work either. "Incorrect! Insufficient! Inept!" complained the tiger. "This is worse than the password on my academic departmental computer."

"We're never getting through this wormhole!" moaned

Tuni. "It's hopeless, Princess! Let's just rip the tail off Tiktiki One and call for reinforcements!"

The bird had its beak hovering near the squawking tiktiki's tail when, suddenly, another possibility occurred to me.

"No, wait, I've got it!" I said, snapping my fingers. "Bunty, try 'home.'"

"No way, too obvious," sniffed Tuni. "I vote we rip this lizard's tail off and tell Mati Didi to send a rescue party."

"No, I cautiously consider Princess Kiranmala might be correct," said the tiger. "That's good PhD-dissertation-level logic there!"

The tiger jumped down to the *H*, and when we made it to the key, we all cheered. Then Bunty went up to the *O*, and down to *M*. Only, before we reached the *E*, Bunty's paws seemed to slip—or did the key itself tip?—and we all fell into the dark void between the keys.

"Ahhhhhh!" screamed someone. I'm pretty sure it was me.

We started falling down a long, long tunnel. Except, I soon realized, it wasn't any ordinary tunnel, but the dirt-packed rabbit hole of a very familiar children's story, the one about the girl who travels to a magical wondrous land. I fell off Bunty's back, and the bird and lizard slipped off mine, and all four of us tumbled, head over paws over tail.

"We're gonna die! We're gonna die!" shrieked Tuni, as if out of habit. But then, a second later, the bird remembered that he knew how to fly, and just flapped his wings alongside us as the rest of us fell like stones.

Tiktiki One, for its part, was pretty quiet on the way down, but Bunty and I pretty much yelled like the world was coming to an end. Which, for all we knew, it was.

We fell for so long, I soon felt like maybe we'd be falling forever. We fell past rakkhosh masks and ancient paintings of snakes on the dirt walls. We fell past floating lemonade stalls and self-twirling jump ropes and skateboards without wheels whizzing by through the air. We dropped past giant billboards advertising romantic films with giant, colorful song-and-dance numbers. We fell past books that were turning their own pages, pirates with shiny swords, and a blinking solar system night-light that looked a lot like the one I'd destroyed recently in a fight with Neel's mom, the Rakkhoshi Rani. We fell past desert fortresses and idyllic castles, blond Princess Pretty Pants™ dolls and brown-skinned ones too. We fell past stories that were familiar, some old and some brand-new. We also fell past butterflies of all colors, shapes, and sizes. Butterflies so bright and magical, they lit up everything around them.

I started to doubt that we'd ever make it to Parsippany at this rate. At one point, I stopped being terrified and just got used to the feeling of being out of control and falling like some kind of unhinged-from-the-sky star.

But finally, we landed with a hard thunk on the floor of the rabbit hole. "Ouch!" I complained. The floor wasn't soft dirt, like I'd anticipated, but covered in hard black-and-white tiles.

"Let's not do that again," squawked Tuni.

"What are you complaining about? You just flew!" I rubbed my aching side.

Bunty was running a paw over an ear, and moaning a little. Tiktiki One just sat there, blinking and flicking its tongue so long and retracting it so fast, it kept hitting itself in the eyeball like it had before. I took this to mean it was upset.

"Do we get to have a tea party with the white rabbit now?" I wondered, looking around at the vaguely familiar surroundings—the chairs and tables hanging from the walls of the tunnel.

"Nope, we're in a different part of the story." Tuni pointed a wing. In front of us were three tiny doors, far too small to get through in our present size. Pointing at the doors were all sorts of arrows on stands. All the arrows said the same thing: *TO NEW JERSEY.*

"Well, that's not how it goes," I murmured. In the original tale, the girl Alice was not on her way to Jersey, and besides, she only had to deal with one tiny door. How was I supposed to deal with three?

CHAPTER 8

Rude Riddles

I stared at the three teeny-tiny doors in the wall. The first was brown-red, like earth, with intricate white alpona all over it—in the shapes of leaves and mangoes and vines. The second one was bright blue like the sea with the shapes of block-print fish stamped all around it. The third door was green like the leaves on trees with a painting in the center of two angry-looking peacocks. The strange thing was that the peacocks seemed to be dancing over an old-fashioned record player, the kind people had to crank before the music came out through an attached funnel-thing. Above the first door was a sign that read:

Three locks for three keys,
How many tries max for you to see

Which one to which door be?

A second sign, above the second door, read:

If you answer me right,
You big clodpole
Then you'll get safely through
This here wormhole!

And then the third sign read:

And if you don't you'll die a horrible, squishy death
And be super sorry you ever lived
So there, you big loser
Plus your feet stink real bad too.

"Okay, that's not comforting," I said. "Besides being rude."

"That third one doesn't even rhyme," Tuntuni sniffed.

"Perhaps we should attempt to turn the doorknobs regardless," Bunty said.

It was hard to do, since they were so small. Neither Bunty nor I could grab on to the tiny doorknobs, but when Tuni tried to turn them with his beak, they didn't move at all.

"Locked, all of them!" announced the little yellow bird,

landing on one of the road-sign arrows in an overly dramatic way. "I told you, we're never getting to New Jersey, no matter what these arrows say. Besides which, we're probably going to die."

"Not like we could have fit through them if they were open anyway," I replied, studying the signs again. "So where are the three keys the poem's talking about?"

"A pointless distraction! It's just a trick to keep us from realizing the fact that we're going starve to death in this room!" Tuntuni grabbed at his throat with his wings and gasped dramatically. "How long have we been down here anyway? How long since we've eaten? A week? A month? Not a year? The days are blending into each other! I have no sense of time anymore!"

I patted the panicky bird on his feathered head. "We've been down here about five minutes, dude."

Bunty ignored Tuni and instead turned their big head toward me. "There is of course the possibility of there being a smallness potion somewhere in this room. That would be narratively consistent with the original tale."

Tiktiki One just sat there wetly on the tile floor, swiveling its eyes and sticking out its tongue. Wait a minute, the lizard was actually sticking out its tongue at something! Something important!

"Thanks, Tiktiki!" I held up a small purple bottle that the gecko had pointed out. In broad, elaborate handwriting, it said *Slug Me!* "This must be the smallness potion!"

"Slug? A rather uncouth turn of phrase!" sniffed Bunty. "Bit of a lowbrow wormhole, this."

"Give it here! Give it here!" shouted Tuni. "I'm about to die of dehydration!"

"Wait, Tuni!" I snatched the bottle back from the frantic bird. "What if it doesn't work the way we want it to?"

"What choice do we have?" argued Bunty. "You do want to make it through the wormhole to New Jersey, don't you?"

"You're right." I uncorked the bottle, wrinkling my nose at the smell. "Well, here goes nothing!" I said, and took a quick gulp before passing the bottle on to Tuni, Tiktiki One, and, finally, the tiger.

Only, I was right. The magic potion didn't exactly work the way I was expecting. Because, even though I grew smaller, but still me-shaped, as soon as they drank from the bottle, the tiger, bird, and lizard transformed into small gold keys that clattered noisily onto the tile floor.

"Whoa! What the . . . ?" I let out a frustrated breath. "Bunty! I told you it might not work right!"

The key that used to be Bunty said nothing in reply. And neither did the other keys. Because of course they couldn't in their current state. Lacking mouths and whatnot.

"Well, I did ask for three keys, I guess," I sighed.

The three keys on the floor bounced and jiggled, as if the animals were impatient for me to get going with solving the riddle. I picked them up in my hands and saw that one had a little tiger shape on the top, the other a little bird shape, and the third a little lizard shape. "Okay, guys, any of you got any bright ideas about how I'm supposed to solve this one now?"

When the keys just lay there in my palm, I took it for a no. "All right, I guess I'm on my own, then."

I reread the signs above the doors yet again. Well, at least the first one. The second two were downright insulting, and I didn't really need the negativity right now.

Three locks for three keys,
How many tries max for you to see
Which one to which door be?

"Okay, so I've just got to figure out how many tries max I'd need to find the right key for each of the doors," I murmured to myself, looking carefully at each key and then each keyhole. But there weren't any identifying marks on the doors, like little tiger-, bird-, and lizard-shaped keyholes. Noooo, that would be way too easy.

"Is it nine?" I wondered. That seemed like it should be the answer, three keys times three doors equaling nine. But something didn't seem right. What was it? I took a big breath, trying to concentrate on the problem again. I supposed I could just try the keys in the locks and see. But something felt really off. And I'd been in bad situations enough times lately to know to trust my feelings. When the hairs on the back of my neck stood up, I decided to leave aside the riddle a second and take a quick glance around the room.

That's when I noticed something more than a little alarming. The room at the bottom of the rabbit hole felt way smaller than it had been before. How was that possible?

I looked to the left and right, all around me, but everything looked the same. Then I looked up.

Oh no. Where there had been a long, open tunnel stretching out above me, now there was a black-and-white-tiled roof that matched the floor. Only, it wasn't at normal ceiling level but looming super close. When had that happened? And wait, was the ceiling actually moving—edging down even more toward me by the second? I remembered now how the sign on the third door had talked about a squishy death. The keys in my palm rattled and shook, as if in warning. Or maybe they were just scared. Well, them and me both.

"Tuni, you were right, we are gonna die down here!" I moaned.

I ran up to the first door, trying the tiger key. It didn't open. Then I tried the tiger key in the second door, and it didn't open either. The other two keys rattled in my hand, heating up to such a degree they almost burned. Oh no, the ceiling had already moved down a bunch more. Now there was barely enough room for me to raise my arm straight above my head. I hunched down, starting to breathe faster in my panic. Oh, this was really not good. I felt a little bit like Lola Morgana in that awful scene in *Star Travels* when she and her team are inside the trash compactor when it starts up, almost squishing them to death. And I didn't have a robot on walkie-talkie I could call. I didn't even have a Tiktiki cell phone anymore since the lizard had been turned into a magical key.

Think, Kiran, think, I told myself, trying to ignore the rapidly squishifying room size. Okay, okay. If the tiger key didn't work in either the brown-red door or the blue door, it was sure to work in the green door. So that was two tries for the first key.

I jumped as the ceiling hit my head. Ouch! I bent over more, my back aching and vision blurring with the panicky sweat dripping into my eyes. *Hurry, hurry,* I told myself. The keys in my hands were boiling hot now, almost jumping out of my palm. I had to think faster. I tried to take deep breaths, forcing myself to not freak out. But, oh man, did every cell in my body want to just mutiny and run out of my body, screaming in panic.

Breathe, Kiran! Breathe! I thought of Ma, Baba, and Zuzu waiting for me in New Jersey. I thought of Neel, Mati, and Naya relying on me to get to Lal. I thought of the animal keys in my hands, and of the sweet Prince Lalkamal, who'd never get rescued if I failed now. And I thought of Sesha, who was up to no good yet again. I had to make it home, I had to rescue Lal, and I had to return and stop Sesha. As the ceiling closed down even more, I took to my knees, kneeling before the three locked doors of the magical wormhole.

My brain was going a million miles an hour. Okay, so if the tiger key fit the green door, then the bird key was either going to fit the brown-red or blue door. I'd just need one try to figure that out. Two plus one equaled three tries.

The ceiling was almost down on me now. I went from my knees into a totally crouched-down position, my hands braced above my head. But I had the solution. I'd just have one key left and one door left, so that was an obvious answer. The lizard fit the last remaining door. No tries necessary.

"Three tries!" I yelled to the room. "I'd need three tries max in any situation to figure out which of the three keys fit which of the three doors!"

"Please do not mumble, young person!" said a disembodied voice from who knows where. "Please speak clearly and distinctly into the Victrola to halt your imminent death!"

"The what?" I yelled. What in the heck was a Victrola? The ceiling was so low now I was on all fours, crawling around like a baby. A few more seconds and I'd be squished up like all these smooshed-together story threads.

I looked desperately around the room, my eyes lighting

on the third door and the record player thing below the dancing peacocks. Whereas it had just been a flat painting a few minutes before, it kind of popped out three-dimensionally now. Of course! A Victrola was what people called those old-fashioned windup record players!

I crawled over to the green door, almost needing to be down on my belly because of the rapidly moving ceiling. "Three tries!" I yelled as loudly as I could into the Victrola's funnel. "I would need three tries to figure out which of the three keys fit which of the three doors!"

With a thudding screech, the ceiling stopped moving. And then it just up and disappeared, revealing the stretching tunnel again above my head. I breathed a huge sigh of relief. I'd gotten it right! And not gotten squished to a horrible, pancake-like death! Then, before my eyes, the three tiny doors morphed into just one and the three keys changed back into the animals they were originally, just all tiny-sized, like me.

"Well done, Princess," said Bunty the tiger. "A scholarly achievement!"

"I honestly didn't think you'd be able to solve it," said Tuni. "I was sure that was it!"

"I was too there for a sec," I said dryly, even as the little yellow bird flew toward the closed door and grabbed the doorknob with his beak. It opened easily. On the other side was a humming darkness full of promise.

Tiktiki One just stuck out its tongue and blinked its giant round eyes.

I put the lizard and bird on either of my shoulders. Bunty knelt down, and I got up on the tiger's muscular striped back.

"Let's go then, you and I, when the evening is spread out against the sky, like a patient etherized upon a table . . ." said Bunty in a deep, poetic voice.

"Um, could we just go like awake people instead?" I asked, wrinkling my nose at the thought.

"Definitively!" laughed Bunty. "Let us vamoose!"

"To New Jersey!" I cried, my fist in the air.

"To New Jersey!" cried the tiger and bird as we leaped through the one small door and out into the ripped fabric of space-time.

CHAPTER 9

A Boy in a Tree

The thing about interdimensional travel that I've come to realize is that it's way unpredictable. One minute I was on a tiger's back with my bird and lizard friends, leaping through a wormhole in space-time, and the next moment, I was alone, freezing my butt off on the top branch of a giant tree in Parsippany. At least I was me-sized again.

When I'd left the Kingdom Beyond, it was blazing summer. I'd entirely forgotten it was February in New Jersey. Which meant, when I landed in the big tree in front of my next-door neighbor Jovi's house, the branches weren't just covered in snow, but ice. My teeth were chattering, and within a few seconds, I was soaking wet. My summer salwar kameez from the Kingdom Beyond wasn't exactly the warmest winter-weather wear.

I teetered there, looking out at the snowy universe around me—Jovi's house at the bend in the road, and my own house right next door. This had been what my moon mother had said to me, about Lal being in a tree at the bend in the road, and something about my enemy's enemy being my friend. I sniffled, my teeth chattering, even as I realized this had to be where Lal had been held captive by that shape-shifting ghost. Even if I had no idea where the animals were, the intergalactic wormhole had somehow deposited me in the exact place I needed to be. I gave my ruby-red boots a little tap of appreciation. Okay, but how to get the trapped prince out?

"Lal?" I called. "Lal, are you in here somewhere?"

Nothing. I licked my numb lips and raised my voice. "Lal? Where are you?"

Again, nothing. How was I supposed to know if this was the right tree, and even if it was, if he was in here? "Prince Lalkamal!" I shouted, knocking at the icy trunk with numb fingers. This was silly. I was getting nowhere, plus probably getting pneumonia. I needed some serious guidance. Why had I not asked my moon mother how I was supposed to get Lal out of the tree once I got to Parsippany? Wait, that was right, I had the multiverse's most useful textbook to guide me!

But when I reached toward my backpack to pull out my copy of Professor K. P. Das's *The Adventurer's Guide to Rakkhosh, Khokkosh, Bhoot, Petni, Doito, Danav, Daini, and Secret Codes*, my bow and quiver got me off-balance. I struggled to right myself, but soon realized my weapons were actually hooked onto a frosty branch. When I tried with a swing to get them free, I slipped right off the branch on which I was sitting!

"Whoa!" I yelled as I crashed down, knocking down snow as I went. I scrambled for a hold as branch after branch whipped past my face, scratching me, and others slammed painfully into my shoulder, leg, chin, and hand.

I would have kept falling too, maybe down into a broken pile of bones on the ground, had the boy not caught me. His warm hand gripped my frozen one, pulling me easily out of my fall and onto the relative safety of the cold tree branch he was sitting on.

"Hey there, girl, slow your roll!" said a voice that sounded so smooth and confident, I wondered for a minute if I'd found Lal. But it wasn't my old friend at all. It was someone I'd never seen before.

It was a boy of strange handsomeness, with ice-blond hair peeking out from under his ski hat and clear-framed glasses like crystal over blue-blue eyes. He wasn't just handsome; he was perfect—a sculpture out of a museum. I was reminded of the celebrities Zuzu and I liked to look up on websites like Cute Boys of the Ancient World. (I mean who doesn't have a sweet tooth for ancient eye candy?)

"Whoareyou?" I mumbled, my lips too numb to form the question right. My cheek prickled where I'd cut myself in a couple of places on branches.

"Hey! Hey! Hold up. You're bleeding, darlin'!" In a flash, the boy had his bright green scarf off and was dabbing my cheek with it. I realized his matching ski hat had words stitched on it in red letters. The hat read, weirdly enough, *Kill the Chaos.*

"Thanks," I said, grateful but a little worried about whether I should be talking to a strange boy like this. Plus, what the heck was he doing sitting in a tree in Jovi's yard? Then I looked more closely at him. His blond good looks and accent made me wonder if maybe he was a cousin of Jovi's visiting from Norway or something. Maybe that's why he looked so comfortable sitting in this frozen tree. It was way cold up in those countries, wasn't it? Oh, why had Tuni, Bunty, and Tiktiki One disappeared right when I needed backup? "Who're you?"

"I'm Ned Hogar," I thought the boy said. "I imagined you'd be getting ready for the wedding." And then, as if this was any time or place for amateur magic tricks, he did something funny with his hands—making an old-looking coin appear in one gloved palm, then the other.

The wedding? What wedding? I was about to ask him what the heck he was talking about, but just then, my front door opened and I heard Ma's voice calling to me.

"Kiran!" she must have said, but my ears were so frozen, and I was so muddled, it sounded like she was saying "Karen!"

"I've got to go," I told the sculpture boy, who was looking at me with his ridiculous blue-blue eyes. I felt a tingling across my skin, and I wasn't sure if it was the force of his cuteness or if I was just about to die of frostbite. "You haven't seen a boy named Lal, have you? In this tree, I mean? About my height, posh accent, probably wearing red clothes?"

"All I can see in this tree is you, darlin'!" said Ned with a wink that made my stomach do a loop-da-loop. "Be sure now to save me a dance at the wedding reception!"

"What wedding reception?" I asked even as I scooched back on the branch away from him. I snuck a look down, trying to calculate the distance to the ground.

"Well, certainly not *ours*, you cheeky monkey!" Ned drawled. "Man, you move fast! Let a guy get to know you a little! We just met and already you're talking marriage!"

"That's not what I meant!" I was embarrassed, so my words were all uptight. Again, I heard my mother calling out my name. "Look, I better go."

"And just when we were starting to have fun," said Ned with a mocking laugh. "We are, you know, already sitting in a tree, all we need to start doing is . . . How does the rhyme go? Oh, yeah, K-I-S-S-I . . ."

"Um, no thanks!" I muttered, feeling more and more alarmed by the second.

"It was just a joke!" Ned laughed. "Oh, how sweet, you're embarrassed!"

This conversation was getting way intense way fast.

Before the boy could say anything else, I turned to make a graceful exit by jumping off the branch. Like, you know, a prancing gazelle or something.

As it turned out, my leap was less prancing gazelle and more dancing water buffalo. I crashed to the ground in an inelegant heap. I got painfully to my frozen feet, remembering the few other times I'd had to jump down from somewhere like this. Each time, Neel had been there to break my fall. The memory made my heart ache a little.

Ned landed next to me on two feet like some kind of ballet-star-slash-elegant-creature-of-the-forest. "You all right, there, Princess?"

The boy's words made the hair stand up on my neck. "What did you just say?" Why had he called me Princess? How could this guy I'd never seen before know the truth about my life?

"Don't worry your pretty little head about it." Ned grinned, then pointed to my open front door, and my mother's silhouetted figure in the doorway. "You better get going or your mom'll get worried."

I know this is a really vain thing to think, but I got a little bit dizzy at this gorgeous stranger calling me pretty. Then I shook my head. Wait a minute, *don't worry your pretty little head about it* meant that he thought I was pretty but also stupid. That wasn't a compliment at all, or, was it? Ack, what was wrong with me? The frostbite must be getting to my brain!

Without another word to Ned, I ran toward my open front door.

"Bye, Princess!" I heard Ned call mockingly. "You and me-e sitting in a tree-e."

I ran up my front steps to where Ma was waiting for me, just inside the threshold. It was so long since I'd been home, so long since I'd seen her, that I couldn't help but cry out a little as I ran into her arms.

I'd been separated from two sets of friends, almost not made it through a bizarre wormhole, and now survived an encounter with a mysterious boy who thought I was pretty. And also stupid. Even though on different scales, all three of those things were traumatic.

But none of it mattered anymore because I was home. And as the saying went, there was no place like home.

CHAPTER 10

Colonized Beyond Repair

I stood in the front hallway of our house, hugging Ma. Everything was so confusing, and I was so darned cold. But her body was solid and warm and safe. I hugged her even tighter, feeling myself start to warm up. It wasn't until a few seconds had passed that I realized she wasn't hugging me back.

"Who was that boy?" Ma asked, and I wondered if she was upset I'd been talking to a boy we didn't know.

"I'm not sure. A relative of Jovi's maybe?" I wiped my runny nose on my sleeve. "Listen, Ma, I have so much I need to tell you . . ."

"Well, he's very handsome. That blond hair! Those blue eyes! Just the kind of boy you should make sure you catch!"

said Ma in a tone so unlike her usual self that I wondered again if the frost was somehow affecting my hearing. No way was my prim and proper immigrant mother telling me I should "catch" a boy! And just because he was blond and blue-eyed!

But I didn't manage to say anything because, just then, Baba's voice made me look up.

"Karen?" he said, coming down the short set of stairs. "Why were you outside without a coat? What will the neighbors think?" And this time, there was no mistaking it. He'd said "Karen," not "Kiran."

I squinted at him and then back at Ma. My parents had always been weird, but something was way off. This was so not like them at all. They'd never cared what the neighbors thought, and they had definitely never messed up my name before. "Ma, Baba, listen, I need your help. Lalkamal is in trouble . . ."

"Who?" said Ma vaguely.

I squinted harder at her. So weird. What was going on here? My eyes fell on the hall calendar, where Ma always crossed off the days as they passed. It was the same day in early February that I'd last been home. The wormhole must have brought me back to the exact Monday morning I'd gone off to school and then found myself in the Kingdom Beyond. No wonder they were acting all blasé. They probably hadn't even noticed I was gone.

"So much has happened! I can't believe I'm finally home!" My eyes filled with tears as I took in the familiar split-level. Huh, that mini chandelier was new. And why did the house not smell the same? Usually it was either my mother's cooking or her sandalwood incense. Now the house smelled like vanilla air freshener.

"Shake it off! Shake it off, young lady!" Ma said, patting my back with stiff fingers. I took in with a start that her usually short and unpainted nails were long, fake, and bright red.

That's when I realized just how different my parents looked. Ma's long hair was all cut and curled like some kind of American sitcom mom's, and she was wearing an ugly polyester business suit with shiny brass buttons that matched the ones on Baba's equally ugly blazer. I blinked hard, feeling like I must be having a nightmare. I'd never seen either of them in clothes like this. Usually, Ma wore comfortable cotton saris and Baba old kurta-pajamas. And certainly I had never seen either of them wearing their shoes inside the house!

"Karen!" Baba shouted again, stomping a booted foot.

He was holding his mouth so tight as he spoke, his lips were unnaturally thin. "What is the matter with you, my girl? So much inappropriate emotion."

"Wha-at?" I stuttered. Usually, they would be suffocating me with hugs and kisses. Ma and Baba didn't just look different; they were acting ridiculously different too. In fact, their coldness was so opposite to anything I knew, I felt even more tears rising to my eyes.

"You won't believe what happened!" I tried again. "In the Kingdom Beyond!"

"Kingdom Beyawnd?" Ma wrinkled her nose as she typed furiously into her cell phone. "I don't want to hear about that old place! We live here now, in New Joi-sey!"

"I had to save Neel," I tried to explain. "From an underwater detention center. And there was a game show . . . a fight. Wait, but you saw some of that on the satellite. Lal's been captured and is somewhere here in New Jersey. And now it looks like Sesha's up to some new plan. I don't exactly understand, but it has to do with something called an Anti-Chaos Committee."

"Oh, you're right on that score! The Kingdom Beyond's one place that's always chaotic! Such a dirty, old, backward dimension!" Baba said in a fake-hearty way. "Aren't you a lucky girl to be growing up here and not there?"

"What do you mean?" In a million millennia, I would never have expected to hear such negative stuff about the Kingdom Beyond from my parents. They loved their homeland. Their main wish had always been for me to embrace all the different parts of my identity and be proud of my heritage. "You don't believe that!"

"We're Am-ree-kans now." Ma clucked her tongue, fluffing her stiffly coiffed and hair-sprayed hair. "It's the land of opportunity, doncha know!"

"I'm not saying we're not, o-or it's not," I stammered. "But there's nothing that says we can't be proud of all the different parts of who we are!"

"Oh, that hyphenated identity stuff? So old-school! There's only room for one winner! And that goes for countries and identities double time!" said Baba, now occupied with his cell phone too. "If there is an Anti-Chaos Whatchamacallit, then it's exactly what the Kingdom Beyond needs! About time somebody got rid of the chaos and whipped that place into order!"

"We're talking about Sesha here!" I tried to say, but my voice was seriously shaky. I'd faced down monsters and fought demons, but seeing my parents act like this, and hearing them say this awful, self-hating stuff about our home dimension, was more frightening than anything I'd ever encountered.

"Time for school now!" said Ma, snapping the wad of gum in her mouth. "Hop to it!"

"No lollygagging!" added Baba. "And don't worry your pretty little head about the politics over there! Leave that to the grown-ups! There's a girl!"

"Stiff upper lip! Chin up! Pull yourself up by the bootstraps, Karen, darling!" Ma said.

Hearing that name come out of my mother's mouth made me see red. "Stop that! My name's Kiran. Kiranmala! You of all people should know my name!" I shook my aching head, looking from one polyester-blazered parent to the other.

"Oh, that's so foreign-sounding! So hard to pronounce! Can't you understand that, Karen?" Baba said super slow and loud, like the way ignorant people sometimes talk to people they assume are from another country.

"If people can learn to pronounce Tchaikovsky or Lothlórien or Parsippany, they can learn to pronounce Kiranmala! And even if they can't, it's still my name!" I rubbed my aching temples. Oh, what in the world had happened to my parents while I was gone? They were downright colonized beyond repair!

"Oh, pishposh. I mean, tomato, tomahto," said Baba. "I don't have time for this. And look at the time—geez Louise, you've already missed the bus, young lady."

"So chop chop, go dress in some decent clothes, will you?" Ma said, sneering at my kurta. She waved, shooing me up the stairs. "I'm not driving you if you're wearing that foreign other-dimensional stuff!"

I wanted to argue with her, tell her how beautiful clothes from the Kingdom Beyond were, how good they made me feel about myself, but then I remembered how cold I'd just been out in Jovi's tree. Okay, maybe there was something to be said for seasonally appropriate clothing. Still, I was furious as I threw on jeans under my light kurta and a fuzzy hoodie over it. But just to show Ma I wasn't doing it to look less "foreign," I put on a pair of giant jhumko earrings I'd gotten from the Kingdom Beyond. My parents may have lost all sense of identity and turned into self-hating robots, but I wasn't going to pretend I was anything other than what I was.

As I headed back downstairs to find both my parents still tapping on their phones, I started to put two and two together. If their clothes and accents weren't a giveaway that something was up, Ma's and Baba's attitudes should have been. Plus their shoes! Those weird, chipper tones! The fact that they'd forgotten how dangerous Sesha was! These weren't my real parents, or even if they were, they must've gotten mixed up in the wrong narrative thread or something. That must be it.

Even as the realization made me feel a little better, I knew that if that was really what was going on, I needed backup. I had to find Bunty and Tuntuni, but more importantly, I had to find Tiktiki One. I needed to send Mati a message and get some help. If I wasn't in the right narrative, maybe this wasn't even the right tree in which Lal was imprisoned! Plus, how was I going to get back to the story line I should be in?

Gah. What a mess. The kicker, though, came when I asked my parents if they needed to head to work at the store.

"The store?" Baba wrinkled his nose. "Oh, that nasty old place!"

"Don't you remember we sold it?" Ma added. "Why, we're tax accountants now!"

CHAPTER 11

Bizarro Middle School

Things only got weirder when I got to school. I wouldn't have thought anything could be stranger than my parents wearing their shoes in the house and telling me they sold their beloved store to become accountants, but I was wrong. School was a whole new level of weirditude.

My first class of the day was science with Dr. Dixon. Usually, I walked from the bus with my best friend, Zuzu, straight to our lockers, then to class. But because I missed the bus, and my newly uptight parents had dropped me at school, I didn't see her until I was in the science room. There, she met my wave with a stony stare.

I sat down, feeling off-balance. I'd never seen Zuzu look at me like that in my life. Had I done something to make her mad?

I must have looked upset, because the next thing I knew someone was asking me if I was okay. I turned my head, and was shocked to see it was my next-door neighbor and lifelong enemy, Jovi. Even more shockingly, Jovi was looking at me with a big old friendly grin.

"You okay, girl?" Jovi said again, touching my arm.

"Is there a problem, ladies?" asked Dr. Dixon from the front of the room.

"No, no problem!" I said, turning back around. I heard a little snicker from my right. When I looked, I realized it was Zuzu, looking at me with a snide, superior expression. Exactly the kind of expression I would have expected to see on Jovi's face.

I slunk down in my seat, trying not to let my upset show as Dr. Dixon went on with his lesson. Ever since I'd come back to New Jersey through that wormhole, everything had been upside down. First, I'd lost my traveling companions. Then there was that weird boy in the tree and my self-hating parents. I'd made zero progress on finding Lal, had no idea what Sesha was up to, and had no one to talk to about it all. And now my best friend and enemy had somehow traded personalities. Enough already! I just needed to catch a break!

That's when Zuzu unexpectedly solved at least one of

my problems. She looked down at my partially open back-pack with a sneer. "Is it bring-your-ugly-pet-to-school day or something?" she half whispered.

I looked down to see Tiktiki One winking up at me from my backpack.

"Where have you been, you dumb lizard?" I hissed. "And where are the others?"

I don't know why I tried. It's not like the gecko was a huge conversationalist. Sure enough, instead of answering me, the lizard flicked out its tongue, hitting itself in the eye on the recoil.

With Zuzu looking straight at me, I couldn't exactly take the lizard out of my bag, whisper a message, and pull off its tail. Calling Mati would have to wait. Instead, I tugged the zipper on my backpack most of the way closed, muttering, "Stay in there!"

"You might want to leave it a little open—so your gecko can breathe," someone murmured from behind me. I thought for a second it might be Naya, who'd been sitting in that seat last time I was in this classroom. But it wasn't. Instead, it was that perfect-faced boy from the tree—Ned Hogar!

"What're you doing here?" I blurted, feeling a little weirded out by the force of his cuteness. I mean, Lal was handsome, and Neel had some serious swagger, but Ned was so good-looking it was almost creepy.

"Ungrateful much? I did save your life—or at least save you from breaking a bone in that tree, darlin'." The blond sculpture boy raised his perfect eyebrows over his perfect eyes. Then he reached out toward me, as if he was going to tuck a stray piece of my hair behind my ear. Instead, he pulled his hand back, revealing a shiny coin he'd apparently just "pulled" from my ear. "You and me, sitting in a tree," he started up again.

I felt my face heat up and snuck a look at Jovi. She was

kind of batting her eyelashes at Ned and giving a super-fake gooby smile. Well, I guess there went the theory that they were related. But then, what the heck had Ned been doing in Jovi's tree?

And there was another problem. If that rip in the time-space continuum I'd traveled through had somehow gotten me back to the same day I'd left New Jersey, then Naya should be here in the classroom with me. Where was she?

"Where's Naya?" I wanted to ask Zuzu but forced myself to whisper to Jovi instead.

"Who?" Jovi seemed totally confused.

I looked desperately around. Oh, jeez. No sign of that multi-ponytailed rakkhoshi selfie addict anywhere. What in the time warp was happening here?

"Cool it with the talking, class!" said Dr. Dixon. "Unless you're gossiping about how oxygen and magnesium got together? I mean, OMG!"

A few kids gave little sympathy chuckles at our teacher's dumb chemistry joke (which was supposed to be funny because O was the symbol for oxygen on the periodic table of elements, and Mg the symbol for magnesium). I was relieved that Dr. Dixon was at least acting like his normal enthusiastic-about-science-jokes self. Weirdly, though, he wasn't wearing the same vest as he had the last time I'd seen him. The last time I'd experienced this day, he'd had on his vest with the farting T. rexes on it. It was one of my favorite nerdy vests of his (the farts were these green clouds coming out from under the dinosaurs' tails and it always made me laugh when I saw it). Today he was wearing one I'd never seen before, covered with, oddly enough, multicolor butter-flies. But Dr. D. seemed otherwise the same. I had to assume he didn't remember the last time I went through this day. Back then, he'd chased me as I drove off across the frozen soccer fields in a magical auto rikshaw toward Bangoma and Bangomee's wormhole.

"All right, it's almost time to go down to our special assembly!" said our science teacher. "I can't believe we've gotten such an amazing guest to come here to Alexander Hamilton Middle School!"

The class erupted into noise as people started putting their textbooks in their backpacks and otherwise gathering up their stuff to go down to the auditorium.

"Special guest?" I slung my lizard-containing backpack on my shoulder. "Who?"

"Are you kidding, girl?" Jovi laughed. "Only your favor-ite television science celebrity herself!"

I felt another wave of dizziness. No, it couldn't be.

"Shady Sadie the Science Lady!" said Ned the perfect sculpture boy.

"Shady Sadie? Here? In Parsippany?" I goggled. "But last time, we just watched her video on the computer."

"Last time?" snorted Zuzu with a meanness unlike her normally sweet disposition. "Keep dreaming, Turnpike Princess!"

Jovi swirled her blond ponytail in Zuzu's direction, then linked her elbow with mine and dragged me out of the room. "Haters to the left!" she said, but kind of teasingly, as we passed by.

"Shady Sadie the Science Lady is here?" I asked. "In Parsippany?"

"Well, sure," said Jovi. "I mean, her atom-smashing labs are here in town, so I guess it's not a long trip for her to come by our school."

"But . . ." I didn't finish the sentence. More than one thing had obviously changed since I'd last been in Parsippany. Shady Sadie the Science Lady had a national science television program that I'd been watching and obsessing over forever. And I knew for sure she didn't work in an atom-smashing lab—or anywhere else—here in Parsippany, New Jersey! (Please, I was her biggest fan. If she'd worked in Parsippany, I would have been at her door every day begging for an autograph or something.)

Man, since I'd managed to solve the riddle of the three keys and traveled through the wormhole's tiny door, I felt like I had been in a strange bizarro version of my life. But whereas most of the other weird things that had been happening seemed like nightmares—my parents' behavior, my best friend and frenemy changing places, Naya disappearing—this seemed like a dream come true. My scientific idol—the rock-star scientist of the multiverse—was actually in my school!

And maybe, if I could figure out how to get a moment alone with her, she could help me understand what was going on, and get back to the right version of New Jersey, where poor Lal was trapped!

CHAPTER 12

Rock-Star Scientist of the Multiverse

Jovi pulled me into the auditorium, which was super loud and rowdy as usual. When Principal Chen came up to the podium, though, the whole auditorium quieted down in less than a millisecond. Even the worst middle school bully knew that our principal took no prisoners and gave no second chances, and only a total idiot would mess with her short but lethal form. I noticed that Principal Chen looked just as pregnant as she had last time I'd seen her, when she'd chased me in her SUV down the icy soccer field. I really, really hoped she didn't remember that.

"Why, thank you, students. Thank you so very much for quieting it down to a dull roar," said the principal. "I was hoping against hope you wouldn't further embarrass yourselves before our esteemed guest. At least all my hopes were not in vain." Principal Chen looked at us over her pink cat-eye glasses with the deceptively cute rhinestones at the corners. She looked just the same as always, only with one major difference—her normally bone-straight hair was in double-helix-like curls about her face. Huh, when had our oh-so-serious principal gotten a perm?

"I know that some of you only appreciate the importance of scientific subjects when they are diluted by the false light of celebrity," Principal Chen went on. "But so be it. In our solipsistic, selfie-obsessed culture, of course the only scientists given any respect are the ones with their own television programs!"

"*That's* an interesting introduction. I don't know why, but I'm guessing it wasn't good old P. Chenny who invited Shady Sadie." Jovi laughed.

"P. Chenny?" I repeated.

"Yeah," said Zuzu, plunking down on my other side. "Don't you think our principal is in desperate need of a good nickname?" She reached across me and gave Jovi a high five.

"That kid in her belly is either going to be another Vlad the Impaler, or like Mother Teresa or something," Jovi whispered back.

"She'll probably be a saint," laughed Zuzu. "Just to rebel against her mom."

I looked from Zuzu to Jovi and back again in astonishment. When had they gotten so chummy?

"Just give Zuzu a chance, will ya?" whispered Jovi in my ear. "I know you didn't get along when you were younger, but we're on the fencing team together now and she's actually not that bad once you get to know her."

I felt my head spinning. Zuzu had said almost the exact same thing to me about Jovi not that long ago. Or, I guess, today. Depending on how you looked at it.

"So you guys are friends now or something?" I muttered.

"Yeah, kind of," Jovi agreed. "Actually, yeah, totally."

I wanted to say something more, but Jovi shushed me, while the other kids in our row gave us dirty looks. I slunk down in my seat when I realized the principal was looking right in my direction. No one, and I mean no one, wanted to be on Biggie Chen's bad side.

"Well then," sneered the principal. "Without further ado, let me introduce you to the host of public television's longest-running science program, none other than Shady Sadie the Science Lady!"

As the trombone music for my favorite program blared over our school loudspeakers, I couldn't help but feel grateful to the wormhole for making this possible. In my previous New Jersey story line, this would never have happened. But somehow, magically, I'd made it to a version of Parsippany where my television scientist role model was right in front of me in real life.

"Hashtag awesomesauce," I gushed.

"Hashtag you're adorkable," countered someone in a mocking voice. It was Ned, who, I realized, was yet again sitting right behind me. I turned to give him a dirty look, but he gave me a face-melting smile and then handed me a teeny plastic flower bouquet that he produced from thin air. Jovi and Zuzu giggled as, totally flustered, I took the flowers before turning back around.

And then I was busy drinking in the sight of my own personal superhero. Shady Sadie had danced onstage to her show's theme music and was now standing there beaming at us. Shady Sadie the Science Lady was wearing her signature round dark–rimmed glasses, pantsuit, and bow tie. Today's suit was a psychedelic blue with the outlines of butterflies all over it. Her bow tie too looked like it might be an actual butterfly resting on her throat. Curiouser and curiouser. What was with all these butterflies? That couldn't be a coincidence, could it?

Shady Sadie's short black hair was all spiky in a zillion directions, and she bopped in place like she didn't know how to stand still. "Heya, young scientists!" Sadie boomed as the music finally finished. Just like on TV, the audience yelled back, "Heya, Sadie!"

She pressed a button, turning the projector on behind her, so that she was standing in front of a giant dark screen with a tiny pinprick of light in the center. Space, I supposed. But then the tiny light started to expand more and more, until, taking up the whole screen, it seemed to explode in a shower of light.

"The big bang!" Sadie said, her voice echoing impressively through the auditorium. "The beginning of our entire multiverse! From a tiny spark, it has grown infinitely! And it continues to grow every day! Think about all that life—all those stories—expanding without end!"

"Booo-ring!" singsonged Ned from the seat behind me. I felt him tugging at a strand of my hair and whipped around.

"Stop that!" I hissed. "It's not cute!"

"But I am!" he said all mock-suavely, raising an eyebrow in a way that weirdly reminded me of Neel. He held out his palms all "jazz hands" like—and did I imagine it or did little flames shoot out of both?

Before I could ask what kind of amateur magician could produce fire from his hands, Jovi pulled at my sleeve. "P-to-the-Chen's looking this way again!"

I whipped back around. I did *not* want to attract Principal Chenopolis's attention again, no matter how cute and/or annoying Ned was.

Sadie flicked an image of a boring-looking gray building on screen. Wait a minute, I'd actually seen it before. It was on Route 46, in the shopping center next to my parents' convenience store!

"We at Smarty-Pants Science Corporation are trying to re-create the environment of the big bang so that we can study it and prevent anything that would reverse the expansion of the multiverse!"

"Why do you keep saying multiverse?" someone shouted out from the audience. "Instead of universe?"

"I say multiverse because I have faith ours is not the only story," said Sadie. "I have faith there are universes we can't even see, but that exist in parallel to ours."

"Like alternate dimensions?" asked Sophie Hiller, one of the hard-core comix kids. "Like on that episode of *Star Travels*? When the captain gets transported into the universe of green-skinned warrior women?"

Everybody laughed, but good old P-to-the-Chen turned around to shoot some death lasers out of her eyes. The auditorium quieted down pretty quick.

"Kind of," agreed Sadie, pushing her glasses back up her

nose. "Multiverse theorists used to think that universes were like strings each held in parallel to each other, which vibrated like the strings on a guitar. Now many think it's more like thin membranes all lined up—pieces of bread in a loaf—with us as the jelly on the bread! The only thing is, those of us on one slice can't see any of the other parallel slices."

The image on the screen changed to a loaf of bread being cut by a knife floating in midair. I sat forward. Multiverse theory wasn't just an idea for me; it was a fundamental truth of my entire life. It was how I could be from another dimension and at the same time from New Jersey. It was how I could hop from one reality, one identity, one story of my life, into another and back again. Multiverse theory was what it meant to be, well, me.

Sadie was pacing back and forth across the stage now, waving her arms as she spoke. "Anyway, whether you believe in string theory or what scientists now call M, or membrane, theory, the important thing to know about the origin of the universe is that it began because of chaos."

Wait, what? Someone else mentioning chaos. Why was this word coming up so often? Sesha was working with some sort of Anti-Chaos Committee, and then, I realized with a start, there was that slogan on Ned's ski hat, *Kill the Chaos.*

"Chaos is something that you middle schoolers know a lot about, right?" Shady Sadie was asking.

There was a nervous tittering in the audience, which was shut down way quick by our principal turning around in her seat and giving the titterers a laser-eyed death glare.

The Science Lady looked around at us, the stage lights glittering on her dark-framed glasses. "Well, who can give me a definition of chaos?"

Jordan Ogino raised his hand, and when she pointed at him, he shouted, "My bedroom—at least according to my mom!"

There was more tittering, and more quieting down after even more death-glaring from our principal. Shady Sadie took it in stride and said, "Sure, chaos can mean something that's messy, disordered. What else?"

"Confusion?" shouted Vic Perralta.

"Disorganization?" said Lily Santiago.

"So something bad, right? Something we don't want in our lives?" said Sadie, holding her arms out wide. "But here's the thing—the multiverse needs chaos! In fact, it was born, in a sense, from that initial singularity into chaos! The very fabric of the multiverse, and of life itself, is chaos, unpredictability, diversity!"

"That's not true!" I was surprised to hear the voice coming from right behind me. It was Ned. This time, it wasn't his hands that were shooting fire, but his words. "What about rules? What about those single stories that bind us all together? What about the all is one, a theory of everything?"

That made me sit up. The all is one, that phrase about the interconnectedness of everything. The last time I'd heard it, Sesha had used it. I shivered. I was getting a really bad feeling about all this.

"Ah!" said Sadie, delightedly pacing the stage as she rubbed her hands together. "We have a future physicist in our midst! Or maybe a philosopher! Yes, indeed, many of the greats—Albert Einstein, Stephen Hawking—they were looking for a theory of everything, one master idea that explained everything—gravity, electromagnetics, what have you—in the universe. But we have yet to find such a unifying tale. There is still so much about the multiverse that lies outside of our theorems, our predictions, our understanding."

"What about Laplace's demon?" Now Ned was standing up, and the entire auditorium was looking at him.

"Holy detention slips," Jovi mumbled. "Not-by-the-Hair-of-My-Cheni-Chen-Chen is going to roast him for dinner."

I would have thought so too, but the weird thing was, our normally no-disruptions-on-my-watch principal just kind of smiled as Ned continued to interrupt our guest.

On the other hand, Shady Sadie was the one starting to look uncomfortable. "You mean Laplace's 1814 theory of an intellect who exists outside the universe and therefore can see and understand all?" The scientist laughed a little awkwardly. "That's a bit of an old-fashioned idea, wouldn't you say?"

"No, no, I wouldn't say!" said Ned, practically shouting now. Since Principal Chen seemed willing to let him say and do whatever he wanted, it was Dr. Dixon who stepped over to his aisle—gesturing over other kids' heads for him to sit down. "Young man, I think that's enough for now. I appreciate you're interested in the subject—"

But the science teacher was cut off by our still weirdly smiling principal. "My dear Dr. Dixon!" the Chenmeister admonished. "Don't be such a fuddy-duddy! Remember we reward intellectual passion here at Alexander Hamilton Middle School!" Her newly curly hair boinged around her head as she talked.

Now I was big-time getting the oogly-booglies. This was way the total opposite of how Principal Chen would normally act. There was also something weird going on with this Ned kid, especially with his talk about an all-knowing demon who could see everything going on in the universe. What kind of a spell did he have over our principal? I felt nervously for my quiver and bow, only to realize I wasn't wearing them. Oh no! They must still be stuck in the frozen tree in Jovi's yard!

In the meantime, Ned seemed to be gearing up for a fight. "The universe needs someone who can see all, bring order to all, kill the chaos, and make everything predictable. Bring all these scattered stories and dimensions and realities into one. But I don't think someone like that should be called a demon; I think someone like that should be considered a god!"

He said these last words with so much force, I could swear I heard lightning outside. And now Principal Chen was standing up too, her curly hair all fringing out around her. But she didn't look angry at Ned; rather, she looked happy. Oh, this was really, really not good. I bent down and quickly lifted Tiktiki One out of my backpack and whispered some instructions. The lizard scuttled away under the auditorium seats.

As I straightened up, something drew my eyes to the stage. It was Sadie, who seemed to be looking straight at me as she said, "There cannot be light without darkness."

I shivered. The merchant of shadows, Chhaya Devi, had said this phrase about light and darkness to Neel and me once, and it had become the organizing principle of my life, as I'd struggled to keep the light and dark forces of my existence in balance.

Sadie didn't break eye contact with me but continued, "There cannot be singularity without multiplicity. There cannot be creation without chaos."

Ned made a sound, deep in his throat. His handsome face was so furious, I thought he was going to yell again. Principal Chen too was starting to look murderous.

But at that exact moment, the fire alarm went off and all was pandemonium.

CHAPTER 13

The Principal Is Not Your Pal

Ever seen one of those Godzilla movies where the whole town runs around screaming their heads off because a giant man-eating lizard is on the loose? Well, you could have mistaken our middle school auditorium for the set of one of those movies right then. The fire alarm system set off the overhead sprinklers, which sprayed water all over everything, transforming the auditorium into a bad imitation of an indoor water park. But what made it even worse was all the super-shrill, super-earsplitting alarm noises, combined with all the yelling, and of course all the pushing and shoving. And I'm just talking about the teachers here.

"Who is the juvenile delinquent who set off the alarm?" yelled P-to-the-Chen, water streaming down her face and then bouncing off her planet-shaped belly. Her hair now seemed to be standing out from her face as if in a halo, and her tongue flickered a little weirdly out of her mouth. "You're going to wish for detention when I'm done with you! The rest of you, get immediately to your fire stations! Some decorum, please! You're embarrassing yourselves!"

She might as well have been speaking in a different language, or from a different membrane dimension, because no one listened to her. Tiny sixth and seventh graders were falling over in the aisles and getting trampled on by giant eighth graders. Teachers were pushing to get in front of students. Kendrick Johnson body-slammed Theresa Ozuah, in response to which Theresa Ozuah clocked him with her giant Hello Kitty book bag.

"Man down!" Kendrick yelled as he fell to the already-soggy auditorium floor.

Mademoiselle Morrow, the French teacher and fencing coach, held off some kids trying to barrel over Kendrick's fallen form, and helped him up. "S'il vous plaît! Keep your eyes on the prize, team!"

But the shrieking and yelling just got louder, and the pandemonium more pandemonious. I turned around just in time to see Shady Sadie the Science Lady being rushed offstage, her intense eyes shining behind her glasses like beacons in the chaotic, sprinkler-induced storm.

"Calmly, students! This is probably nothing, just an unfortunate accident," Dr. Dixon called from the door, where he was trying to organize kids into a single-file line.

"Who did this? I want names, ranks, and serial numbers!" P. Chenny was shrieking again from the front of the room. Her face was all twisted, and even though she was otherwise soaked, her hair now stood out straight from her head. Wow, that must be one really fancy perm. "Suspension and expulsion are too good for the criminals who did this! You're going straight to juvie! You hear me? Straight to reform school! Do not pass go! Do not collect your diploma!"

"Come on, Kiran!" Jovi was holding out her hand as my row filed out, pushing and shoving, toward the door.

"I'll be right there!" I called as she was swept away by the tide of panicky students.

In the confusion, no one saw me bend down to pick up the gecko that scuttled back toward me from under the rows of chairs. "Thanks, little dude. Good job pulling that fire alarm."

The lizard flickered its tongue at me in what I can only assume was a *you're welcome*.

All right. Now that the auditorium was on its way to becoming empty, for the next part of my plan. I wasn't about to follow my classmates out of the auditorium. Four months ago, I would have convinced myself this was all coincidence and that if I just kept my head down, and acted in ways that were unnoticeable, everything would spontaneously fix itself and all would be fine. Now I knew better. I wasn't the kind of person anymore who waited for bad situations to get better, hoping someone else would take charge. I was the kind of person who stepped up, fixed things, and made them right. Which is why I'd had Tiktiki One pull the alarm. There was clearly something strange going on here, and I had to get to the bottom of it. I needed to talk to Shady Sadie one-on-one and get her to explain to me this stuff about the multiverse, chaos, and demons. I knew it had something to do with everything that was going on. I just didn't get how yet.

"Come on, students, everyone out of there!" I heard Mademoiselle Morrow call. I ducked down beneath the rows and started crawling so that she couldn't see me. The sprinklers were raining on my head and the lights were kind of blinking too, but I crawled along the wet floor without stopping. I was on a mission.

"Be smart. Take care of each other, folks!" I heard Dr. Dixon's booming voice in the hallway outside the auditorium. "Walk, don't run, students. Get outside to your meet-up places to join your homerooms!"

The sprinklers were still going and alarms still blaring, but I was pretty sure from the quieting down of the auditorium that it was finally empty. Now was my chance to find Shady Sadie before she left the school grounds. But when I grabbed my backpack and straightened up, I was shocked to find myself nose-to-nose with Not-by-the-Hair-of-My-Cheni-Chen-Chen.

The principal's clothes were wet and her pink glasses so water-streaked I couldn't see her eyes, but her hair was even more twisty-curly and standing out from her head than before. She swiveled her neck, like she wasn't looking *at* me but somehow *around* me, hissing, "Illegal!"

I took some serious offense, sputtering through the sprinkler water, "Illegal? I'm a human being! No human being is illegal!"

"Illegal! Trespasser! Dimensional interloper!" Principal Chen shrieked to make herself heard over the alarm. Her teeth were kind of bared now in a creepy way. I mean, I knew she was strict, but this was ridiculous.

"Dimensional interloper? What do you mean?" I blinked through the water streaming over my face, trying to stall for time. Now I hoped Dr. Dixon or one of the other teachers was still hanging around and would see us. I was starting

to think there was something really not right with old
P. Chenny.

"You dropped into the wrong story, girl!" Principal
Chen hissed as she clamped an alarmingly clawlike hand
over my wrist. "But never mind, we'll make do!"

"Let me go!" I shouted, trying to pull away from my surprisingly strong principal. Even as I did, her words started
to take hold in my mind. Wait a minute, what did she mean
I was a dimensional interloper? That I'd dropped into the
wrong story? Oh, jeez, maybe my suspicions were right!
This wasn't some temporary story-smushing thing—like
what had happened to Neel or my moon mother or Bunty.
This was something to do with string, or membrane, theory! I bet I'd dropped into a parallel dimension that was
near my own, but not quite. Maybe that dysfunctional
wormhole had dropped me and Tiktiki One into a close but
ultimately wrong version of New Jersey!

Principal Chen was pulling me along now, despite my
best efforts to get away from her. "Let me go! Let me go!" I
demanded as she dragged me down the empty hallway outside the auditorium. I was so off-balance, trying to break free
from her, that I almost slipped on some soggy Valentine's
Day decorations that had fallen to the wet hallway floor

because of the overhead-sprinkler rain. I slipped and skidded on construction hearts and overly fat baby cupids with bows and arrows, which seemed to be mocking me. Man, now was a really bad time for me to have left my weapons in a frozen tree. I needed some help. Like, pronto.

As if in answer to my call, Tiktiki One slipped out of my backpack and onto my shoulder. The lizard flicked its tongue, hitting me in the ear.

"Tell Neel and Mati I'm in trouble!" I yelled. The time for secret messages had obviously passed. "Tell my friends I need help!"

Even as Principal Chen whipped her head around, I yanked off the gecko's rubbery tail with my free hand and watched my lizard friend go scampering down my side and off along the tiled hallway.

"No one can help you, girl!" sneered my obviously unhinged principal as she yanked me along at a frightening pace out the front doors of the school.

As soon as we were outside, with the freezing February air hitting our cheeks, the principal ran, flat out, away from the flagpole, which was the emergency meet-up place for most of the sixth grade. As she booked along, her big belly not slowing her down one whit, she dragged me with her.

"That's not the right way!" I tried to break my hand free

of her grip, but it was steel. Even my thick-soled combat boots were slipping in the muddy, frosty grass, and my backpack swung crazily back and forth on my shoulders. "I've got to go find my homeroom teacher!"

"No worries, you're with the principal!" cackled Principal Chen in a disturbing way. "You know how to remember the spelling of principal, don't you? The *principal* is your *pal*!" She cackled again, and I felt goose bumps come up across my arms. And it wasn't just because I was freezing in my sopping clothes.

I half tripped, half stumbled as Principal Chen pulled me along the cafeteria-side wall of the middle school, out behind the building to where the giant metal dumpsters stood. Within seconds, I couldn't feel my lips or fingertips. My nose was running something fierce. Principal Chen was wearing her normal office suit with no winter jacket but didn't seem to be feeling the cold at all as she yanked me along with alarming strength. I mean, I'd heard of pregnant women's hormones making them powerful, but this was beyond beyond!

On the way along the edge of our middle school, we passed a few students running in the other direction, but no one thought to stop us. The screaming fire alarm was still bleating from inside the building, and now, from a distance,

I could hear the whine and screeching tires of fire trucks speeding toward the school.

The principal didn't stop power-walking and yanking until we were out behind the cafeteria dumpsters, where the reek of lunchtime garbage was vomit-inducing. Finally, in the smelly shelter of the giant garbage area, I shook myself free of her grip.

"Who are you?" I built up my courage to ask. I stomped my feet and rubbed my arms. I could barely feel my face from the cold.

To my alarm, Principal Chen turned on me with a decidedly non-Principal-Chen-like look. To tell the truth, she looked a bit like a very familiar villain from a very familiar myth. Her curly hair was weaving around her head like it had a mind of its own. It looked alarmingly like, well, a headful of snakes.

"Haven't you guessed who I am?" she hissed. Her eyes glinted dangerously behind her pink cat-eye glasses. And her hair was looking more and more snaky by the second. "I thought you knew your Greek myths!"

"Medusa?" I squeaked, thinking of the story I'd read about so many times with Zuzu. But if this was Medusa, why wasn't I already turned to stone?

"Wrong!" Principal Chen—or who I still thought of as

Principal Chen—sneered and spit on the ground. She went on in a whiny voice, "Everybody's so terrified of my sister. It's always about Medusa . . . I mean, MEDU-SA, MEDU-SA, MEDU-SA! What about me, huh? What about Stheno and our other sister Euryale? Just because we can't turn people to stone, no one remembers to fear us—oh, nooooo. We're just the cut-rate Gorgons, aren't we? I'm just the middle sister, aren't I? I mean, like, it's so unfair!"

What? Maybe she wasn't Medusa, but standing before me was one of her Gorgon sisters! I was starting to really freak, my body shaking not just from the freezing February temperatures, but from fear. I didn't have my weapons, I didn't have my friends, I didn't even have my lizard anymore. What was I going to do?

Principal Chen, aka the Gorgon Stheno, approached me with her claws out and teeth bared. I nervously retreated, my back almost against the brick wall of the school.

"You're not even really pregnant!" I said, pointing at her suddenly flat belly.

Stheno couldn't reply, because just then, a voice came out of the skies. "Unhand that princess!" someone yelled, and then there was a torrent of arrows raining down toward the Gorgon-slash-principal. Under the assault, the Chenmeister turned more and more into her Gorgon form, her body becoming more lionlike, and great big wings sprouting from her back. With her skirt suit and jacket still on, she looked seriously strange. Plus there were what looked like horns peeking out from under her snaky locks!

I turned around, hoping that my rescuer was somehow, miraculously, Neel; that he'd gotten the lizard-gram and made it across the dimensions in the last few minutes. But of course, it wasn't. Instead, for whatever shocking reason, the person wielding a very familiar-looking bow and shooting arrows at our Gorgon-slash-principal was none other than the too-perfect-looking boy Ned, riding on, of all things, a giant eagle!

Yo, this was some wacky sort of magic trick.

CHAPTER 14

Middle School Monsters

"Unhand that princess!" Ned shouted again. At some point, I'd have to figure out how he knew about my identity. But first, survival and getting away from this principal-slash-mythical-beast-monster.

"You!" shrieked the Gorgon formerly known as Principal Chen. "A year's worth of hard labor detention! Suspension by your teeth in midair! Off-planetary expulsion!"

"Oh yeah? Well, how about a haircut, you googly goon?" Ned let a few more arrows fly with his words.

"What are you doing with my weapons?" I recognized the arrows as well as the distinctive ash-colored bow in his hands. "You stole those from me!"

"Um, how about I brought them back after you lost them in a tree? Don't worry, darlin', I'll return them just as soon as I finish saving your life," said Ned as his eagle flapped its giant wings, creating even more freezing wind to add to what was already swirling around us.

Out of the corner of my eye, I thought I noticed some blue butterflies flying by over Ned's shoulder. But that couldn't be right. What would butterflies be doing in New Jersey in February?

Principal Chen roared, far more of a monster than a school administrator now. "Go away, you pale yellow tree monster! Your country's food is terrible, and your stories are gross! That one about the eyeball! UGH!"

"Worry about your own gross stories, you cut-rate excuse for a Gorgon!" Ned's eagle swooped down and then up in the nick of time as Principal Stheno's grasping claws almost caught the bird's legs. As the bird banked hard right, huge against the gray-white sky, I saw that it had snatched the principal's bright pink handbag with its claws. With a loud caw, the eagle dropped the overstuffed purse, making used tissues, chewing gum wrappers, and a giant sheaf of detention slips roll out onto the icy ground.

The rolling detention slip bundle crashed into some other trash near the dumpsters. Stheno shrieked and recoiled. Surprised at her reaction, I looked more carefully. What her detention slips had bumped into wasn't anything too scary—just a lighter with a drawing of an atom on it. In fact, I recognized that lighter. It was the same one Dr. Dixon sometimes used to do chemistry demonstrations for our science class. But seeing Stheno's reaction, I got an idea. I took two quick steps backward, then grabbed it. I waved the tiny object at the principal-slash-snake-haired-monster.

"You don't like fire, huh?" I yelled, shoving the lighter at her face. I could hear it still had a little fluid left in it. "You're not scared of it or anything, are you?"

"Stop that! You bully!" shrieked Medusa's less capable sibling, trying to knock the lighter from my hand. "You're as bad as my sister! It's not my fault I'm scared of fire since that aromatherapy candle incident!"

Fear seemed to make Stheno faster. Before I knew what was happening, she was on me, scratching and punching. Okay, just waving the lighter around wasn't going to be enough. I tried to avoid her blows as I looked desperately around for a better weapon. My eyes fell on just the thing: an old half-broken field hockey stick poking out of the dumpster closest to me. With a yell and a superhuman leap, I grabbed it, swishing it through the air like a staff. This bought me a few minutes, but I needed something more. I glanced at the lighter still in my other hand. Of course. Swishing and spinning the staff like a fighter in a movie I once saw, I got Stheno off-balance. Then I followed through on my new plan. It took me a few tries—I'd never used a lighter before—but I got the bendy side of the wooden hockey stick to finally light. Trying not to freak out at the flames, I spun the fiery staff at the Gorgon, swishing it first above my head and then down. I spun around to give myself more momentum, leaping through the air to lunge at the monster with the flaming end of the field hockey stick.

Stheno hissed and spit at me but started to back off. "Put that out! Put that evil thing out!"

"No chance!" I yelled, bringing my flaming hockey stick down from the right, then from the left. In the midst of all this, a blue butterfly flew down between us, landing on one of Stheno's snaky hairs.

"I'll get you, my pretty!" snarled the Gorgon, and for a flash, she looked just like a green-skinned witch from a different story. Pointy black hat and everything. Then the butterfly flew off her, and she was herself again.

The distraction gave me an idea, though. The witch in that other story had melted when water was thrown on her. Judging from how wet we'd both gotten from the auditorium sprinklers, Stheno seemed fine with water. But clearly, she had a thing about fire.

"Ned! Flame up those arrows!" I yelled. "Let's see if she likes that!"

"Oh, you meddling dimension trespasser!" Stheno shrieked. She was so mad, there were drops of spittle flying from her lips, so she looked like she was almost frothing at the mouth. "I'll make sure this goes on your permanent transcript! You'll never get into college!"

The Gorgon formerly known as my principal was moving fast now, eyes huge beneath the pink cat-eye glasses, nostrils flared, raining angry spittle. She was doing roundhouse kicks toward my stomach, leaping side kicks toward my head. I backed up fast, brandishing my flaming hockey stick. The body of the stick was burning now, and I was afraid my weapon wouldn't last too much longer.

"Ned! Come on!" I yelled again. What was taking him so long?

"Your boyfriend's too scared!" Stheno shrieked, jabbing at me with a one-two punch.

"He's not my boyfriend!" I don't know why I felt the need to correct P. Sthenny on my romantic status even as she was mauling me. Then I watched with horror as her jaw unhinged from her face. As it opened up, razor-sharp teeth reached out in my direction!

"Oh, shove it in your hockey puck!" she snarled, knocking the wind out of me with a super-agile jumping front kick to the gut. Her teeth, more like long-stemmed tentacles—or maybe snakes—practically swarmed out from her giant, unhinged maw of a mouth even as her hair snakes hissed and bit at me.

Beside the large green dumpsters were a few regular-sized metal garbage cans. I picked up one of the round lids just as the Gorgon leaped toward me, both hands outstretched. I held the garbage lid up like a shield to keep her claws and hair and teeth from me. At the same time, I kept waving the flaming hockey stick at her around the side of my makeshift shield.

"Ow! You made me break a nail!" yelled the ex–Principal Chen, her wiggling teeth and giant mouth making it hard to understand her. "And I just got a manicure!"

"Ned!" I yelled again as I pushed the metal lid out against the Gorgon's body. Her flailing snake-hairs and tentacle-teeth snuck around the top and sides of it, snapping at me, taunting me. "Some help, like, now would be perfect!" I looked up long enough to see that the blond boy had finally nocked an arrow in my bow and was aiming at Principal-My-Teeth-Are-Alive.

I held up the still flaming hockey stick. "Here!" I shouted.

"Flaming arrows coming right up!" yelled Ned. "Princess, you might want to take some cover!"

"UGH! Flaming arrows!" shrieked Stheno. "I hate those!"

Ned's eagle flew down close enough so that he could light each arrow from the flaming hockey stick before he shot it at the Gorgon. Where the flaming arrows hit her, they burned her skin, hair, and teeth, making parts of her begin to shrivel like pieces of burning paper.

Okay, so Ned was probably more than an ordinary sixth grader. But then again, so was I. I gave a loud whoop of victory. To be perfectly honest, the only other person I'd felt this sense of heroic teamwork with was Neel. It felt strange to experience the same emotion with a totally different boy.

"You tween troublemaker!" the Gorgon groaned, trying to hold the now-falling-apart parts of her body in place. "You Norse nincompoop! Why couldn't you just leave this dimension thief to me? You'll pay for this, you Scandinavian show-off!"

And with that, Stheno-slash-Principal-Chen seemed to disintegrate into a pile of ash on the snow. Before I could even fully put down my garbage pail lid of a shield and investigate, the eagle swooped down, landing on top of one of the giant dumpsters. The force of its beating wings made a swirl of ice and snow dance all around us, and the Gorgon's gray ashes caught the breeze and floated away.

"Well, thank goodness for that!" I tossed the burned-out hockey stick and garbage lid aside with a clatter, then rounded on Ned. "Who are you, anyway? She seemed to know you!"

"Aw, shucks. I'm just a guy." He shrugged, turning the force of his smile in my direction. "Just a guy saving a girl from a Gorgon."

"Saving!" I sputtered. "How about following her suggestions and plan, a little late, but still successfully while she got the stuffing beat out of her?"

"That doesn't have quite as romantic a ring to it," he said with a heart-stopping grin. I was going to snap off a fast response, but as he tossed me the bow and still-full magic quiver, the spells my moon mother had filled them with seemed to radiate into my skin, soothing me. Okay, yes, things were a little bit off and I just had to fight a monster disguised as my middle school principal. And yes, Ned had taken a while, but he'd come through with the flaming arrows in the end. Plus, I was alive, so that was a thing.

"Thank you for helping me," I said sincerely. "But

seriously, you owe me some kind of explanation. Where are you really from?"

"Don't you of all people find that question annoying?" Ned asked, his blond brows arching above his perfect eyes. His eagle kind of arched its nonexistent eyebrows too, so they both wore the same expression. "Where are you from? No, where are you *really* from?"

The mocking way that Ned asked these questions made me give a short laugh. "Yeah, I guess I do find those questions annoying, but I don't mean it that way. I know you're not just a regular sixth grader from Parsippany. So who are you?"

Instead of answering, Ned got off the bird's back and walked toward me. He reached his hand out toward my ear, like he had before. This time, though, instead of pulling out any loose change, he simply tucked a piece of hair behind my ear.

"*Hey* there," he said in kind of a growly way. He was looking at me so weirdly, so intently, I had two totally conflicting feelings: (1) totally gooey and flattered and (2) like I wanted to punch him in the nose.

I decided to go with the second emotion. I mean, who did this guy think he was? Plus, I was a Jersey girl, and so I had a reputation to uphold as not so easy to impress. "Get your hands off me," I snapped, even as I felt my cheeks heating up and heart thumping kind of offbeat.

Ned didn't have a chance to answer, though, because just then the cafeteria double doors behind us banged open, and somebody yelled, "You heard her, creep—back off!" while someone else cried, "En garde!"

CHAPTER 15

Speak Friend and Enter

I whipped around to see Jovi and Zuzu in fighting stances, their fencing foils drawn and pointing at Ned.

"You giant jerk!" Jovi yelled. She turned panicky eyes toward me. "Kiran, are you okay?"

"Ladies, relax! Relax! I think you have the wrong idea . . ." Ned began, reaching out an arm like he was going to wrap it around my shoulders.

"Get away from her!" Zuzu flourished her sword in Ned's direction. "Now!"

"Hey there, ho, there." Ned put his hands up and backed away a little from Zuzu's pointed foil. The sword made little zipping sounds through the air as she waved it at him.

"What did he do to your face?" Jovi pointed at the cuts

bleeding hotly on my injured cheeks. I touched my sore jaw. I was definitely going to be black-and-blue there.

"Enough talking, Jovi, move aside so I can cut this patriarchal pig to ribbons!" Zuzu yelled. "How dare you hurt her?"

As weirdly unnerving as Ned was, I knew I had to stop Zuzu from attacking the guy. "Hang on, I know what this looks like, but Ned didn't hurt me, he was helping me. It was actually . . ." I gestured to the pile of ashes, but then I realized Principal Chen was no longer exactly a piece of material evidence. I'd have to explain that part later. "Someone else," I concluded, adding, "Wait, what are you two doing here?"

"We heard you were in trouble and that you needed help!" Jovi explained. "I mean, I was surprised, I admit, to have a gecko talk to me at first, but I figured it must be an emergency for you to send it."

It was only then that I saw what was sitting on her shoulder. Or rather, who. It was Tiktiki One, looking all pleased with itself as it absentmindedly boing-boinged its tongue in and out of its mouth. Oh man, the lizard-gram had totally malfunctioned. I had sent Tiktiki One off to get Mati and Neel, not Jovi and Zuzu. But I was really touched by how worried both of them looked.

"I'm okay, but thanks for coming." Even if Ned hadn't

been the one to attack me, I was relieved Jovi and Zuzu had come right when he was getting all suave and weird.

"If you say so." Jovi lowered her sword, but she took a little "fake-out" punch-step toward Ned, who gamely backed up. "But watch it, pretty boy!"

"Do I even want to know what's going on with that giant bird?" Zuzu pointed her sword at the eagle.

"Let's just say it's been an interesting day," I sighed.

After Jovi and Zuzu had finally lowered their fencing foils, Ned raised an eyebrow at me. "Shouldn't you stop fooling around and be getting on with your heroic agenda?"

"Heroic agenda?" I repeated, my teeth chattering from the cold.

"Did you forget about your friend stuck in the tree?" As he spoke, both Ned and his eagle cocked their heads again and looked at me.

At the question, my limbs got all liquidy. How did this kid know so much about my life? He must be from the Kingdom Beyond too. It was the only explanation.

"How do you know about my friend Lal?" I demanded, trying to inconspicuously wipe my nose on my sleeve. "He's here, then? In this dimension?"

"In the same tree where first I met you, darlin'," drawled Ned.

"You have a friend stuck in a tree?" asked Zuzu.

"Is Lal okay?" said Jovi almost at the same time. It was so weird, having my BFF and my frenemy in opposite roles. Obviously, in this version of New Jersey, it was Jovi who knew about my identity as a princess from the Kingdom Beyond, not Zuzu.

"It's a long story," I said, my teeth chattering more than ever. "A little bit hard to explain. But I have to go help him."

"Oh, how rude of me." Ned whipped off his ski jacket and wrapped it around my shoulders. He had on a green fleece under it that matched his ski hat and scarf.

"Thanks." I felt both grateful for the jacket and a little flustered. I remembered once, last fall, when I'd worn Neel's jacket just like this. But somehow, the two situations felt really different. Neel's coat had felt warm and smelled like soap and clean-boy smells. Ned's jacket smelled like antiseptic or medicine.

"Anyway . . ." I tried to get my brain back on track. "Ned, how do you know about my friend being captured by a ghost and stuck in a tree?"

"I'll tell you on the way," Ned said. "For now, you better get on the eagle already before someone finds us out here and makes us go back to class. Girls, you can go make our excuses to the attendance office."

For who knows what reason, the thought of getting on the giant eagle alone with Ned was a little uncomfortable. Thank goodness, though, Zuzu and Jovi weren't having any of it.

"Um, I don't think so. (A) Don't call us 'girls'—what are you, our weird uncle? And two, we're not letting you go anywhere alone with her!" Jovi snapped. "I know she says you didn't hurt her, but I don't see anyone else out here, and I see her hurt. So it's a little hard not to jump to conclusions."

"As Principal Chen would say, you're on probation," added Zuzu, making a V from two fingers, pointing to her own eyes and then at Ned's. "We've got our eyes on you."

And so, I found myself on the back of a giant eagle holding on to the waist of a way-too-good-looking blond boy who was clearly something more than just a way-too-good-looking blond boy. Behind me on the eagle were Zuzu and Jovi, their fencing swords in hand, and Tiktiki One still perched on Jovi's shoulders. For two totally normal girls from the Jersey burbs, Zuzu and Jovi were accepting the weirdness of the situation—i.e., the flying giant eagle and whatnot—with remarkable calmness. I wondered how they'd take the knowledge that our principal was really a Greek Gorgon. Well, I'd have to cross that bridge when we came to it.

As the eagle took off, away from Alexander Hamilton Middle School and toward Jovi's and my neighborhood, I gave a little whoop. No matter how many times I did it—on a flying pakkhiraj horse, in a magic auto rikshaw, or on the back of a giant otherworldly bird—I would never get over it. I loved the magical feeling of soaring high in the sky.

I pumped my fist in the air and shouted the slogan from the story about the three musketeers: "All for one and one for all!"

Ned kind of looked skeptically over his shoulder at me, but Jovi and Zuzu laughed, echoing, "All for one and one for all!"

"The all is one!" cheered Ned. His words, so like Sesha's, gave me the creeps. All the stuff I'd recently learned about the beginning of the universe, and chaos, and the demon who saw all and controlled all was swimming around in my brain, but like pieces of a giant table puzzle, I couldn't see how everything fit together just yet.

But there was no time to dwell on this, because we were soon landing at the base of the giant tree in Jovi's front yard. I glanced to my own house and saw the lights were off. My parents must still be at their boring accounting office jobs. That was a relief, at least.

"Nobody home at my house either." Jovi pointed to

her own darkened house. Her mom, Dr. Berger, was our neighborhood dentist, so I'm sure she was busy filling somebody's cavities.

"Okay, so let's take a look at this tree," I said, dismounting and walking toward the giant ash. "Lal? Lal, can you hear me?" I called, knocking on the trunk. There was no answer.

"That's strange. I've played under this tree my entire life, and I never noticed that." Jovi touched a knot in the giant trunk that looked weirdly like a door handle, and then promptly gave a little shriek. The moment she had put her hand upon the big bump, an arched doorway appeared around the knot.

"Whoa, this is some fairy-tale-level stuff happening here," Zuzu said, approaching the tree with her sword raised.

The snow crunched under our feet, and our breath made frosty designs in the air. Our suburban street was lifeless and gray on this February midmorning. Something about all this wasn't feeling right. Quick as a wink, I whispered a message again in the gecko's ear and pulled off its already regrown tail. It scampered up the tree trunk and out of sight.

And then my eyes filled with wonder as mysterious

glowing letters in some ancient script appeared above the tree trunk doorway. "Wait a minute, I've read about this in a story before. Plus I've seen this movie way more times than I should."

"Then what do those letters say?" Ned asked. I was too distracted at the moment to think too much about it, but there was something kind of hungry and excited in the way that he asked the question.

"How are we supposed to know? That's not in any known language." Zuzu frowned as she ran her gloved hand along the unfamiliar lettering. "Believe me, I would recognize it if it was."

Well, that at least sounded familiar. The Zuzu I knew and loved was way into languages and was teaching herself to speak a bunch from a website. But the Zuzu I knew and loved would also have recognized this language, since it was she who had watched the movie so many times with me.

"The letters aren't in a real language. They're in a story-book one: Elvish," I whispered.

It was happening again. The smooshing-of-stories thing. Like when Neel and I had fallen into this very same story back on the shores of the Honey-Gold Ocean of Souls.

"You mean, like from the movie with the blond elf guy?

And that tough dude who's heir to the throne of Bondor or Gondor or whatever?" Jovi asked.

"Veeery good!" Ned watched us carefully as he practiced a silly magic trick, making a playing card appear and disappear from between his fingers. I noticed the design on the card was a bright blue butterfly. "But can you tell me what it says?"

Zuzu whipped her sword around toward the boy. "Wait, Kiran, I think it's a trick!"

"Suspicious much?" Ned waved his hand so that the butterfly card disappeared into the frosty air with a pop.

"Of course I know what it says!" I scoffed.

"Kiran, do you think . . ." began Jovi, but I was on a roll, wanting to prove myself somehow to Ned.

"It's Elvish for the phrase 'Speak, friend, and enter!'" I said.

Despite Zuzu and Jovi's warnings, nothing weird happened when I said the words from the movie. Well, nothing more weird than had already happened. The magical doorway was still there, the glowing letters arching above it.

"I love that elf dude with the ears," Jovi mumbled, coming over to examine the doorway with me.

"What about that elf queen lady?" Zuzu added as we all three ran our hands over the door. "She's so cool, talking about how she's going to be beautiful and terrible and everyone will love her and despair."

"Self-confidence goals!" I agreed, and the other girls laughed.

We were all examining the frosty tree with its funny doorway, basically ignoring Ned. It had been weird to accept this new, nice version of Jovi, and the slightly meaner version of Zuzu, but we were starting to feel like an all-girl crew. Like a female version of three musketeers, only without moustaches. Like the Pink-Sari Skateboarders, only without pink saris. Or, like, skateboards. Like Charlie's Angels, but without the 1970s feathered haircuts or disembodied dude on the speakerphone.

So that's why, when Jovi and Zuzu both lost their footing at the same time, I was looking at them and not at Ned. "Whoa, are you okay?" I asked, before I felt my own ankles suddenly stiffen, like someone had clamped a giant hand around them. I looked down to realize that, as my friends were being pulled underground, one of the tree's giant roots had wrapped its strong length around my ankles! What was going on?

The girls were screaming now, and while I tried to reach them, I couldn't move. The tree's gnarled roots had me fixed in place.

"This better not be one of your magic tricks, dude!" Zuzu yelled, her feet entirely hidden now under the frosty lawn. Ned laughed, but as he did, he kind of hissed at the same time.

I turned, almost in slow motion, toward Ned and saw that his eyes were a lot more yellow than blue. And his perfect pale skin strangely scaly.

I gave a startled yelp of recognition. "You're a serpent?" I shrieked. I was pulling my legs with my hands now but with no luck.

Ned shrugged, letting out a little lick of flames from his vicious mouth. Then he transformed into his other, far more terrifying self—complete with scales, teeth, tail, and slit-like eyes. "Dragon, but close enough."

"I knew there was something seriously off about you!" I screamed.

But my realization was too late, because before the words had finished leaving my mouth, the doorway in the tree trunk slammed open. With a slurping gulp, the roots of the huge tree shoved Jovi and Zuzu in through the doorway, a bit like hands shoving food into a giant mouth. One second, I was hearing my friends' screams, and the next, all was silent.

And then I was alone, face-to-face with the dragon boy.

CHAPTER 16

The Death of Difference

What have you done with my friends?" I had my bow and arrow out and was aiming right at Ned's smirking yellow eyes. "And who the heck are you for real?"

"Can't you guess?" With a pop, Ned transformed back from his dragon-self to looking more or less like a boy. Then, with a suave little flick of his wrist, he pulled a flat magician's hat out of thin air and flicked his hand again to pop the hat open. The dude had style, I had to give that to him. He was wrong, but he had style.

Perching the hat on his head at a rakish angle, Ned went on, "I'm hurt, Kiran! You knew about the Gorgon, but I suppose the U.S. educational system is sadly lacking in teaching storied diversity. Not that diversity of any kind is going to be important for much longer."

"Stop talking in riddles," I snapped. "Who are you?"

The still-somehow-perfect-looking dragon boy gave me a swaggery bow. "I told you, I'm Ned Hogar! Or perhaps I should pronounce it the Norse way, Nidhoggr. I'm the dragon that guards the base of Yggdrasil." Ned gestured to the tree in front of us.

Wait a minute. What?

"Yggdrasil . . . are you trying to tell me that this tree on the Bergers' lawn is actually the mythological Norse tree of life?" I demanded. "Yo, are you kidding me?"

"Nope, sorry, darlin', not kidding at all." Nidhoggr raised a perfect blond eyebrow and gave me what I'm sure he thought was a devastating smile.

"Okay, so you're a dragon from a Norse myth. I don't even care anymore," I snapped. "What have you done with my friends? Get them back, now!"

"Your friends are safe enough. They're being held inside Yggdrasil along with your friend Prince Lalkamal," Ned drawled.

I looked at the seemingly solid tree trunk that had now captured three of my friends. "How did Lal get captured by a bhoot from the Kingdom Beyond but end up in a Norse mythological tree?"

"It's all a part of the greater plan," Ned said, a mysterious smile playing at his lips.

"What plan?" I made my voice as firm as I could and sighted my arrow right at his chest.

Ned raised his eyebrow again, finally noticing I was aiming my bow at him. "Well, that's rather rude." With a little flick of Ned's hands, another of the tree's roots wrapped around my wrists, making it impossible for me to use my weapon.

"Let me go!" I twisted my wrists, trying to get myself free. "Tell the tree to let me go!"

"And why would I do that?" Ned, or rather, Nidhoggr, then murmured, "The mythical poems do foretell of three maidens deep in knowledge. Could one of these be the mythical völva foretold?"

"Oh, yes!" I blurted out. My hands and feet now all bound, I had no weapon available to use but my tongue and brain. "Zuzu, Jovi, and me—we're you're three mythical maidens! You better let us go if you don't want the Volvo thingy to . . . to . . . smite you!"

"A völva is a female seer, not a vengeful station wagon!" Ned laughed, spitting out little sparks of fire from his mouth as he did. Annoyingly, it didn't make him any less handsome. "The ancient poems may tell of you, but they don't say that I can't kill you."

"Kill? Kill?" my voice squeaked painfully high. I couldn't believe I was having this conversation with a cute but deranged serpent-dragon boy right on Jovi's front lawn in Parsippany, New Jersey. It was too surreal. I looked desperately up and down the deserted suburban street. Everyone was at work or school, and there wasn't even a postal person or garbage collector around to help. Tiktiki One had vanished and not returned yet. I was on my own. I had to think fast and try to get inside this dragon kid's head. I remembered his love of magic tricks. This guy was proud of his skills. He'd probably love a chance to show off.

"You don't want to kill me! What's the fun in that?" I tried to coax a laugh out of my numb lips. "I mean, you could have killed me back behind the cafeteria or let Principal Gorgon do the job. But you didn't, did you?" My voice was shaking now, but I pressed on. "You must have had a reason for saving me back then, right?"

"You know, the AC Committee's party line is that we're all supposed to smush into one big happy story, but I've got to tell you, I really hate those Greek mythical creatures." Ned pulled what at first looked like a rabbit but turned out to be a squirrel out of his magician's hat. I was afraid for a minute he'd turn into a dragon again and tear the poor animal apart, but he let it go, and the animal scampered up the tree trunk and out of sight, in the same direction Tiktiki One had gone. I wondered what was taking the darned gecko so long.

"The Greek stories get so much more play than us Norse stories do," continued the boy dragon in a pouty drawl, "and it's just not fair. Unjust, I tell you! But then again, you know what that's like. I mean, your stories are practically forgotten."

"What do you mean?" I was trying desperately to get my limbs free without him noticing, but no matter how much I wiggled my arms and legs, I couldn't seem to get out of the tree Yggdrasil's rooty grasp. I had to keep Ned talking while I figured out a plan.

"How often do you hear people who aren't from the Kingdom Beyond talk about your dimension, your stories?" Ned pulled three half shells out of the hat now, sort of like giant acorns. He held one out to me before waving his hands and making it disappear into the air and then reappear. "But it won't matter much longer. The ACC is going to take care of all that. Soon, your stories won't exist at all."

That got my attention. "What did you just say?"

"You asked me why Lalkamal was captured by a Kingdom Beyond ghost and ended up in a Norse tree." Ned flexed his own bicep, shamelessly showing off for me even as he held me and my friends captive. "Haven't you figured it out yet? All the stories from less important places are getting forgotten, or collapsed with more important stories. Soon, there won't be any more stories from the Kingdom Beyond at all. Soon, there won't even be a Kingdom Beyond to have any stories."

"What are you talking about?" I felt everything inside me go cold and still. All the rich culture from the Kingdom Beyond—it was disappearing? Our stories? Our history? Our people—all disappearing? How could this be happening?

"We're gonna kill all the chaos, Princess, and bring harmony to the singular universe." Ned spread out his hands wide. "You of all people should be grateful you don't have to be all mixed up anymore!" He made a mock baby voice, probably supposed to be me. "'Oh, I'm so culturally confused! Am I from here? Am I from there? Who am I? What am I?'"

"I don't sound like that!" I sputtered, but he just interrupted me and went on.

"When the ACC has its way, the multiverse will fade into myth, and difference will disappear. That's an act of love, Princess. That's the end of prejudice and discrimination and everything." Ned laughed in a seriously maniacal way. "The all will be one."

There it was again, that terrible expression that Sesha had used when he was talking about the Ouroboros myth, the one about the snake eating its own tale. "Taking away our uniqueness and killing our stories aren't acts of love!" I protested. "Ending difference isn't an act of love!"

Even as I said these words, I remembered my moon mother's poem:

> *Your enemy's enemy*
> *Is your friend*
> *Find your prince*
> *Where the road bends*
> *A tree between worlds*
> *A serpent's friend*
> *Hate not love*
> *Makes difference end*

"Killing our unique stories is an act of hate!" My mind was whirring. A tree between worlds. A serpent's friend. Hate, not love, makes difference end.

I looked again at the slogan on the dragon boy's hat. *Kill the Chaos.* Hadn't Shady Sadie been saying that the universe needed chaos and diversity? And "Ned" had been arguing . . . what? That diversity was a bad thing—that there should only be one story ruling the multiverse. He'd been all excited about some demon who could be like a god, seeing all, understanding all, uniting all the stories into one. And he kept using that dratted expression—the all is one. Oh man, I was getting a really bad feeling about all this.

"Nidhoggr," I said, trying to keep the panic out of my voice. "What is this ACC you keep mentioning?

"Hah! Do you seriously have to ask?" Ned smirked even as he reproduced that one disappeared shell, then started juggling with all three. "Well, I guess you're not exactly bes- ties. Not since you keep trying to kill him. AC is short for the Interdimensional Multivillain Anti-Chaos Committee. And its chairperson is your dear old daddy, Sesha, of course."

My stomach gave a serious nosedive off a metaphoric cliff.

"I knew it . . ." I breathed. "So he's working with all you serpents from other stories to try and destroy diversity? He wants to make all the different stories of the multiverse the same, and become, what, some kind of all-seeing demon-god?"

"Ding-ding-ding went the princess!" Ned gave me

another of his oh-so-charming grins, this time along with a broad wink. "You got it *right*, beautiful snake girl."

Ugh. I ignored Ned calling me beautiful and thought about what I'd just learned. That's why Neel had turned briefly into that other king, why my moon mother had transformed temporarily into that wand-waving good witch, why I'd fallen down another storybook girl's rabbit hole. It was all the work of Sesha, Nidhoggr, Stheno, and this Anti-Chaos Committee. This was horrible. Were all the stories from the Kingdom Beyond going to be lost— smushed forever into other, more dominant tales?

"If you hate the Greek myths," I said, remembering the dragon boy's words about some myths getting more play, "you don't want your own story to become smushed with my Gorgon principal's, do you?"

"Don't you worry, Princess, I didn't survive all these millennia by being stupid. I'll figure something out." Ned was playing with the three acorn shells now on a root so thick and flat it was like a table. He put a penny under one of the acorns, then kept moving them around in front of him like roadside hucksters do in the movies, showing me how the penny was now under one, now under another of the shells. "You, on the other hand"—he laughed in a not-so-friendly way—"are in a bit of trouble, my girl."

Oh man. There was no one to help me. I had to get myself out of this mess and stop Sesha and his Anti-Chaos Committee goons. I had to save the multiverse and save our stories. But first, I'd have to save Jovi, Zuzu, and Lal. And I didn't have much time to figure out how.

CHAPTER 17

A Game of Wits

"So you're pretty smart, are you? Pretty good at games of illusion?" I asked the dragon Ned as cheekily as I could. "But how good at magic are you really?"

The Anti-Chaos Committee wanted to smush stories together, huh? Well, two could play at that game. I had just remembered a movie Zuzu and I had watched a whole bunch of times and loved. In it, a brave hero had outwitted a villain and saved a captured princess with a game of wits.

"Let me put it this way. Ever heard of Houdini, Copperfield, P. C. Sorcar?" asked Nidhoggr as he shuffled the acorn shells in front of himself faster and faster.

"Sure." In truth, I hadn't heard of any of the names but the first. But I figured they must be other magicians.

"They're all kids' birthday party magicians compared to me," spat Ned.

"Is that so? Well, then how about a challenge?" I said, trying to act all confident even though my hands and feet were totally trapped by Yggdrasil's roots. "I challenge you to a battle of illusions and wits!"

"For your friends' lives?" the dragon snarled.

I nodded.

"To the death?" he added.

I nodded again, trying to do that trick that Neel did where he raised one eyebrow. From the confused way that Nidhoggr was looking at me, I'm not sure if I was doing it right. But finally, eyebrow raise or not, he took my offer.

"All right, darlin', why not? I accept!" he said. "I've never been stumped by any game of wits!"

"I don't know, though," I fudged, hoping Ned's ego was as huge as it seemed. "I don't know if you're a good enough magician to get me the things I'll need. They're pretty random."

"Name them and I'll get them!" the dragon boy said airily.

"First I'll need two glasses and a pitcher of Thumpuchi!" I said, naming a kind of soda from the Kingdom Beyond.

"Done!" Nidhoggr snapped his fingers and pulled out of

his hat two goblets as well as a pitcher of cola. Waving his hands, he made two little tree stumps appear on either side of the thick root he had been using as a table. He gestured like I should sit down. With my arms and legs still tied up in tree roots, it wasn't that easy, but I perched myself on the edge of the stump.

"Okay, now pour the soda," I said.

Nidhoggr grinned, obviously excited by the challenge. "I think I see where this is going!" He poured the liquid from the pitcher into the two goblets. "Now what?"

"Now I'll need you to get something pretty hard to get," I said, hoping that Nidhoggr could do it. "It's called Bhuvanprash. It's a special . . . uh . . . poisonous paste from the Kingdom Beyond. Oh, and I'll need a spoon too."

"Hard to get?" Nidhoggr waved his hands and produced a container of the paste from his hat, along with a spoon. "Maybe for other magical beings, but not for me."

I smiled in what I hoped was a mysterious way. The familiar gloppy black goo was of course not poison at all, but something Ma had made me take as a vitamin supplement (along with my gummy chewables) for years! My entire plan rested on the assumption that Norse dragons' moms didn't make them take Bhuvanprash too.

"You'll have to undo my hands for the next part," I said.

The dragon gave me a skeptical look and first moved my bow and arrow way out of my reach. Then, with a wave of his hands, he had the roots binding my hands wrap around my chest and shoulders instead.

"Great, so much more comfortable," I muttered. My arms were free, but the pressure of the root across my body was so great I couldn't even take a deep breath. "Not."

"What did you say?" snapped Nidhoggr. "You know, I don't have to play along with this. I just am because of your snaky heritage. And also, I can't pass up the chance to show Sesha that I beat his daughter."

I tried to keep my face blank even though I was cheering on the inside. It was working! I had him by the vanity. Thank goodness Ned was so overproud of being smart and clever.

I picked up the container of Bhuvanprash and opened it. Then I dipped the spoon in, making a big show of being careful, as if the substance inside was super dangerous. "When I mix the paste into the Thumpuchi, it will become odorless and undetectable!"

"Now you're talking my poison! I mean, poison is my poison! Get it? I mean, I really dig poison! Buah hah hah!" Nidhoggr said in what I supposed he thought was a dastardly-villain-type voice. I wondered for a second if I wasn't the only one acting here.

"It's a deadly poison, I suppose?" he added as I turned around as best I could and fiddled with the Bhuvanprash and two goblets.

"We'll see, won't we?" When I turned back around, I made a big show of switching the goblets in front of us a couple times. "I've put the poison in one of the goblets only. And now begins the test. Where is the poison?" I cleared my throat, trying to remember the line from the movie. "Our contest ends when you decide which one to drink from, and we will see who is right . . . and who is dead!"

"Well, this is simple enough." Nidhoggr gave me a skeptical look with his narrow eyes. He licked his thin lips with a pointed tongue. "All I have to do is figure out what kind of a person you are. Are you the kind of sixth grader who would put the poison in her own cup or her enemy's?"

I nodded, willing myself not to give anything away, willing myself not to look at one cup or the other.

"Now, only a total ding-dong would reach for what they're given. So I can't drink the goblet in front of me." Nidhoggr tapped his finger on his lips. "But you would have known I wasn't a complete ding-dong, and so I obviously can't choose the soda in front of you."

"So you know which cup you're drinking from?" My

heart was hammering in my chest. Would my plan work?

"Not even! You know that I'm a dragon, and you probably know the stories about us being suspicious creatures, and so I obviously can't choose the soda in front of me."

"Done yet?" I asked, noting the frenzied expression on Nidhoggr's face.

"No way, I'm just getting going! You must also know that dragon stories are really popular in England, where they drive on the left. And you brought that goblet around in your left hand, so I can obviously not choose the soda in front of you!" Nidhoggr's eyes were getting a little glazed.

"This is super impressive. I'm sure you get really high scores on all your standardized villain tests," I said in as patient a voice as I could manage.

"Aha! Your reference to standardized tests implies you're a good student. So you know it's wise to keep danger and death far away from you, so I obviously can't choose the soda in front of me!" The dragon boy was panting now in agitation, shooting little flames out of his mouth and nose as he talked.

"You must be a blast at parties," I muttered, hoping this wouldn't go on all afternoon. I had friends to rescue and things to do!

Nidhoggr rambled on, "Being a good student, you must also have heard the expression 'Keep your friends close and your enemies closer.' And a deadly poison is the worst sort of enemy, so you would have kept it close. So I obviously can't choose the soda in front of you!"

"You're trying to trick me into giving something away!" I smirked, remembering the cute pirate boy from the other story. "It's not going to work!"

"It's already worked." Nidhoggr's eyes glowed yellow even as his skin was growing obviously scalier. "You've given everything away! I know where the poison is!"

"So choose already!" I pointed at the two soda-filled goblets.

"Of course! I'm ready! I choose . . ." Nidhoggr suddenly pointed behind me. Boy, he was a terrible actor. "Oh, look, it's your friend Lal!" he said in a super-fake voice.

"Where?" I turned my head, pretending to believe him, but turned back fast enough to see the dragon boy's hands on the two goblets. He'd obviously switched them yet again, but I didn't let on that I knew that.

"Okay, drink up!" he said with a totally creepy smile. His sharp teeth glistened in the winter light.

I picked up my soda and made a little "cheers" motion,

and then started to drink. I noticed that he didn't put his lips to his goblet until I did. And then he downed his Thumpuchi with one long, loud slurp.

"Hah, you fool!" he yelled as soon as our goblets were down. "I switched the sodas when you weren't looking! It's such a classic mistake!"

"Oh, really?" I wiped my sticky lips with the back of my hand.

"Yes, the first being never get involved in a firefight with a bunch of plucky villagers who own a dragon-piercing crossbow! But only slightly well-known is this—never go in against a mythical Norse dragon masquerading as a middle schooler when death is on the line!" Nidhoggr laughed so hard, he almost choked.

When he fell off his stump, I looked over casually. "Hey, are you all right, dude?"

"Oh, my stomach feels terrible!" the dragon boy moaned. Then his face grew downright alarmed. "Oh no! I think I need an outhouse! And fast!"

"I'll tell you where the park is with the public bathrooms if you untie these roots!" I said helpfully. I could hear his stomach churning even from where I was, loud and obnoxious like a washing machine.

"Fine, fine!" Nidhoggr moaned. He was doubled over, clutching his stomach, but he waved his hands, instructing Yggdrasil to let me go. "Now tell me where the park is!"

"How about you let my friends go too?" I said, studying my cuticles with an air of calm.

"Ohhhhh!" groaned Nidhoggr, clutching his stomach and bending over in two. "You drive a hard bargain, snake princess! Your father would be proud!"

With another wave of his hand, there was a groaning and popping noise, and the tree trunk popped open, depositing a dirty but otherwise okay-looking Jovi and Zuzu.

"What about Lal?" I was starting to feel a little bad about how miserable Nidhoggr looked, but comforted myself with the fact that the "poison" obviously wasn't "poison" at all, and while he might need to live on the potty for a couple days, the dragon would eventually be fine.

"Oh, all right! All right!" yelped the green and moaning creature boy. With a flick of Ned's hand, Yggdrasil deposited a very dirty and very confused-looking prince on the frozen ground. Lalkamal looked around, yawning and rubbing his eyes, as if he'd been asleep for a very long time.

"Lal!" I yelled, running over to my friend and helping him to his feet.

"Just Kiran?" Lal looked around wonderingly at the icy landscape. "Where are we?"

"New Jersey—I'll explain everything!" I promised.

"I did what you asked! I brought him up!" Ned growled, now doubled over in pain. "And now you have to show me the little dragons' room!"

Obligingly, I pointed in the direction of the public park. As Nidhoggr ran down the street, desperately holding on to the back of his pants, Jovi burst out, "How did you manage that without getting sick yourself?" Her face was streaked with mud, but her eyes were all sparkly with interest.

"We could hear everything from inside the tree," added Zuzu as she pulled clumps of frozen earth out of her hair.

"I put the Bhuvanprash in both cups," I explained. "I've spent a lifetime building up my immunity. It's not poison, but boy, it'll mess your stomach up good if you're not used to it!"

Zuzu and Jovi laughed, high-fiving me. Lal looked at all three of us in confusion and wonder.

CHAPTER 18

The Dirt-Biking Musketeers

Being trapped in a tree so long had left Lal confused, shaken, and cold. Plus, he had a wicked twisted ankle from when the ghost had originally tripped him, before stealing his identity. So the first thing we did was help him limp up Jovi's driveway and into her warm mudroom. Jovi threw a blanket over Lal's shoulders, and Zuzu gave him a big glass of water. Jovi's black lab Loki tried to get in on the act too by jumping up on Lal and giving him big-tongued licks all over his face.

Even though Lal was out of it, I expected Jovi and Zuzu to be peppering me with questions—about the Kingdom Beyond, about Nidhoggr, about how Lal had been captured in another dimension by a ghost but held in a Norse tree in this dimension. I wasn't sure about that last one myself, to be honest, but after their recent life-threatening experience, I was certainly expecting Zuzu and Jovi to be demanding some answers. What I couldn't understand was why they weren't.

That's when I noticed that my friends were each giggling and staring at Lal, making up stupid excuses to touch his sleeve or brush the tree dirt from his hair. Their voices were like three octaves higher than usual and I kept trying to signal to them to cut it out, but they both avoided meeting my fury eyeballs. It's not like I couldn't understand. Even I was seriously dumbstruck at Lal's movie-star handsomeness when I first met him, so I guess I got what they were feeling. But they were acting like such total dorks. It was like they were seeing half-naked fat cupids floating around above the prince's head or something.

"I really like that jacket!" gushed Zuzu, running her finger down Lal's arm. "Did you, like, get it at the Kingdom Beyond mall? You guys do have malls in your dimension, right?"

"What kind of conditioner do you use? Your hair smells, like, really good," babbled Jovi, taking a big embarrassing sniff of Lal's head. "I mean, a little like the inside of a tree trunk, but also really good."

"Here, rest your leg," said Zuzu, shoving Lal in the direction of a bench. "Sit here!"

"No, sit on this chair!" Jovi insisted, pulling in a kitchen chair. "It's much more comfortable."

"Thank you for all your kind attentions, ladies," said Lal, who looked exhausted, but still somehow turned on his hundred-watt smile for my friends as they pushed and prodded at him.

"So there's a lot I have to tell you all," I said, hoping it would stop Jovi and Zuzu from making fools of themselves. Quickly I explained how the Raja had disappeared and Neel had been crowned (Lal gasped), how I suspected Sesha was at the bottom of smushing various story lines together (Zuzu and Jovi gasped), and how Stheno and Nidhoggr had therefore escaped from their Greek and Norse stories and appeared in New Jersey (everyone gasped, which made Loki howl). The one thing I didn't go into, though, was how I was worried that the wormhole might have landed me in the wrong membrane dimension. I didn't think I could bring myself to explain how my parents were acting, or how, in my real version of reality, Jovi and I were enemies, and Zuzu and I friends.

Lal looked thoughtful as he petted Loki's head and nose. "Then the first thing we must do, Just Kiran, is to get back home to the Kingdom Beyond. But how? Are there any automated wormhole makers here in New Jersey?"

"Automated wormhole makers?" echoed Zuzu in a goofy voice, still acting like her eyeballs had been replaced by hearts.

"Just Kiran?" asked Jovi, a little less goofily, grinning in my direction.

"It's a long story," I mumbled. "But I think I have an idea of who can help get us back to the Kingdom Beyond."

"Who?" the girls and Lal asked, almost all in unison.

"The smartest scientist in this dimension, of course," I said. "We've got to get to Shady Sadie's atom-smashing lab. From all the stuff she was saying at the assembly today, about black holes, chaos, the light and dark—I think she was trying to send me a message."

"Oh, come on," started Zuzu. She was still petting Lal's coat sleeve and I wondered if she just didn't want me to take him away.

"No, really," I said. "Unless you have any better ideas, I think it's our best chance."

"Then let us go! We must not waste any time!" Lal was starting to sound a bit more like himself. Jovi had also heated up a plate of nachos and he was digging in, so that might have had something to do with it. He crunched loudly, mumbling through a cheesy mouth, "I must get back to the Kingdom Beyond! My people need me! Also, what kind of salsa is this? It is very delicious!"

"Jovi, you said her atom-smashing lab was somewhere here in town. That picture Shady Sadie showed us in school looked like a building right near my parents' store." I stole a nacho from Lal, earning a dirty look from both my friends.

Jovi furrowed her blond eyebrows. "You mean your parents' old store, before they sold it."

"Right." Yet another thing that was wacko about this dimension. I scratched Loki's ears while the big dog licked my elbow. "So how are we going to get all the way out to Route 46 from here?" I asked, turning my mind to practical problems. "It's too far to walk. At least in this cold. Especially with Lal's twisted ankle."

"Either of you know how to drive?" Zuzu had the door open to Jovi's garage and was staring at her parents' extra car.

I thought about my experience driving the auto rikshaw. And then the fact that I'd crashed and totaled it. "Nidhoggr almost just killed us all. I'd rather not finish the job for him."

"Never fret, I have the solution." Jovi was pointing at something in the garage. "How about some nonautomated wheels?"

I looked to see that Jovi was pointing to two incredibly small dirt bikes, obviously the property of her little stepbrothers.

"There aren't enough for all of us!" I eyed the tiny dirt bikes with the huge thick rims. "And those seats are so small, there's no way we can ride double!"

"Well, don't you have a bike too at your house next door?" Jovi asked. "I trashed mine last year and never got a new one, but you've got to still have yours in your shed, right? The one with the big banana seat? That should be big enough to take Lal on too, right?"

"Prince Lal can't ride alone with his twisted ankle!" Zuzu said, adding hopefully, "Maybe I could take him on your bike!"

"No, I'd be happy to!" volunteered Jovi.

In the end, I rode my own bike, the embarrassingly pink and sparkly Princess Pretty Pants™ one with the crown streamers on the handlebars and the unicorn flippety-floppety inserts on the wheels. It was a little awkward, since the bike was so small, and Lal's weight on the back of the banana seat didn't make it very easy to pedal. Still, within a few minutes, we were biking away through our neighborhood, everybody's knees practically up around our armpits. It had taken a minute to convince Loki to stay at home instead of coming with us, but we'd finally managed.

We were off! I'd grabbed an old jacket from my house, since I'd left my own winter coat at school. It was a little bit

small on my arms, but it was better than wearing Ned-slash-Nidhoggr's ski jacket. (I didn't want his dragon cooties!) I was actually feeling kind of like a kid again, the wind whipping by my face, the handlebar streamers flying. I even cring-cringed my rusty Princess Pretty Pants™ bell for good measure.

Jovi and even Zuzu were doing little tricks on and off the curb on their bikes, but it was a lot of effort for me to just keep my little pink bicycle steady and straight down the road. Lal was holding on to my waist and giving me incredibly unhelpful suggestions.

"Watch that ice patch, Just Kiran!" he yelped. "Slow

down! Not so sideways, my lady! Not so straight! Ring your bell! Perchance might you have any snacks in that basket?"

"Stop holding on so tight, Lal!" I griped. "I can barely breathe!"

"I have snacks!" Zuzu enthused, tossing Lal a granola bar from her pocket. She was standing up to pedal and looked like she was having a ball.

"Good thing we decided to come with you two!" said Jovi, maneuvering her bike on the other side of me and tossing Lal some gummy bears.

Embarrassingly, Lal lapped up all the attention even as he ate up all the snacks.

We were at the top of a big hill, and before I had time to think about it, my friends were convincing me to stop pedaling and see who could coast down the hill fastest. "Princess Just Kiran, be careful!" Lal yelled as we careened down the icy road. He scattered a bunch of gummy bears into the air in his agitation.

I was reminded of zipping along on a skateboard behind an auto rikshaw with the Pink-Sari Skateboarders what felt like ages ago. Even though I was nervous at first, soon I was whooping and hollering along with Zuzu and Jovi. Even Lal seemed to get over his fear.

"All for one and one for all!" the girls cheered as they

started pedaling again at the bottom of the hill. For good measure, they even waved their fencing foils around in the air.

I thought about how much that musketeer rallying cry was like Nidhoggr and Sesha's favorite: *The all is one.* Both sayings were talking about how people were connected, but our phrase, as opposed to Sesha's, didn't necessarily mean that we had to all be exactly the same to be on the same side.

Lal cheered. "I like your friends, Just Kiran!"

I laughed. "I'm fairly sure they like you too!"

Unfortunately, we were all so giddy from the rush of our adventure that no one really considered the route we were taking from our neighborhood to Smarty-Pants Science Corporation. The way we were going would not only take us in front of my parents' old convenience store, but around the back of Zuzu's family's Greek diner. We were already biking through the adjoining parking lot, the one that goes between the pet grooming place and the Bennigan's Coat Factory, when the fiercest employee of Mount Olympus Diner spotted us: Zuzu's grandmother.

Zuzu's yiayia was well into her eighties, but she still worked every day at the family's restaurant, making the world's best spanakopita and baklava, chatting up customers, and basically keeping Zuzu's entire family on their toes. And our bad luck, she swung open the back door to the diner just as we were skating by.

"Oh no!" breathed Zuzu, but it was too late to turn around.

Yiayia stood there in her head scarf, apron, and ortho-pedic shoes, a bag of garbage in her hand. She squinted at us for a second, as if she couldn't believe what she was seeing, and then, in a move worthy of any intergalactic superhero, she threw the garbage bag. The smelly plastic sack hit Zuzu in the legs and knocked her off her bike.

"What kind of babushka'd monster is this?" Lal thun-dered, taking out his sword and brandishing it around.

"That's not a monster—that's Zuzu's grandma!" I warned, and my friend put his sword away quickly.

In the time it took Zuzu to pick herself and her bike up off the icy ground, Yiayia got to us. You wouldn't think that someone so old and stout could run so fast, but Yiayia was a marvel. Even more remarkable was when she started yell-ing. The parking lot was crowded with the lunch rush, but Yiayia didn't care. With speed I wouldn't have expected from such an old lady, she caught Jovi by the arm, forcing her off her bike. Then, with her other hand, she caught Zuzu by the ear, twisting hard.

"Ow, Yiayia, stop! Please!" Zuzu begged.

"Kakó korítsi!" yelled her grandmother.

"Madam, please, let go these nice ladies' ears!" Lal was sputtering. We were the only ones still on our bike.

I didn't understand half of the Greek scolding Yiayia was giving us, but I certainly understood the word *school*, which seemed to be coming up a lot. I also understood the words *Mama* and *Papa*, and understood from Zuzu's reaction that Yiayia was about to drag her by the ear to her parents. Never mind our principal had turned out to be a Greek Gorgon and Nidhoggr the Norse dragon snake had not only been masquerading as a Parsippany middle schooler but had also tried to kill us; we were all about to be in some serious trouble with Yiayia.

"Kiran, Lal, get out of here while you can!" Jovi hissed, and I knew she was right. Zuzu's grandma only had two arms, and while she was including me and Lal just as ferociously as the other two girls in her half-Greek–half-English chewing-out, she didn't have a physical hold on us. I didn't want to abandon my friends, but I couldn't think what else to do.

"Go, Kiran!" Zuzu urged as Yiayia started to drag both girls toward the door.

"O-hee! Kiran!" Yiayia exclaimed as she saw what I was about to do. "Who that boy?"

"Thank you! I love you guys!" I yelled as I pushed off with my ruby-red boot, banking a hard right by the parking lot curb to get away from Yiayia's grasping arm. I pedaled as hard and fast as I could. "Sorry, Yiayia, but there's a good explanation for us being out of school! I promise!"

I'm not sure if she understood me, but the old grandma lunged, like she wanted to chase me through the icy lot. I watched helplessly as her orthopedic shoes gave out from under her, and she slipped. Luckily, Zuzu and Jovi caught her under her arms before she fell flat on her face.

"Go stop that snake dude!" Zuzu called as she supported Yiayia, who had begun her multilingual yelling yet again.

"Bye, Lal, come back and see us soon!" added Jovi, almost off-balance from supporting Yiayia's considerable weight and size.

"Skipping school no good!" shouted Yiayia in my direction. "Kiran, you are a good girl!"

I had no choice. I felt like a total rat, but I zoomed Lal away on my bike before Yiayia somehow grew another two arms to haul us inside.

"Hang on!" I yelled as I flew down the service road behind Route 46, leaving my friends behind me.

CHAPTER 19

Science, Sports, and Wedding Cards

A few minutes later, we had made it safely to Smarty-Pants Science Corporation. We got off my ridiculous bike and pushed open the front door. There was no receptionist in the outer offices. Instead, there was a dusty black desk with the company's logo (a massive exploding supernova), a few totally mismatched office-type chairs, a chipped foosball table, and a miniature Ping-Pong table that looked like it had seen a lot of heated games.

"I guess space scientists like to blow off steam by playing office sports." I touched a basketball hoop hanging crookedly from one nail.

Lal nodded. "Apparently so, Just Kiran. Although I am more of a cricket fan myself."

After waiting a few seconds for anyone to show up, Lal

hobbled over to the desk and called out a tentative "Hello?" Then we heard it. The telltale *dum-dum-DA-dum* noise of people playing table tennis nearby. There must be another table somewhere. From the speed they were playing, it sounded like some scientists had a seriously vicious tournament going.

Following the sound, I pushed open the first set of big double doors to our right. The inner office was decorated in the same style as the outer one, with another, much bigger Ping-Pong table, an air hockey table, a water cooler, and a sofa so comfy and worn I was sure it was meant for napping in between sports matches. When I realized who it was involved in the high-intensity table tennis game, I almost fainted from surprise.

"Bunty? Tuni?" I gasped at the sight of my tiger friend with a table tennis racket in their giant teeth and Tuntuni the tiny yellow bird on the opposite side of the table with one in his beak. But what really shocked me was who their doubles partners were.

Playing alongside Tuni was Shady Sadie herself, her bow tie askew, her glasses slipping down from her nose with sweat. She stuck her tongue out and grunted every time she hit the ball, like the famous tennis players do. On the opposite side of the table was Professor Khogen Prasad Das, the elderly author of the Kingdom Beyond textbook *The Adventurer's Guide to Rakkhosh, Khokkosh, Bhoot, Petni, Doito, Danav, Daini, and Secret Codes.* He had his dhoti gathered up in one hand and was darting this way and that as he played, diving, jumping, and practically sailing for the ball. He sliced a killer ace, making Sadie slam down her paddle in frustration when she couldn't return the shot.

"Getting soft from all that scientific grant money, Professor!" K. P. Das taunted, his eyes huge behind his dirty Coke-bottle glasses.

"Lucky shot! Just like your gold medal from the Royal Demonological Institute!" griped Shady Sadie before launching into a wild volley again.

"K. P. Babu and Shady Sadie know each other?" I breathed.

"I suppose knowledge belongs to all," Lal said. "And scientific progress knows no borders."

While they might be good at sharing their knowledge, when it came to their Ping-Pong, both scientists were super greedy. In fact, they were ball hogs, jumping for shots that were clearly meant for their doubles partners. But because of this, my bird and tiger friends actually noticed when we walked in.

"Princess!" roared Bunty.

"Prince Lalkamal!" squawked Tuni. "I know someone who's going to be very happy to see you!"

"Who?" I looked confusedly around.

When the huge tiger moved aside, I realized who else was in the room. He'd been pacing around behind the Ping-Pong table, biting his nails. He stopped pacing as he saw us, a stunned expression on his usually confident face. Wow, it was good to see that face again.

"Brother!" Lal launched himself at Neel, almost like he was still a little kid.

"Kiran, you did it!" Neel was hugging his brother, but his smiles were just for me. "You found him! You saved my little bro!"

"Did you doubt I could?" I scoffed. I was so excited to see Neel that the words came out way harsher than I intended. I tried to soften my tone. "How long have you been here?"

"I just got here with K. P. Babu," said Neel. "I wanted to go out and look for you right away, but the professor wanted a quick game of table tennis first."

Wait, what? "So . . . you decided just to hang out here and let him play instead of looking for me while I was, oh, I don't know, fighting for my life?"

Neel looked surprised and guilty. "Sadie said she had

seen you in your school, and that there had been some kind of a fire drill, and that you were probably still there."

"It wasn't just a fire drill. And I seriously could have dealt with some help, you know. I was only battling mythological creatures from multiple different cultures!" When Neel blanched, I sighed. "But hey, at least I was able to rescue Lal."

Neel turned to his younger brother with a protective glance. "Are you all right? Dude, look at the size of your ankle!" Then he turned back to me. "I'm really, really sorry, Kiran, that I wasn't there to help you."

"Sure, whatever. I guess it all worked out in the end." I had to raise my voice a little to make myself heard over the endless *dum-dum-DA-dum* of the table tennis game, which was still going on. "But, Neel, what are you doing in this dimension in the first place? Did you get my lizard-gram?"

Neel waved for the scientists to stop playing so that he could respond, but they had such an intense volley going that they still didn't notice us.

"Take a break, scientists!" Tuni yelled. When neither Sadie nor Professor Das stopped their playing, the bird jumped up and caught the next shot in his mouth. Both players looked at Tuntuni in surprise.

"That is against intergalactic table tennis regulations!" sputtered K. P. Das. "No player on either doubles team may

eat the Ping-Pong ball while in play! Your team forfeits the point! It's my game, set, and match!"

"Wait a minute, don't be such a stickler!" protested Sadie, who seemed very upset at the possibility of losing. "Those regulations are only applicable on Sundays during an intergalactic apocalypse!"

"We very well might be in the middle of an intergalactic apocalypse!" said K. P. Babu triumphantly.

"Ha ha, the joke's on you, then!" crowed Sadie. "Because it's *Monday*!"

I decided to ignore the bickering players and turned back to Neel, happy to be able to hear myself. "Seriously, what are you doing here?" Then I turned to Tuni. "And how did you and Bunty make it here? I thought for sure you were back on the other side of the wormhole and we'd lost you!"

Since Tuni couldn't exactly reply with a giant Ping-Pong ball in his beak, he shot it out at me with a *ptu* sound. I caught the little missive in midair.

"Say, Princess!" squawked my birdie friend. "Why was Cinderella kicked off the soccer team?"

"Tuni, seriously?" Neel was helping his limping brother into a chair, playfully messing with Lal's hair as he did. I felt bad for being so snippy before with Neel. He was obviously super happy to see his brother again. And I guess he couldn't have known I would be battling a Gorgon and a dragon right here in Parsippany.

"Who is this Cinderella?" Lal heavily sat down, wincing as Neel helped him prop up his injured foot.

"She's a 2-D-story princess," I explained. Then, to make up for my bad mood before, I guessed, "Um . . . Cinderella got kicked off the soccer team because her glass slippers weren't cleats?"

Tuntuni landed on my shoulder, squawking, "No! Because she kept running away from the ball!"

I laughed at the bird's silly joke, then realized Shady Sadie was waving her hands maniacally, gesturing for me to throw her the Ping-Pong ball. Ugh, I couldn't stand them starting up again.

"It's time for a Ping-Pong intervention!" said Bunty. I tossed the plastic ball at the tiger, who promptly crunched down on it and ate it in one gulp.

"Aw! That's not fair!" protested Shady Sadie.

When Bunty responded with a loud roar, both players looked a little sheepish. "Okay, maybe it's a little fair," amended the television scientist.

"I'll dock your grade for this, Prince Neel!" grumbled K. P. Das. "You too, Prince Lal! And no hope of extra credit!"

Lal looked a little worried, but Neel rolled his eyes. "We're not even in your class anymore, Professor. And we've got more important things to worry about right now. Could we stay on topic?"

Both scientists seemed to get their acts together at the scolding. "Sorry, perhaps we got a little carried away," said Shady Sadie.

"Ping-Pong always brings out the worst in the scientific community," agreed K. P. Babu.

Finally realizing who was in the room, Shady Sadie came over to me and started shaking my hand so hard I thought it would fall off. "I knew you'd make it, young scientist!" she said, her eyes dancing behind her glasses. "Your friends the tiger and tia bird were doubtful, but I told them to give you time, that you'd heard my message about the darkness and the light and you'd make your way here!"

So Shady Sadie *had* been looking at me during the end of the assembly! "You showed that slide of the Smarty-Pants Science Corporation building on purpose so I would know where it was!"

"That's why I set up that visit to your school in the first place," explained my scientist idol. "When your tiger and bird friends got dropped here by the wormhole and told me about you, I assumed your coordinates were somewhere close by and you would make it to your school somehow."

"But then Shady Sadie came back without you and we got worried." Bunty padded over to me and rubbed a big head against my side. "She wouldn't let us leave to go look for you either!"

"Said it would be hard to explain a talking bird and a giant tiger roaming around Parsippany," Tuni sniffed.

That was actually fair. It would be a problem to explain a talking tiger and bird wandering around Parsippany. Weirdly, I didn't feel as irritated at Tuni or Bunty for not coming to help me as I did at Neel.

"But then why did you and K. P. Babu come to New

Jersey, my brother?" Lal asked. "I heard you were canvassing the countryside, looking for support from our people. That you got crowned temporary Raja."

At Lal's words, Neel got a funny expression on his face. "Now that you're free, we'll make sure the crown goes to you as soon as we get home, okay?"

I was hoping Lal would say something wise and magnanimous, about how their father should never have stripped the crown prince title from Neel anyway, and how Neel should hang on to the crown, but instead, the younger prince just said, "Okay, sure." He was holding his lips a little funny, and I wondered if he was in pain or just upset that Neel had been made Raja instead of him.

I took a quick glance at Neel, wondering how he was taking his brother's reaction. Unfortunately, his face got all still, like he'd brought down a mask over it that refused to let through any emotion. "Cool, cool, cool," he said. "You'll make a great Raja, Lal. Plus, I can't wait to get rid of the responsibility."

"No surprise there," said Lal, more teasing than mean, but I could tell the words hit his brother like a slap. Neel winced a little and turned around, busily putting away all the paddles and balls.

As I was trying to figure out what to say to take down the tension in the room, Tuni squawked, "Hey, Princess, what did Delaware?"

"I don't know, Tuni, what did Delaware?" I asked, a little too loud and a little too happy. Neel gave me a look like he thought I'd lost it.

"A New Jersey!" Tuni bellowed, flying in a circle around Neel's head.

I guffawed way too loud at the dumb bird, not knowing what else to do to make Neel feel better. For his part, Neel rolled his eyes, but I did see a hint of a smile on his lips.

"So are you going to tell me why you're here or what?" I asked Neel. "Did Tiktiki One find you?"

"Yeah, the lizard passed on your message." The prince stopped putting away the Ping-Pong stuff and gave a grimace. "That's how I knew where you were. But I was already planning on coming because of the wedding invitation."

"Wedding invitation?" I was relieved to hear Tiktiki One was okay, but at Neel's mention of an invitation, I remembered Ned/Nidhoggr talking about someone getting married too. "What is this wedding I keep hearing about?"

"I knew I had to come find you as soon as I got it," Neel went on, chewing on his nail.

"What kind of a wedding invitation could send you all

the way across the dimensions to find me?" I looked from one face to another, but no one seemed to be willing to spit it out. The animals were suddenly eager to clean their whiskers and feathers, the scientists seemed busy staring at the ceiling and floor, and Lal looked just as clueless as I felt.

Without a word, Neel reached into a beat-up old leather shoulder bag and pulled out a bright red-and-gold wedding card. The outside of the folded card was decorated with the shapes of butterflies, fish, and peacocks—traditional wedding card fare. But there were also a number of twisting snakes weaving in and out of the other animals that gave me a little bit of a start. The address on the wedding invitation reminded me of a different letter in a different story.

HRH Raja Neelkamal (Substitute King
Though He Is)
Big Elephant's Back
Roaming the Countryside, Looking for Support
from His People
The Kingdom Beyond Seven Oceans and
Thirteen Rivers
Soon to Be Part of the Singular
Universe

When I opened the top and bottom folds of the card, I almost yelled at what I found inside. It was a beautifully decorated invitation, gold lettering on a red background:

The Late Shri Sapendronath Shapu and
the Late Smt. Snakeswari Devi
of
No Address Since We're Dead Lane
kindly request your august company at the
auspicious occasion of marriage of their
all-powerful and all-knowing son
Sesha
the Great and Beneficent, Soon to be Supreme
Ruler of the Singular Universe
with
Pinki
D/o the late Smt. Ai-Ma
Rakkhoshini, former Rani of the Kingdom Beyond
and ex-wife of the scaredy-cat runaway Raja
Fatteshwar Orebaba (Rontu)
on
this coming Saturday evening
at
the former palace of Raja Fatteshwar Orebaba

(across from post office, right at panwallah
and diagonal from cinema hall)
Dress code: Your fanciest of the fance
wedding clothes squared!
No rakkhosh except the bride. No
bride's family or friends either. No exceptions.
Precious gifts required.

It took me at least three times of reading the card to let all the information sink in. "My dad is marrying . . . Neel's *mom*?" I finally sputtered.

"It sure looks like it," squawked Tuni.

"How could this happen?" Lal was downright shocked. "Anyway, Just Kiran, isn't Sesha still married to your mother, the moon?"

"I think her turning him to ashes with her moonbeams counted as some sort of divorce. She mentioned they weren't married anymore." I spoke slowly, still processing the news. "The last time they were together, Sesha was trying to kill Neel's mom! How could they be getting married? Is this the rumor that Mati heard—about them allying with each other?"

Then something else occurred to me. "Wait a minute, if our parents are getting married, Neel, that's gonna make you my . . . !"

"Stepbrother," said Neel grimly.

At that, Tuni started singing the theme song from an old 2-D TV show about a blended family. Who knows where he learned it. "That's the way they all became the Snaky Bunch!" the bird warbled, adding, "You guys can fight about bathroom time and get into funny hijinks with the family dog!"

The thought made me want to puke. I spit out the word more than said it. "Gross!"

"Super gross!" Neel nodded.

Well, at least we finally agreed on something.

CHAPTER 20

Black Holes and Singularities

Not willing to think about Neel and me living as happy-go-lucky stepsiblings, I turned my attention back to the invitation. I shook the envelope and out fell two more cards. One card inside the envelope was labeled *Pre-Wedding Festivities*:

Monday-night engagement party (Dress code: black and white)
Tuesday-night gaye holud (Dress code: yellow—DUH)
Wednesday-night mehendi (Dress code: carnival—including giant stilts)
Thursday-night sangeet (Be prepared with a world-class musical number you will perform with

your nearest and dearest to honor the bride and
groom. If you're bad, you may be thrown in the
dungeons. Or killed. Or both.)

There was also a small RSVP card that read:

Value My Life, so Attending Wedding
Happily [ ]
Don't Care about My or My Family's Safety,
so Rudely Skipping Event of the Millennia [ ]

"How could this be for real?" I sputtered. Was this
another bizarro-parallel-dimension thing happening
again? But I couldn't imagine there being any dimension in
the multiverse where Sesha and Neel's mom actually loved
each other.

"They hate each other," Neel said, as if reading my mind.

"Maybe that hate has turned to true love!" chirped Tuni.
He'd gotten a flower garland from who knows where—the
kind that people exchange when they're getting married in
the Kingdom Beyond—and was humming a wedding song.
"Mala badal hobe ei raate!"

"Could such a wedding be real?" Lal looked confusedly
from me to Neel to Tuni.

"Of course it is!" Tuni declared. "You all are way too cynical! I blame it on your generation using too much social media."

"No such thing as true love," said Bunty. "Only heteronormative rituals created by a capitalist patriarchy to reinscribe its institutional power."

"Um, right," Lal agreed uncertainly. "What the tiger said."

"Whatever this is," I said slowly, "it can't just be them deciding to get married because they fell in love. There's clearly some evil plan going on here." I whirled around to face Neel. "I know! Your mom must be a part of this Anti-Chaos Committee!"

"What?" Neel looked startled. "I don't even know what that is."

"That whole being on our side and rescuing us stuff must have been an act before!" I sputtered. "Maybe she was faking wanting to save you so bad from demon detention. Maybe she and Sesha staged that whole fight in his undersea detention center . . ."

"Wait. Hold it right there, Kiran. You think it was an act that my mother was willing to give up her life—sacrifice her soul bee—to save mine? And that she staged the fight with Sesha, the fight where Ai-Ma, her own mother, died to save her?" Neel snapped. "No way. That's sick!"

"Well, I don't know. I don't know how supervillains think!" I protested. My brain was working hard trying to put all the pieces of the puzzle together. "It would be gullible of us to think Pinki's suddenly become all nice and heroic, wouldn't it? I mean, the Anti-Chaos Committee is all these baddies from all different cultures trying to collapse the diversity of the multiverse's stories. It would be just like her to be a part of that!"

"But I can't imagine my mom would be involved in something like that!" Neel countered.

"Brother, she did try to eat both me and Mati," Lal reminded him. "Only a few months ago."

"And she is kind of mean," Tuni added. "Plus cruel, sadistic . . ."

"Not to mention seriously bloodthirsty and power-hungry," I volunteered.

"Okay, great, thanks, everybody, for your input," Neel snapped. "Never mind I was just starting to think I could have some sort of relationship with my mom, what with Ai-Ma being gone and everything. Way to point out how that's never going to happen."

Lal, Tuni, and I exchanged guilty looks. I wasn't sure what to say to that. There were a few seconds of awkward silence before K. P. Babu came to our rescue.

"Yes, well, never mind all that now. Supposition will only get us so far. It's time to gather some more data and then send you all back home to do some hypothesis testing!" the elderly professor exclaimed.

"All right, gang, so let's go gather some data and test some hypotheses!" said Sadie, clearly all pumped up at the science talk. "Time to go to the atom smasher! Woot!"

From who knows where, she produced a wheelchair with a Smarty-Pants Science Corporation logo on the back. We helped the injured Lal into the chair, and Sadie took charge of pushing it out of the break room and down a long lab hallway.

As we all walked, K. P. Babu turned to Bunty and asked, "Now, tiger, tell me the secret to your killer serve. How do you get that topspin?"

Lal and Sadie were at the lead, while Bunty, K. P. Das, and Tuni were chatting in happy tones about table tennis. So that left Neel and me to walk quietly together at the end of the group.

He wasn't looking at me, and I felt a twinge of guilt at how upset he seemed. "Neel, I didn't want to hurt your feelings, really, but I can't think of another explanation as to why Pinki would want to marry Sesha."

"Feelings hurt? My feelings aren't hurt, what makes you

say that?" snapped Neel in a way that kind of proved the opposite point. "No, Kiran, you're right, as usual. Once a villain, always a villain. My mom's obviously marrying Sesha to be a part of his latest dastardly plan. I'm probably just not thinking straight. Being in that detention center obviously messed me up bad. Gosh, I can't even trust my own judgment anymore."

"Hey, I didn't mean any of that," I protested.

"No, seriously. I'm so, so glad you're here to set me right," Neel said, still refusing to look at me.

"It's just a theory," I said, trying to be nice. "Like K. P. Babu said, we should gather some more facts or whatever before we assume our theory's right."

"Your theory," Neel muttered. "Not mine."

Ugh. How could he be so gullible? I crossed my arms over my chest. "I wonder where my invitation went? There's a strict 'no rakkhosh' policy on the invite, but they still sent you a card."

Neel snorted. "Are you seriously upset that your killer of a serpent dad didn't invite you to his wedding?"

"No, I just—well, maybe," I said, feeling unnecessarily flustered. "I don't know. I hate him, but he's also my bio dad. And also, well, I hate him."

"Yeah, I know how that one goes." Neel looked down at his feet. "It's hard to figure out how I feel about my mom too. Obviously."

I didn't have a chance to respond, because just then Sadie pushed open the steel double doors to the atom-smasher laboratory.

"Whoa!" I glanced at Neel, who just shrugged and moved away.

But Bunty the tiger heard my words. "Impressive, is it not? I felt the same way when I first got here."

I felt torn, like I should go after Neel and make up with him, but I also didn't want to make a scene in front of the others. So I just ignored the grumpy prince and looked around the room some more. Impressive was an understatement. The room was dark and cool, with ceilings so high I wasn't even sure how far up they were. There were pipes and tubes—blue, silver, red—running in twisting patterns over the wall, all toward a big mechanical eye at the far end of the room.

"That's the atom smasher." Sadie pointed at the eye thing. "Where my colleagues and I try to re-create the conditions of the big bang. Conveniently, it can also double as an interdimensional wormhole maker."

The atom smasher had a bright blue sphere at the center

of a bunch of complicated gears and clock innards that moved constantly around it. Interlocking, shifting, opening, refitting together, the movement of the gears was absolutely mesmerizing. And just to the side of the giant eye-clock thing was a very welcome old friend.

"Raat!" I cried, running over to the winged horse and putting my arms around his neck. He was Neel's horse but had served me well on my last adventure, when I was shutting down Sesha's evil game show, *Who Wants to Be a Demon Slayer?*

Princess! the midnight-black horse said into my mind. *I brought my boy to you across the dimensions.*

"Yes, I know you did, my wonderful friend," I murmured, sneaking a look over at Neel. The prince was standing alone, looking into space, chewing on a nail. I felt a confusing flood of emotions rush through me at how sad Neel was looking. My face felt so hot, I pressed my nose into Raat's velvety temple. His wings expanded and contracted in pleasure.

And then I heard the familiar, accented voice right above our heads. "Ev-ry-sing is connected to ev-ry-sing."

"But how?" I responded. Raat whinnied, looking up too. We were staring into the face of the scientist I'd met on my first trip to the Kingdom Beyond. He was floating in midair, legs folded, like he was meditating. Just like he'd been the first time I'd seen him.

"Smartie-ji!" chirped Tuni, flying up to give the floating scientist an affectionate peck on the cheek. "How's it hangin'?"

That's right, it was Albert Einstein, one of the world's most famous scientists, hanging out in this atom-smashing lab in Parsippany, New Jersey. Never mind he was defying gravity. Also never mind he was actually dead.

"How are you, Einstein-ji?" I said respectfully, putting my hands together in a namaskar. "Can I introduce you . . ."

"No need, no need!" said Albert Einstein in his distinctive accent. "I've spent a most pleasant day being taught ze rules of foosball by your tiger and bird friends here. And of course I know ze Princes Lalkamal and Neelkamal."

Lal waved happily at the scientist, but Neel just gave a little head nod.

The scientist went on, "Ze good pakkhiraj horse and I just had to take a small break from the fray when, ahem, some people started to get rather competitive with ze table tennis!"

Competition stresses me out, Raat admitted into my mind.

Shady Sadie and K. P. Das looked guiltily at the floor,

but they didn't say anything. Everyone seemed a little bit in awe of the famous scientist. Maybe it was the fact that he'd discovered important scientific formulas like $E = mc^2$ or maybe it was just that he was the only one among us who wasn't supposed to be alive.

The other strange thing about Einstein-ji (well, other than him just being there) was how he was dressed. The last time we'd seen him, he'd been wearing a turban, kurta, and pajamas. Now he was in gray robes and a floppy gray wizard's hat, and carrying a wand that he kept twirling and tossing in the air like some kind of overage marching band baton twirler. His outfit reminded me too much of a certain wizarding headmaster from another famous story, but I decided to keep quiet about the scientist's fashion choices.

"How are the star babies, Smartie-ji?" Neel asked. He was referring to the fact that the last time we'd seen him, Einstein-ji was teaching star nursery school in an outer space nebula known in the other dimension as Maya Pahar. "I didn't ask you before, but did you retire from teaching?"

"Oh, I'm just here temporarily, so I got a substitute!" Albert Einstein flipped, so his folded legs were up and his head was down. Despite this feat of gravity, his wizard's hat stayed on his head. "Dr. Hawking is very popular with ze star babies! He is most excellent at remembering ze nursery rhymes and playing ring around ze rosie."

"Dr. Hawking?" I asked. "Like Dr. Stephen Hawking?"

"Ze one and ze same!" said Einstein-ji, pointing at me with his wand.

Okay. Why not. Stephen Hawking, the world-famous scientist who had recently passed away (at least in this dimension!), was now teaching star babies in an outer space star nursery in Maya Pahar.

I squinted at the floating scientist-slash-wizard. "No offense, Your Smartness, but how are you here? I know you can exist in Maya Pahar because of, um, something to do with the fabric of space-time . . ." My voice trailed off.

"Oh, pfft! Death! Just transfer of matter from one plane of existence to another, you know!" Einstein flipped back around in midair.

"He shouldn't be able to be here, actually, and certainly not in that outfit," said Shady Sadie as she typed something into a computer keyboard. "But because of the work of the Anti-Chaos Committee, many interdimensional and intercultural stories are slipping into one another. The boundaries between stories, but also dimensions, seems to be weakening. It's probably how all of you ended up in this slightly wrong version of New Jersey."

"You know about that?" I breathed. "My parents, and Jovi and Zuzu . . ."

Neel shot me a confused look. I raised my eyebrows and shrugged back at him. He might be mad at me for thinking his mom was a villain, but I still had totally good reasons to be mad at him too. I'd been all alone, dealing with this bizarre version of New Jersey, while he was—what? Planning how to have a fuzzy and warm new relationship with his monstrous mama?

"Science and stories are not so different, my young friends," said K. P. Babu. "They both ask the big questions of life and both seek answers to make sense of the mysterious world around us."

"But now Sesha and his Anti-Chaos Committee are trying to simplify those answers!" Einstein-ji added. His accent made it so that he pronounced "chaos" like "kah-os."

"But I thought you and Dr. Hawking didn't believe the universe needed chaos, Professor Einstein!" I said, remembering back to what Ned-slash-Nidhoggr had been arguing about the need for a universal theory, one singular story. "I thought you were both looking for a theory of everything!"

"Yes, that is true," Einstein-ji agreed, giving his wand a toss before impressively catching it with one foot. "But we never found such a theory, did we? It was in the very search that our knowledge grew."

"What do you mean?" I looked from one scientist to the next, and then back to my friends. The animals, Lal, and Neel all just shrugged.

"Let us go back to ze beginning, Prinzess," said Einstein-ji, waving his hand vaguely at Sadie. She typed some more stuff into the keyboard, pulling up an image of a black funnel-type thing—kind of like the drawing of the Victrola in the three-doored room. "Do you know what a singularity is?"

I wrinkled my brow. "No?"

Bunty cleared their throat. "Do you mean, the idea of a superhuman artificial intelligence that will outstrip human intellect?"

"Show-off," muttered Tuntuni, and Neel gave the bird a glare.

"No, tiger-ji, not that sort of singularity," said K. P. Babu patiently. "Dr. Einstein means in the context of space science."

"Well, then, no, I don't know," admitted Bunty with an embarrassed cough.

Everybody else, for their parts, looked just as clueless as I felt.

"A singularity is a one-dimensional point from where the entire multiverse was born. Think about a huge amount of mass being mashed into an infinitely small space." K. P. Babu took a piece of paper and crumpled it tightly in his hand, holding out the small ball he had made when done.

"Kind of like what almost happened to us at the bottom of that squishifying rabbit hole," muttered Tuni. I shuddered at the memory.

Einstein-ji twirled his wand in one hand as he continued, "A singularity is something scientists haven't been able to see, but think exists in ze middle of black holes—what you know as rakkhosh in the Kingdom Beyond. It's ze point from where ze big bang happened."

"So, something inside a rakkhosh is why the entire multiverse was started? Sir, can you possibly be saying that rakkhosh are responsible for the birth of everything we know?" Lal gave his brother an amazed look, which Neel returned with a raise of one eyebrow.

"You all got a problem with that too?" snapped Neel.

Lal looked incredulous, but I remembered back to when Neel's mom had once opened her mouth and I'd been sure I'd seen planets, stars, moons—entire galaxies—in there.

"It's a theory, of course, but with good evidence to support it," said Shady Sadie. "We think of a black hole as only destructive, something that gobbles up energy and life, but that's a simplistic idea, just a singular story about rakkhosh."

Neel gave me a pointed look. I scowled. It was not simplistic to think that his mother was mostly evil and destructive. No matter what these scientists said.

"Despite my efforts to find the beautiful simplicity of the multiverse," Einstein-ji went on, "ze truth is, there is also beauty in its complexity and ambiguity. As much as we work to understand it, there are parts of the truth that always slip through our fingers, lie always beyond our understanding." He flipped this way and that in the air as he spoke, now up, now down, dancing to an invisible cosmic music in the flickering light of the lab's giant atom smasher.

"And this is what the Anti-Chaos Committee is trying to destroy?" I asked.

"The multiverse may have started from a singularity, but it started expanding outward and outward immediately after the big bang. It's still expanding—think of all the different, diverse stories being born every day. Well, that is, unless . . ." K. P. Babu's words drifted off.

"Unless someone puts a stop to it. Unless someone stops

the chaos and kills the diversity of the multiverse," Neel finished.

"And causes it to begin shrinking," said Einstein-ji. "As there was once a big bang, there might indeed be a big crunch."

"But what does all this have to do with the Serpent King and Rakkhoshi Rani getting married?" asked Lal.

"Love, exciting and new . . ." crooned Tuni. This time, Neel took a swat at him but missed when the bird flew up and out of the way.

"We fear Sesha's efforts to destroy and demoralize Demon Land by rounding up rakkhosh, khokkosh, doito, and danav recently were just the tip of the iceberg. It is through the power of rakkhosh that the multiverse was born, and it is by destroying rakkhosh-kind that the multiverse can die. Or at least, collapse from its wondrous complexity into one reality, one single story," K. P. Das said.

Sadie went on, "Sesha realized that killing or imprisoning rakkhosh from all the different clans one at a time was not enough of an energetic shift to begin the universe shrinking. To jump-start the big crunch, Sesha must control the Rakkhoshi Rani's power, the power that stems from being the elected leader of all the rakkhosh from all the different clans."

"I'm getting married in the mo-orning," sang Tuni tunelessly.

"Zip it, Tuni," I muttered, looking from one serious scientific face to the next.

"Mawage!" chirped Tuni. "That bwessed awangement! That dweam within a dweam!"

"Tuni!" I snapped, while almost at the same time, Bunty growled, "Desist, birdbrain!"

"So Sesha is marrying my mother because he's trying to steal her power—the power of all rakkhosh-kind!" Neel gave me a triumphant look. "It's what he tried to do before with those neutron stars. So she must be his prisoner. I was right—she's not agreeing to this marriage voluntarily!"

"Perhaps," said Einstein. "But perhaps she has an agenda of her own."

I raised my eyebrows, giving Neel an "I told you so" look. "Yeah, like maybe she *wants* the Anti-Chaos Committee to use her power so she and Sesha can, like, rule the singular universe together or whatever."

Neel gave me a murderous look.

I let out a frustrated breath, but before I could say anything, Einstein beckoned us both over to him. "Come here, my young friends," he said gently.

As we approached him, he handed me a little book—a

hardback volume bound in fading silver with vague images
of rakkhosh, khokkosh, pakkhiraj horses, and even a tiger
on the outside. I read the title carved into the spine.

"*Thakurmar Jhuli.*" I sounded the Bengali lettering out
slowly—then looked up at the scientist. "This is the book of
Kingdom Beyond stories my baba always read to me." I
flipped through the familiar pages, the illustrations of
various stories about ghosts and demons, clever owls and
silly monkeys, brave princes and princesses, all from the
Kingdom Beyond.

"My mom used to read it to me too," said Neel in a low
voice. I shot him a surprised look. I'd never figured Pinki
did ordinary mom things like tell Neel stories. "She was a
great storyteller," added Neel defensively. "She'd do all the
voices and everything."

Einstein-ji tapped his finger on the side of his nose mysteriously. "You asked me how I can be alive and also not
alive. Here and also not here. It is because I, like these stories, operate outside of *time*." He emphasized the last word
kind of unnecessarily.

"What do you mean, Smartie-ji?" Neel asked.

"My children," said the old scientist, "keep zis volume
close to you, and if ever you have need to go backward into a
story, back in time, even, just open the pages and dive right in."

Neel and I exchanged troubled glances. "Back in time?" I repeated.

"Just so! Just so!" Einstein burbled, flipping again through the air. "Wormhole travel is not bad, but story travel is the best kind of travel of all! Beyond the reaches of linear space and time! Stories are the most powerful way to journey in the multiverse!"

Neel raised his eyebrow at me, like he wasn't sure the old scientist was all there in the head anymore. I mouthed, "Cut it out," before finally turning my face up toward Einstein-ji again.

"Um, okay, we'll do that," I said, tucking the book into my backpack. "Thanks, Professor Einstein."

"Perhaps you might even go back in time to settle your little quarrel about why your parents are getting married," said the scientist mysteriously.

"You should all get ready! The wormhole will be operational momentarily!" It was Sadie, who was punching something into her keyboard. I realized that while Neel and I had been talking to Einstein-ji, the atom smasher at the end of the room had started spinning the opposite way, gears and locks whirring around it.

"No one has told us, though, how we're going to stop this wedding?" Neel asked. "Whether my mom's Sesha's prisoner"—he raised an eyebrow in my direction—"or something else, we can't let the wedding continue, can we?"

"Oh no, absolutely not!" burbled K. P. Das. "The wedding must be stopped! The big crunch must be avoided at all costs!"

"We have been discussing it, and we think the first thing to do is enlist an army to infiltrate the wedding party and slow down the wedding festivities!" Shady Sadie was shouting to be heard over the whirling wormhole maker.

"No offense, Your Smartnesses, but you put the greatest scientific minds of the multiverse together and that's what you came up with?" Tuni twittered. "An army of wedding crashers?"

"Just so," agreed K. P. Babu. He was holding tight on to his dhoti to stop it from lifting off in the wind being generated by the spinning wormhole. Or pre-wormhole. Or whatever that thing was at the end of the room. "Already your friend Mati and the PSS are gathering their forces. You must help everyone get primped and dressed appropriately to blend into the crowd!"

"And if that doesn't work," shouted Shady Sadie, "use the butterflies!"

"What?" The wind was battering against my face so hard it felt like there was a storm brewing inside the room.

"Butterfly effect!" Einstein-ji was talking, but I could barely make out his words, everything was so loud now.

"The butterfly effect?" Neel echoed. He helped his brother onto Raat's back and climbed on after. Raat stepped this way and that, trying to stay upright in the face of all the wind.

As Tuni jumped on my shoulder, Bunty crouched down in front of me. "Your carriage, my princess!" the tiger purred. I got gratefully on, holding tight to Bunty's thick neck fur.

Then Bunty roared to the scientists, "Isn't the butterfly effect the idea that a butterfly flapping its wings in Maya Pahar can cause a tornado in the Kingdom Beyond?"

At the end of the room, the wormhole was spinning faster now, shooting off light around the room.

"Something like that," shouted Shady Sadie. "It's the idea that no matter how accurate or advanced our science is at predicting weather, say, there's always something beyond our understanding. That's the beauty of the universe. That's the butterfly effect."

"No matter how sure you are, things change!" K. P. Das clapped his hands as Bunty reared back, getting ready to leap at the whirring wormhole. "A butterfly might move a wing across the world and change your entire reality."

I had no idea how the butterfly effect was going to help us stop this wedding, but it was too loud to ask. The noise of the whirling wormhole was so tremendous I couldn't hear myself think, and the shooting lights flying out of it hurt my brain. Then Sadie pushed a button on her control panel, and the vortex of the wormhole cranked open like a mechanical eye. The room shook like a spaceship taking off.

"Now off with you!" said Einstein-ji. Or at least, I think that's what he said. The force of the wind coming off the mechanical wormhole had blown away his words, even as it blew off his hat, making his crazy gray hair fly this way and that. He made a gesture with his hands like a book opening and pointed to my backpack, where I'd stored the copy of *Thakurmar Jhuli*. The last words I heard him say before we leaped into the wormhole were "Trust in the power of stories!"

CHAPTER 21

The Return of the (Other) King

The Smarty-Pants Science Corporation atom-smasher-slash-wormhole obviously had super-powerful GPS. Not only did it get us all intact to the Kingdom Beyond, but it deposited us exactly where we wanted to be—at the entrance to the cave complex that was the PSS resistance headquarters. We were greeted there by a very angry Sir Gobbet, followed by a sheepish-looking Buddhu and Bhootoom. Buddhu, I was surprised to see, was wearing Neel's paper crown on his furry monkey head.

"You came to find me and left Buddhu in charge?" I whispered to Neel as I got off Bunty's back. I mean, what was Neel thinking? The monkey prince could hardly be trusted to be in charge of his own hygiene.

"Not just him," Neel argued as he petted Raat's nose. He sounded a little defensive. "Bhootoom too."

I rolled my eyes. The owl prince Bhootoom was even worse than Buddhu. He hardly talked, ate rodents, and could only fly backward. They were not exactly a crack team.

Apparently Sir Gobbet agreed, because within minutes of us coming through the wormhole, and Neel helping a limping Lal off of the pakkhiraj horse's back, the minister ripped the paper crown off the monkey prince's head and slammed it down on Lal's perfect curls.

"There, we have a new Raja now!" announced the man unceremoniously.

"I graciously accept the honor," said Lal.

Neel gently helped his brother sit down on a rock. "Better you than me, Bro," he said, but his words were the opposite of the hurt expression on his face. I looked away, not wanting to see how upset Neel looked. I knew I was responsible for a lot of it, but I didn't know how to undo what I'd done.

"Where are Mati and Naya?" I asked the monkey prince.

"Arré, top sekrit PSS meeting, yaar," drawled Buddhu in his characteristic laid-back tone. "Beyond my pay grade, you know. Nice to see you, brother Lalkamal. Glad to see that little vacation in the tree trunk didn't hurt you any, yaar!" Lal acknowledged Buddhu's comment with a smiling nod.

"Thank goodness you are here, Raja Lalkamal!" Sir Gobbet sputtered. "And you too, Prince Neelkamal. You won't believe what's it's been like since you've been gone."

"I've been gone for a day." Neel frowned. "What could have happened?"

"What could have happened, you asked? Oh, your princely brothers just hacked into the Thirteen Rivers satellite, interrupted the kingdom's favorite soap opera, and started telling those terrible jokes on live national television!" Sir Gobbet wailed. "Just in the course of a day, they have lost the support of half the kingdom and turned the other half of the kingdom more in support of Sesha!"

"Arré, yaar, am I to be blamed if the people here aren't sophisticated enough to appreciate my banana jokes?" Buddhu said while scratching an armpit.

I petted the monkey's furry shoulder. "Not many people are."

"And what about the leaving of banana peels all over the capital city?" Sir Gobbet demanded.

"You didn't!" I tried to keep myself from laughing. "Buddhu, no!"

"No one has any appreciation for physical comedy these

days, yaar!" He wiped his fat tears with his tail. "Arré, there's a real elegance in a classic pratfall!"

Obviously angry, Bhootoom hopped off his monkey brother's shoulder to peck at Sir Gobbet's turnip-shaped turban. Then, unbeknownst to the little minister, the little white owl spit out a giant regurgitated pellet of food on the man's head. The rest of us looked the other way, hoping Sir Gobbet wouldn't notice.

This seemed to make Buddhu feel better, because the next thing he did was jump onto Bunty's back. He screeched a little, chattered his teeth. "Hey, tiger, what kind of key opens a banana?"

"A turnkey, a latchkey, an academic index—that's a sort of a key, you know!" said Bunty.

"Dorky, hokey, malarkey?" drawled Neel, earning a dirty look and smothered laugh from me.

A donkey? asked the horse Raat into my mind. I patted the pakkhiraj's neck. "Not a bad guess, buddy," I said to him.

"Key lime pie!" shouted Lal, his handsome face beaming with confidence. Neel and I both gave him a funny look.

"What?" asked the younger prince, looking back at us with a confused expression. Sometimes Lal was so adorably clueless.

"Nothing! Nothing!" said Neel. I couldn't help laughing

but then swallowed down my chuckles when I realized Sir Gobbet's face was going from red to purple with outrage.

I didn't want the minister to get even more annoyed than he already was, so I said quickly, "Tell us, Buddhu, what kind of key opens a banana?"

Buddhu jumped from Bunty to me, then flipped upside down, hanging from my forearm by his tail. "Arré, a monkey of course!"

The animals and Lal all erupted in peals of laughter.

"Oh, that's good. Puerile, but good!" laughed Bunty. Raat stomped his hooves with pleasure. Neel and I tried to contain ourselves, but it was a challenge.

"You see what I mean?" the minister sputtered.

Neel tried to stop laughing and look serious. "You're right, it was a pretty terrible joke."

"Enough!" sputtered Sir Gobbet. He beckoned to some other ministers, lords and ladies, and palace servants all crowding around the hideout entrance. "We must try to earn the goodwill of the people toward our cause once again."

"All hail the new Raja, Lalkamal!" he and the other courtiers cheered.

Just then, Mati and Naya came bounding out of the hideout entrance as well. Naya threw herself into my arms for a hug, and Lal did the same to Mati. He practically fell over on top of her because of his sprained ankle.

"Whoa there!" Neel helped right his brother, putting a stabilizing arm under Mati's shoulder too. I noticed that my cousin, who used special shoes because one of her legs was a little shorter than the other, was actually using a cane. This was new. I wondered if she'd been overdoing it.

"Try not to kill yourself, Bro, before you go off on campaign," Neel was saying.

"But I just got here!" Lal's eyes were glued to Mati's face. "Do I really have to go on campaign right now?"

To my surprise, it was Mati who insisted. She gave Lal a stern look. "We're never going to win against Sesha and the Anti-Chaos Committee without the support of the people."

"It wasn't my fault everybody hated my jokes, boss! Really it wasn't!" Buddhu wailed. He and Bhootoom had been working for Mati and the resistance as spies for a while now. "Let us make it up to you!"

"You two can go with your brother on campaign and help him," Mati told the owl and monkey princes. "But no more hacking into the satellite signal, and no more banana jokes, all right? And I want to hear that you personally apologized to anyone who slipped on those banana peels!"

Buddhu and Bhootoom looked down at the ground with sheepish expressions. Naya, softhearted rakkhoshi that she was, went to give them reassuring pets on the head. As she did, I realized that there was yet another animal sitting on her shoulder. Tiktiki One!

"What's that goofy gecko doing here?" I asked. "The last time I saw it, it climbed up the Norse tree of life and disappeared!"

"Don't be mean, Tiktiki One's just a prototype," said Naya defensively. "There may be some bugs in the system still."

"I'll say!" laughed Neel as the lizard flicked out a giant tongue, caught a fly in midair, and then swallowed it.

In the meantime, Lal seemed flabbergasted by Naya's presence. "So you're a rakkhoshi," he said slowly, wrinkling his nose.

"Lal," said Neel in a warning voice. "Naya is Kiran's friend. And now mine too."

Naya, cupcake of sunshine that she was, beamed at Neel's words. I knew, even if Neel didn't realize it, that she'd been a member of the flying fangirls gang that had once chased me and Neel, threatening to nibble on Neel's feet. I also knew for a fact she cut out all of Lal's and Neel's pictures, not to mention those of Buddhu and Bhootoom, from the Kingdom Beyond celebrity magazine *Teen Taal*. So I'm sure Neel calling her a friend was the thrill of a century.

Naya turned to Lal with a giant smile. As she spoke, the zillions of perky ponytails all over her head kind of bopped and waved.

"Oh yes, Your Princeliness! I am a rakkhoshi! From the air clan!" At Lal's confused expression, Naya added, "I just happen to have retractable wings—not everyone does. Should I bring them out? They're pretty cool. Do you want to see them?"

"No!" Lal shouted, his hands up. Sir Gobbet and the rest of the palace courtiers were looking nervous too. Lal turned to Mati. "She's not coming with me, is she?"

Naya's face fell. I put a protective arm around the girl's shoulders. "Lal, seriously!" I muttered. I noticed Naya's eyes were already filling with tears.

Neel looked thunderous. "Dude, did you forget *I'm* part rakkhosh too?"

Lal looked even more confused. "But you're different—" he began.

Mati cut him off. "A lot has happened since you've been gone, Lal. If you want to work with the resistance, you're going to have to get used to the fact that we are an interspecies group. You're going to have to get over your prejudice against rakkhosh."

Neel gave me another fiery look, but I ignored him. Unlike Lal's opinion of Naya, my opinion about Pinki wasn't based on prejudice; it was based on knowing what kind of an evil monster the Demon Queen really was.

"I was just saying—" Lal started, but Mati interrupted him again. "I don't want to hear it. But for your information, no, Naya's not going with you. I need her here, helping me. She's my right-hand woman."

Poor Lal looked totally confused by his best friend's reaction. The last time he'd seen Mati, she'd been a loyal and gentle stable hand. Now she was the general of an interspecies resistance army.

"I'm . . . sorry," Lal muttered to Naya. Even as she nodded her thanks, I could tell that Lal was having a hard time understanding that rakkhosh, like human beings, weren't all the same.

Gobbet and his helpers bundled Lal onto the elephant's back, and within less than an hour of us arriving in the dimension, Lal, Budhhu, Bhootoom, Gobbet, and the royal ministers and courtiers were off.

"Good luck, Lal!" I called to the younger prince. "Take care of your ankle!" I hoped that being on campaign would give him time to get used to the new way of things and that he'd learn to be more open-minded about our new rakkhosh friends.

"I'll miss you . . . all," said Lal, but I could tell his words were mainly for Mati. Then he looked down at Neel, his face amused. "Thanks for doing my job while I was gone, Brother! I'm sure you're relieved to hand over the responsibility!"

"Sure," Neel said in kind of a flat way. I noticed a little muscle kind of clenching and unclenching in his jaw. "Good luck, Bro!"

We walked together behind Mati deeper into the PSS headquarters. Both Naya and Neel were super quiet, and I could tell they were each thinking about what Lal had said.

As Naya moved in front of us, to walk with Mati, I poked Neel teasingly in the side with my finger. "He's been trapped in a tree for a long time. He'll figure things out."

Neel let out a breath, batting my poking hand away. "A lot of people have prejudice against rakkhosh. Some who even think they don't."

"Ugh, enough," I said. "Look, let's just agree to disagree right now on why your mom is marrying Sesha, all right?"

"Fine," snapped Neel.

He was so darn pigheaded! I really wanted to scream, or knock him in the head, or both.

CHAPTER 22

Demonic Wedding Crashers

The main part of the PSS headquarters was overrun with rakkhosh. Fire clan, air clan, water clan, land clan—they were everywhere. I gave a little gasp at all the demons surrounding us. I was still not used to seeing so many rakkhosh and not having a freak-out fight-or-flight-type response.

"Relax. Remember they're on our side," Neel said under his breath, like he knew what I was thinking.

I felt my face heat up. Okay, maybe I was a little more like Lal than I was ready to admit. I too seemed to be having a hard time getting over stereotypes about rakkhosh. But of course, that didn't mean I was wrong about Neel's mom.

"Operation Demonic Wedding Guest is well underway!" Mati told us, spreading her hands around her with pride.

"The wedding invitation clearly says no rakkhosh," Neel said, looking around at all the potential wedding guests. "How are you planning on getting all these demons to pass as human?"

"These rakkhosh are going to pass as human the same way I passed as a regular Parsippany sixth grader!" explained Naya. Tuni was sitting on her shoulder, casually nibbling on the birdseed she held out in her hand. "Nothing that a little manicure, pedicure, dental filing, contact lens insertion, haircut, dermabrasion, and wart peel can't solve!"

"What about for air clans—the ones who can't hide their wings like Naya?" I pointed to a bunch of rakkhosh waiting around, who had huge dragon-type wings, smaller insect-type wings, feathered eagle wings, and everything in between.

"Oh, that's nothing for the legendary fashion designer Gyanendrachandra Mukherjee!" Mati said. I followed her gaze and realized there was a little mini fashion show going on in one corner of the cave. A long-bearded, gray-ponytailed fashion designer with a cape, gloves, and dark glasses was clapping his hands and showing off models wearing futuristic backpacks over their evening gowns, giant feathery capes over their saris, and even elaborate hat-scarf sets that draped all the way down the backs of

their tuxedo jackets. All were designed, I guessed, to hide wings.

"Clever," Neel said, but I wasn't convinced any of those outfits wouldn't draw more rather than less attention to the person wearing it.

"Exploitation of the sewing proletariat," sniffed Bunty. "Although I do like those snazzy capes."

"You should see some of these engagement party pictures!" said Tuni, dropping a copy of the *Seven Oceans Gazette* in my lap. "We missed a wild party while we were traveling through that wormhole!"

I looked at the party photographs on the front page of

the *Seven Oceans Gazette*. I noticed a couple of tall cape-and-scarf-draped partygoers, and realized they were probably rakkhosh in disguise.

"The plan is to send out just a few scouts at a time to each of these pre-wedding events, to see if their disguises hold," explained Mati. "Last night, all of our spies came home safe and sound."

"Why are you being so cautious?" Neel asked. "I thought our plan was to infiltrate the wedding and stop it."

I couldn't help but agree with Neel. "Plus, I didn't travel through all these dimensions just to sit around and watch other people go up against Sesha," I said. "I'm ready. I want to face him."

"We can't just rush in there, Kiran. I want to make sure we have a plan that works," said Mati. "We can't risk everybody's lives because you're impatient."

I glanced at my cousin's cane, wondering again if she was overdoing it. "You should take it easy, Cuz. Is your foot bothering you?"

"Are you implying something?" Mati's temper went from about zero to sixty in a second. "Because if you are, you need to step off with your ableist assumptions. I've been running this resistance group this whole time, and I'm going to keep running it."

"I'm not implying anything!" I said, holding my hands up in an "I give up" gesture. Wow, the multiverse potentially coming to an end really had everyone on edge.

"Sorry." Mati rubbed a tired hand over her eyes. "You're right. This whole leading-a-revolution thing has been a little stressful. I didn't mean to snap at you like that."

"No worries," I said in a somewhat milder tone, even though I was still irritated inside.

To stop myself from saying anything I'd regret later, I studied the huge front-page newspaper photo of Sesha and Pinki, the Demon Queen. They were posed in kind of a fancy-perfume-ad style, her flinging her hair and staring off into the distance, him flexing his bicep as he kissed it.

"Weird," I muttered. "I still can't believe they're getting married."

"Because marriage is an antiquated symbol of the hetero-capitalist patriarchy," asked Bunty, "or because you can't believe they're marrying each other?"

"That second thing you said," I told the tiger.

"Wait, I've got video!" gushed Naya. I was glad to see that being in the PSS resistance hadn't squelched any of my friend Naya's natural enthusiasm for all things glamorous. She pulled up the Thirteen Rivers television anchor Miss Twinkle Chakraborty's MeTube channel, where Twinkle had done a little segment on the fancy engagement party. Tiktiki One, who was sticking to Naya's shoulder like glue, flicked out its tongue as if in excitement to see the clip.

"I'm livestrooming from the event of the milloonium!" squealed the nose-ringed and heavily mascara'd anchor, her face mere inches from her camera screen. "I'm here with my handsoom date, ex–Kingdom Beyoond cricket captoon Suman Rahamoon."

"Heya, Kingdom Beyond superfans," drawled Suman Rahaman. He was wearing a glittery black sherwani, and Miss Twinkle was in a white chiffon sari. Despite being in a high-collar jacket, "Sooms" had still managed to keep enough buttons undone to show a bunch of chest hair and his gold chain necklace.

"Gross," I muttered.

"Oh, come on, I think he's dreamy," drawled the rakkhoshi Priya in a sarcastic voice. The effect of her words was even more ruined by the fact that she scratched her bald head with her long-taloned hand as she spoke.

"The doonce floor is hoopin'! They're dooing the cain-cain, the macaroona, *and* the elooctric slide," said Miss Twinkle, mispronouncing dances so old-fashioned I wasn't sure I even really knew what they were. "And look, there's the looscious snaky bridegroom himsoolf doing the flooss!"

"Oh, I don't think I can unsee that," I groaned. I squinted at the screen, watching Sesha do the side-to-side hip-swinging dance that looked like someone, well, flossing their teeth. It was super weird.

Besides the dancing, Sesha looked just like he always did—green-black hair, perfect skin, piercing eyes, and a-little-too-sharp-for-comfort teeth. He was the only person not dressed according to the engagement party's black-and-white dress code. His green velvet jacket was close enough to black to pass in some light, but its snaky color still shone through.

"Thank you so much for celebrating our joy with us!" Miss Twinkle's cell phone camera panned violently left, and caught, through a bunch of other people's arms, Neel's mom giving what sounded like a heartfelt speech. She was dressed in a black-and-white sari studded with diamonds. Her hair was flowing lusciously over her horns and shoulders, and her eyelashes were glamorously silky and long. Jewels glittered at her neck, arms, and ears, and she looked like she was actually glowing. Of course, the fancy effect was a little bit ruined by the fact that she kept rubbing her chest and burping as she spoke. "I'm just over the moon to be starting my new life soon, with my all-powerful new husband, ruler of the singular universe! So much better than that last human husband of mine, jerky runaway chicken butt that he was!"

"Is there anything better than a blushing, burping bride?" gushed Suman Rahaman. "Even a blushing, burping bride who's been known to cannibalize entire villages?"

At these words, Miss Twinkle's cell phone went all sideways and diagonal.

"Hey, we're members of the press, and very good-looking besides! We can too have our cameras here," I heard Suman say. "Do you know who I am? I'm Sooms! Ex–cricket captain and intergalactic heartthrob! Darn it! Don't you recognize me? I'm the host of *Lifestyles of the Rich and Monstrous*!"

The camera still didn't right itself despite all his protests. All we could see was an image of the dance floor and a bunch of feet. In the background, a song about posing like a statue was blaring through the loudspeakers. Some of the partygoers were dancing, and others chanting, "Down with Chaos! Down with Chaos!" as they stomped their feet.

"Yoo coon't take my phoone!" sputtered Twinkle Chakraborty's voice. "I'm a moomber of the prooss, you goon! Give it boock!"

But apparently whoever it was didn't seem to care about her press credentials, because that was the end of the video.

"Dang, that was harsh!" Tuni said.

"Attacking the free press is the first step in establishing authoritarianism," said Bunty as they cleaned their whiskers.

"Well, that is reassuring, isn't it, Your Princeliness? Your mother looked . . . happy?" said Naya in an unsure voice. I could tell she was trying to cheer Neel up.

"Yeah," I confirmed. "She kinda did seem super happy. If a little burpy. Doesn't that convince you that she's getting married to Sesha willingly?"

"I don't believe it. Maybe the recording was doctored. Or she's been brainwashed," said Neel. "Or maybe that's a body double."

"Or maybe your mother really wants to marry Kiran's evil dad," suggested Tuni.

Neel sighed, running his fingers so harshly through his hair it all stood up. "Or that."

"As much as I respect all of your input, the truth is, we don't have time to debate the Rakkhoshi Rani's motivations right now," said Mati matter-of-factly. "But if you want to try and smuggle a note in to her, Neel, we can do it with the tottho."

"The what?" I asked.

"You know, Your Royalness, the tottho!" Naya pointed

to a bunch of beautifully decorated trays already arranged in lines on the ground. I saw packets of sweets, jewels, saris, fish, and more. "The presents that one side of the wedding party sends to the other! But because Sesha is, well, a greedy Gus, he's expecting tottho presents from everyone in the kingdom to commemorate the day of the gaye halud ceremony!"

"So that's the ceremony where the bride and groom get smeared in turmeric paste—like for purification or whatever, right?" I asked.

"Very good, Your Highnosity!" agreed Naya. "Growing up in another dimension and everything, I know things can be confusing, but you catch on quick!"

I remembered Ma had told me stories about her cousin-sister's gaye halud. How she and her other young cousins had all worn yellow. How they had watched as all their aunties had laughed and ulu-ulu'ed and smeared the bride-to-be's face, arms, and legs with Va-va-voom Turmeric Cream, a product advertised to help clear up your complexion and make you look, according to their company jingle, "va-va-voomilicious!"

Neel, I noticed, was scribbling something on a piece of notebook paper that Naya had helpfully handed him. In

classic Naya style, she'd also given him an assortment of sparkly and fruity-smelling markers to write his note. For who knows what reason, Neel was going along with her suggestion to write each word in a different color. I looked over his shoulder and saw that his note was simple but direct.

Dear Mother—You may be a killer, but you're no stooge. Are you marrying this goon for real or are you a prisoner?

    Your sometimes-loving son,

    Neelkamal

"Huh," I couldn't help but say, "interesting choice of wording."

"Don't judge," Neel snapped, as with Naya's help, he tucked the note into a gift tray full of fake eyelashes, bobby pins, and nail polish.

Mati came over to me. "The plan is to smuggle some weapons into the wedding venue inside these trays of presents. So that they are there for when we decide to bring in a bigger force."

"Weapons?" I echoed.

"Sure. We rakkhosh can use our strength and nails and teeth. But you human resistance fighters need a little more help. Take that giant sandesh shaped like a fish." Priya pointed at a tottho tray lying nearby, wrapped prettily in bright pink cellopaper. "It's the perfect shape to hide chakus."

"What's the point of smuggling in weapons without anyone to use them?" I asked. "I mean, you're putting knives inside sandesh, but you're only sending in four or five spies at a time to each of these events."

"Weapons are expendable; my team is not," Mati said. "I'm not risking even one PSS life unnecessarily. We have to study, scout, and plan everything out."

"How long are you going to do that? The wedding is at

the end of the week," I snorted. Man, for an important resistance leader, Mati was ridiculously cautious.

"Do you have a problem with the way I'm running things, Cousin?" Mati's voice got tense again as she caught my expression.

"No, no! Not at all!" I said, trying to fix my face.

I caught Naya and Priya giving each other a look. "What are in these saris, then?" Neel asked, pointing to a tray of saris starched and sculpted to look like a bouquet of butterflies.

"Oh, they're not saris at all," explained Mati. "They're poison-proof shields. Armor for the humans on our side if and when there's a battle."

"Wouldn't want to risk someone getting a hangnail," I muttered.

"Kiran, come on," Neel said. Now it was his turn to give me a "cut it out" look.

"The fate of the multiverse is at stake, Cousin," Mati snapped. "I'm not going to just run in there willy-nilly without a plan!"

"If you're so busy planning, maybe you'll never have to run in there at all," I countered.

Just then, one of the younger PSS girls skated on her board into the room and whispered something in Mati's ear.

"Listen, I've got to go deal with some kind of crisis with the rakkhosh pedicures. I'll be right back," Mati said. Her face was tight and tired, and I felt bad for giving her a hard time. "Naya, will you give me a hand? I'm not sure I can always make out all these different demonic dialects."

As Mati and Naya left, I felt ashamed, but also a little irritated. Why was Mati being so darned careful? Were we heroes dedicated to saving the multiverse or not?

"What's that?" I pointed to a clay horse half a head taller than me. It looked like the traditional clay horses from the Kingdom Beyond that Ma had decorating our mantel in Parsippany, only a bunch bigger.

"Oh, Mati had it made to hide swords and bows," said Priya. "It's going to be part of the tottho."

Looking at the big clay horse gave me an idea. "Why not hide the rakkhosh army in there instead of just weapons?" I suggested, thinking of an old story I'd read about at school. "You have a few humans go with it, pretending it's a present for the tottho, and then, at the right moment, they let the rakkhosh out of the horse! No need to worry about all this costuming and manicuring, then!"

"Brilliant!" squawked Tuni.

"It could work," said Neel. "If only to get us enough time

to figure out if my mom's a prisoner and get her out of there."

I rolled my eyes but didn't say anything.

"Cool plan." Priya looked impressed. "Why didn't I think of that?"

"Let's clear it by Mati," Bunty suggested. But I stopped the tiger before they padded away.

"Don't bother her! She said she had to deal with a pedicure crisis!" I knew Mati was a good leader, but what did that make the rest of us, chopped liver? "We can do this on our own!"

"But, Princess . . ." protested Tuni.

"What, don't you trust me?" I asked in an offended tone. "I do have some experience with this being a hero stuff, you know. More than Mati."

"Jealousy is a green-eyed monster," mumbled Neel.

"What did you say?" I snapped.

"Nothing, nothing," said the prince, but his words struck me hard. I set my jaw in a determined line. Just because I had a different way of doing things than Mati, that didn't mean I was wrong.

CHAPTER 23

The Trojan Rakkhosh

While most of the rakkhosh army stayed at head-quarters, working on their manis and pedis and tusk filings, I assembled a crack force. Even though Bunty didn't want us to, Neel and I decided to be a part of the Trojan horse delivery mission.

"I'll go with them and keep them out of trouble," Tuni said. "Don't you worry, you old scaredy-cat!"

Bunty roared in annoyance at the bird, batting a giant paw. Wisely, Tuni flew out of the tiger's reach and perched on a jutting rock near the ceiling.

"You're not leaving me out of the fun!" said Priya. "You're right, Kiran. I'm getting tired of all this prepping and planning. I want some action!"

"Perhaps it is more prudent to wait until a bigger horse

can be prepared," mused Bunty. "I estimate no more than about six rakkhosh are going to fit inside that!"

"I've got to go see if I can find my mom, talk to her." Neel was chewing on his fingernail again. "Even if this isn't a perfect plan, it's better than sitting around here doing nothing."

Neel and I gave Priya and her friends on the inside our weapons. Then we dressed up in some excellent yellow designer duds from Gyan Mukherjee. Since both Neel and I were pretty recognizable, we made sure to hide our faces. Neel had on a weird fake beard and I a full face scarf.

"Most likely Mati is going to be livid!" said Bunty, but Tuni flapped his wings in the tiger's face.

"You're just mad you can't join the army!" said the bird to the tiger. "Not only do I get to go along, my yellow feathers perfectly match today's dress code!"

"With only six rakkhosh within," said Bunty again. "It's hardly an army."

"The six of us are as good as an army!" roared Priya, clapping her fellow rakkhosh on the back. They roared and drooled and cheered, waving long-nailed fists in the air.

"I've got to find a way to talk to my mother." Neel scratched distractedly at his fake facial hair. "It may not be a perfect plan, but if she's Sesha's prisoner, I've got to free her."

I said nothing but exchanged a rolly-eyed look with Tuni.

"I have a great deal of concern for your lack of cautiousness," sniffed Bunty.

And with that, we were off.

The area surrounding the palace was an absolute zoo. It seemed that everyone from all over the Kingdom Beyond, the Kingdom of Serpents, and beyond had been invited to the pre-wedding festivities. Everyone except me, I thought bitterly. From servants to farmers to bankers to schoolchildren—everyone was crowding the streets, dressed in their fanciest yellow and red clothing for the gaye halud ceremony. There were horses and carriages, elephants and rikshaws, prettied-up bicycles, and even a painted bullock cart or two.

As I saw the throngs of people swarming around, I wondered how Sesha, enemy of the Kingdom Beyond, had convinced an entire country to trust him so quickly. Had it been that stupid *Who Wants to Be a Demon Slayer?* game show? I'd heard from Naya that he'd started his own MeTube station, where he said the most outrageous things. Most of his rants were about how much he hated rakkhosh, and how rakkhosh were responsible for all the ills of the kingdom. Was it really that easy? Just to give a group of people someone different than themselves to hate and blame for their problems? And how did that even make sense if he was marrying the queen of the rakkhosh? But apparently, everyone was so swept up in wedding party fever, no one was bothered by the contradiction.

As soon as I thought this, of course, I squirmed a little inside but quickly convinced myself that my view of the Rakkhoshi Rani was based on *facts*, not opinion. So it definitely wasn't the same thing.

"Check those out," Neel breathed. As he spoke, his moustache fluttered a little, making him sneeze.

"Jiu—bless you!" I looked where he was pointing, at the billboards decorating the streets. I was grateful that he hadn't seen the ones that had been up only a few weeks ago, those fake images for the game show that showed Lal and me killing rakkhosh, looking glamorous, and being in love.

But now the billboards were all of Sesha. The weird thing was, all the images seemed borrowed from other stories. In one picture, Sesha was wearing a knight's armor and helmet, riding on a horse like he was going jousting. In another, he was in military uniform, saluting at a row of tanks and airplanes dropping bombs on Demon Land. On yet another billboard, he was wearing a suit and tie, sitting behind a presidential desk, his fist poised over a big red

button that read *Blow Up the Rakkhosh.* In the background in about half the billboards was the Demon Queen, at her most glamorous and beautiful.

"Why do they look so different, Sesha and my mother?" Neel wondered aloud. "They don't look like themselves."

"It's got to be the effect of the story smushing," I said. Neel was right. Not only were the images in clothing from other cultures, both his mom and my bio dad looked way paler in most of the images, like they weren't even themselves anymore. "Whatever they and their Anti-Chaos goons are up to, they're moving us more toward the singularity."

Neel made a noise in the back of his throat but didn't say anything.

All this weirdness didn't seem to bother the people in the streets at all. There were tottho gifts coming from all directions. People danced, sang, clapped, and chanted as they brought their beautifully decorated trays of offerings toward the palace. We joined a procession of people playing the conch shell and ulu-ulu'ing. Despite the fact that it was a little unnerving to see everyone so happy about this particular wedding, it was hard not to get caught up in the party atmosphere. I was feeling so confident and pumped that, when Neel started to whisper at me, I didn't know what he was going on about.

"Guards," I heard him muttering. "There are guards doing spot checks on the gift trays. And I don't recognize any of them! Sesha must have hired a whole new crew to replace my father's people!"

"Kill 'em!" hissed Priya a little too gleefully from inside the horse.

"We're gonna die!" burbled Tuni, who'd hitched a ride to the party on my shoulder.

"Relax, no one is killing anyone," I whispered, tucking the scarf more firmly around my face. "Everyone chill and keep quiet!" I gave Tuntuni a quick pat. "Especially you, birdie. You shouldn't have insisted on coming if you couldn't take the stress!"

I looked cautiously around and realized that Neel was overreacting. The guards walked right by us, waving us on.

"That was close," Neel muttered as a lady carrying a wrapped tray of oranges, mangoes, and bananas walked by.

"What was close?" hissed Priya from inside the horse. "Did you split their jugular veins with your teeth in a silent but deadly attack?"

"Shh! Keep quiet in there already!" I ordered, pushing the wheeling horse along. I turned to Neel, lowering my voice even more. "Are you okay?"

I'd never seen Neel looking so nervous. He was more the overconfident type.

"I just can't get over the feeling that my mom is a prisoner," Neel admitted. His eyes were darting this way and that, like he was sure someone was going to capture him and throw him in detention again at any minute. I wondered if he had a case of post-demonic stress disorder or something. "I can't help but think that Sesha's got her trapped in this engagement just like he had me trapped in that prison."

I gave him what I hoped was a supportive look, without fighting with him again, like I was trying to say "Buck up, little buckaroo!" with my eyes. I'm not sure it worked, as Neel squinted at me and asked, "Do you have something in your eye?"

I sighed. Sesha was awful, that much we both knew. And I also knew how monstrous the serpent king had been to my moon mother when they were together, turning her first seven children into snakes, forcing her to send me into hiding in a different dimension with adoptive parents. And I understood why Neel thought Sesha might be being the same way to his mom.

But I couldn't forget what I knew of the Queen too, as someone with a less-than-perfect moral compass. Plus, she had looked so happy on that video report by Twinkle Chakraborty. Anyway, the Demon Queen was a tough cookie, unlike my delicate moon mother, and more than capable of taking care of herself.

"I think we should abort the mission," Neel muttered from behind his beard. "I don't think this is going to work."

"Chill," I said to Neel in an easy tone as some more guards strolled by to our right. "You're making me nervous."

"You're making us nervous too!" It was one of the rakkhosh from inside the horse. Without a word, I banged on the side of the clay animal.

A voice I recognized as Priya's said from inside the horse, "I'm not nervous!"

"I am!" burbled Tuni again, earning himself a stern look from me.

"I don't have a good feeling about this, Kiran," Neel mumbled, chewing on his fingernail.

I couldn't help it, but I almost laughed at how much our roles had reversed. When I'd first met Neel, I'd known nothing of what it took to be a hero, and I'd been downright allergic to taking risks or standing out. But learning about myself, and where I was from, had changed me. Now I was more than willing to see this pre-wedding invasion through until the end. The problem was, the end came a lot sooner than I thought.

The twisting line of dancing, singing, ululating guests had slowly made its way toward the palace. We walked in past the outdoor guards easily. They waved us on with good-humored jokes about the size of the horse and whether or not it would take off into the sky when we weren't looking.

"We're in!" I whispered to the hidden rakkhosh inside the horse as soon as we were in the grand marble courtyard of the palace. Musicians played from every corner, and everything was decorated with yellow flowers—mostly thick marigold garlands that draped richly, in strands of three, six, twelve, and more in every possible direction. In addition to the flowers, which made the air sweet with their heady smells, there were delicate white alpona designs everywhere, along with silk tapestries and rows of colorful flags waving in the breeze.

"You see?" I poked Neel in the ribs with a sharp elbow. "You were worrying for nothing."

"Oh, really?" Neel was looking around the decorated marble courtyard. "We're still not in the inner courtyard, and if anything happens here, we're absolute sitting ducks!"

"I don't wanna be a roasted chickadee!" moaned Tuni.

I followed Neel's gaze and realized he was right. I'd forgotten that the Raja's palace had not just one courtyard. We'd made it into the outer courtyard but still had to pass through more sets of guards before we made it to one of the inner ones. And unlike when we had been outside in the square, here, we were trapped in on all sides by the prettily decorated balconies and breezeways. Now, none of this would have been an actual problem had each of those balconies and breezeways not been populated by a whole mess of guards. Then there was the serious problem of the guard at the front of the courtyard.

"Uh-oh," I whispered, not wanting to believe what I was seeing. At the front of the tottho line, checking each and every gift that went through the gates of the palace, was Stheno—back from the dead!

"I can't believe it!" I breathed. "It's my principal! I knew that fink Ned didn't really kill her!"

"What?" Neel's eyes darted this way and that. "Your undead middle school principal is here? Are you sure about that?"

"She's not really my principal!" I hissed. "She's a Gorgon! And yes, I'm sure!"

"Your middle school principal is a Gorgon?" chirped Tuni, his voice high and taught with fright. "That has got to be against the teachers' union rules!"

Neel's hand reached for his sword, but of course we'd both put our weapons inside the horse with our friends, where we could get to them later. Which meant we had no way of getting to them now.

"Let's go, Princess. Let's get outa here!" The bird on my shoulder was squawking and losing tail feathers in his agitation.

I couldn't help but agree with Tuni this time. I was already wheeling the horse in the opposite direction, trying to look inconspicuous. Word to the wise: It's really hard to look inconspicuous while wheeling around a ten-foot-tall horse filled with rakkhosh in the middle of a crowded palace courtyard.

"Stop that horse!" I heard Stheno shriek.

"Don't stop!" muttered Neel, now pushing the horse on the other side. I noticed his fake beard was kind of falling off, but there was no time to fix it now. We were both doing that fast-walking thing like when neighborhood moms want to exercise but are afraid they'll look silly running. Only we weren't afraid to look silly. We were just trying to pretend that we weren't getting the heck out of there as fast as we could.

The act only lasted so long. By the time Stheno yelled, "It's a trick! I know this story! Stop that Trojan horse!" we were flat-out bolting.

"Get them out of there! No point in trying to hide now!" I yelled to Neel as I ripped off my face scarf.

I grabbed a shehnai from a musician to the side of me. Ignoring the man's protests, I flung the long metal horn at the clay horse. A little hole formed. Neel didn't bother with stealing an instrument but just shoved his fist through the hole I'd made in the clay, ripping it wider. I saw Priya's taloned hands and a few others helping him from the inside too. And then the hole was big enough, and our rakkhosh friends came pouring out of the horse.

"Get them! Get those monsters!" shrieked my monster of an ex-principal.

The same musician whose instrument I'd stolen made a grab for me, but Priya whirled on him, fire lashing from her mouth. In her full rakkhoshi form, she shrieked, "Wedding yellows ain't so mellow! Get lost, you creep, or I'll eat your feet!"

All around us the other rakkhosh who had been inside the horse began to emerge in their full demonic forms.

"Back off or your throats we'll tear! And make you soil your underwear!" screeched one rakkhoshi.

"From horse's belly we are born! We'll kick your butts, then toot a horn!" yelled another.

"Get them! Stop them!" shrieked Stheno. Her hair tentacles and teeth tentacles had come unhinged and each was chasing our demon friends.

"Any more fire clan with you?" I yelled to Priya. "She hates fire!"

Priya and another fire rakkhosh started blasting flames out of their mouths at the Gorgon. Unfortunately, unlike the time we were behind my middle school, Stheno had a lot of help here at the palace. At her cries, supervillains from a bunch of mythological traditions and stories came rushing out into the courtyard. There were horse-men and selkie women, card soldiers, wicked witches, orcs and goblins, Rodents of Very Big Size, and bankers in business suits. None of them belonged in the Kingdom Beyond, but here they all were.

"What are all these storybook baddies doing in my house?" yelled Neel. "This is seriously not cool!"

"My fellow members of the Anti-Chaos Committee— get them!" shrieked Stheno.

When the evil flying monkeys started dive-bombing us, I knew we were in trouble.

"Outnumbered we are, Princess, ma'am!" shouted one of the water rakkhosh who'd been in the horse. "We need a new plan—we'd better scram!"

I was firing off arrows as fast as I could, trying to hit Stheno's tentacle hair and teeth. The only problem was, as quick as I hit one of the tentacle things, two more seemed to grow back in its place.

"Sssissster!" I heard the voice coming from behind me. Without even thinking, I whirled and shot at Naga. My seven-headed snake brother was such a jerk. Also, a ridiculous glutton for punishment. No matter how mean our father was to him, Naga never seemed to get the message.

"Ugh, Naga, why don't you get a life already?" I snapped, firing at his ugly head. "How'd you manage to untie yourself after Ai-Ma tied you up?"

"You can't be into this idea of our parents getting married!" Neel said, his attention somewhat occupied in a sword fight with three different guards.

"Dad can marry whoever he wantsss!" Naga whined, all seven of his tongues shooting out at me. "He said I could be best snake!"

"That's not even a thing, you loser!" I snapped, shooting two arrows into a couple of his heads at the same time.

Stheno, on seeing my face, was yelling bloody murder. "You meddling middle schooler! I'll get you for this, my pretty!"

Neel, suddenly free of enemies, swung around to help me with Naga. I kept shooting arrows at his seven heads as Neel slashed at Naga's tail.

"Ow!" yelled Naga. "Butt-brain! I'm gonna tell Daddy you're hanging out with the cute prince again!" The seven-headed snake slithered up a banister and disappeared down an upstairs breezeway.

"Cute prince, huh?" Neel seemed way too pleased at this. And while it was nice to see some of his old confidence restored, this was really not the time.

"Let's scram before Sesha gets here!" I yelled.

Neel turned, his sword whirling so fast now I could hardly see it. His back was up against mine, and he was working hard, trying not to injure but rather disarm the pack of human guards attacking him. In the meantime, I started shooting arrows at the flying monkeys dive-bombing us yet again. Man, were those exploding bananas they were lobbing down at us?

"Now would be a good time to fly out of here!" Neel called, slicing mercilessly into a disgusting, smelly-furred and yet kind of mechanical-looking Rodent of Very Big Size.

"Where are the air clan rakkhosh?" I looked desperately to Priya, who was still keeping Stheno at bay with buckets of fire-vomit. The rakkhoshi shook her head no. "Didn't you think to bring any fliers so we had an escape plan?"

"Fire clan and air clan don't get along!" Priya yelled, whirling around to fire-blast a charging orc with a cudgel. "They always beat us in the rickets league! I wouldn't ask those guys for any favors!"

"Now you tell me!" I shrieked, shooting off two, three, and now four arrows at a time at some drooling goblins. I could not believe we didn't have an escape plan because fire and air clans were enemies in rakkhosh cricket!

"We're goners! Absolute goners!" Tuni squealed as he flew around, pecking at the eyes of the vicious monkeys, flapping in the faces of the green witches. There were so many evildoers from so many different story traditions, I felt like an entire fairy-tale library had been blended up and dumped over us.

I looked desperately around. We were hemmed in from

all sides. Now there were white-sheeted and chain-clanking ghosts, long-toothed vampires, ratty zombies, and green-skinned Frankensteins coming out of the woodwork. The Raja's courtyard looked like some deadly, out-of-season Halloween party store. None of these creatures belonged in the stories from the Kingdom Beyond, and yet, here they all were. This was a serious problem.

"Not to be a downer or anything," said Neel, now fighting what looked like a family of trolls, "but we might be in a little bit of trouble, Kiran. Unless you have some kind of secret weapon you haven't told me about."

Neel's words made a light bulb go off in my head. "Priya, do you have that Lola Morgana thermos with you still?" I demanded as I dove right to avoid an evil-looking clown with a chain saw.

"Oh, yeah, I do!" Priya pulled out the thermos from some hidden pocket in her pink cape. "Take this, ya second-rate villains! Get a load of what a real ghost is like!"

The rakkhoshi unscrewed the lid to the *Star Travels* thermos and released the terrible bhoot who had captured Lal and taken over his identity, fooling all of us for so long.

Unlike ghosts from other cultures, bhoot from the Kingdom Beyond are seriously powerful creatures, and the bhoot-formerly-known-as-Lal was no exception. It whooshed shriekingly from its container and flew right at the Halloween villains that were chasing us.

"Go back to your own stories, you interlopers!" yelled the bhoot. "I'll toast up your liver and eat it like a crumpet! I'll make a thorkari with your thyroid! I'll use your toes to flavor my morning tea!"

"You bought us a little time with these baddies, but there are more where those came from," Priya muttered, pulling at my arm. "Not to mention the ghost himself! We better get out of here before good ol' Bhoot-Baba-ji remembers it was you who put him in that thermos!"

"But how? We've still got no rides!" said Neel, sounding seriously worried.

And then I felt him, Tiktiki One, clambering up my leg.

"What are you doing here?" As I grabbed the little gecko and put him on my shoulder, I saw who was flying through the air toward us.

"Naya!" I yelled with delight. "And you brought more air clan with you!"

"Hang on!" Naya's black wings were beating strongly in the wind, and for the first time, I realized what a beautiful sight they were. Or maybe I was just grateful my friend was there saving our butts. She grabbed me under the armpits, and the other flying rakkhosh grabbed the rest of our team.

"I should have realized someone else would know the Trojan horse story!" I yelled to Naya. "Thank goodness you came for us! How did you know we were here?"

"I guessed . . ." Naya began, but then she choked out a little scream and she and I started to spiral unevenly through the air.

"Naya!" I yelled. I realized that one of the flying monkeys had punctured her wing with an arrow, making a giant gaping hole in the middle! We spun through the air, dropping down a few dozen feet. Naya's usually happy-go-lucky face was twisted in pain, and when she gasped, she brought up a frothy mouthful of blood! "Help! Somebody help us!" I screamed.

I'm not sure anyone heard me, or even knew we were in trouble. Priya and the other fire rakkhosh, riding on the backs of two air clan, were still shooting flames in the direction of our pursuers. Two land clan rakkhosh, hanging on to the legs of their air clan rescuers, were throwing spears down to our enemies. From the back of his ride, Neel was beating off some green-faced witches who were trying to chase us on their brooms. The air was dark with smoke, as our enemies on the ground were sending up flaming arrows.

I could still hear Stheno's evil voice, shrieking for my meddling middle-school head.

But Naya and I were lurching through the air, her injured wing making it more and more impossible for her to fly. "Hang in there, Your Princessness," gasped my sweet friend, worried about me even when it was she who was so badly hurt.

"We need help! Naya's been shot!" I yelled as loud as I could. It was finally Neel who heard me. He turned his head, his eyes widening as he took in our plight. He shouted something I couldn't hear, and within seconds, two flying rakkhosh swooped up next to Naya. One—a fierce green-skinned fellow with a scar splitting his face in two—grabbed me out of her hands, and the other—a rakkhoshi with needlelike black teeth—put a strong arm around a flailing Naya's shoulder.

I yelped as I saw the needle-toothed rakkhoshi slap Naya's almost-unconscious face with a merciless hand. Her words were equally strong and fierce. "Sister, we must flee and fly! Lean on me! I won't let you die!"

It was chaos, with the shrieking villains below us and the flying villains behind us, but the entire time we were escaping, the only thing I could think was: If anything happened to Naya, it was entirely my fault!

CHAPTER 24

The Power of Stories

I don't know how the air clan rescue party lost the flying monkeys, green-faced witches, and other supervillains who were chasing us. But somehow they did. Back at PSS headquarters, we got a now-unconscious Naya in with the one physician Mati had found willing to treat hurt rakkhosh, Dr. Jhumpa Ahmed. Dangerously sick, my friend was rushed into surgery. The rest of us paced and fretted outside. Bunty, on hearing about what happened, let out an earsplitting roar. The accusing look the tiger gave me made me want to shrivel up and disappear. Bunty then planted themself outside of the surgery door, refusing to leave. Naya's fellow clan members, the ones who had risked their own lives to come and get us, didn't spare me any sympathy either.

"If our sister dies, it is on your head!" snapped the

rakkhosh who had flown me home. "I really wish it was you instead!"

I shrank back from his snarling face, but I couldn't blame him at all. "Whoa, whoa, whoa there," Neel said, standing protectively next to me. "Let's just all take a big breath and calm down, shall we?"

I felt a warm rush of gratitude for my friend. Neel and I might fight sometimes, but when the going got tough, he always had my back.

"Humans are selfish, with hearts like dumpsters!" barked the black-toothed rakkhoshi. "They hurt us and then call us monsters!"

"Slow your roll, you flighty fliers!" Priya snapped, getting in between me, Neel, and Naya's air clan friends.

"Hothead flamies, burping fire!" roared another air clan member. "We fliers from the resistance retire!"

"No! Please!" It was Mati, rushing into the room with a few other PSS on her heels. When she saw the furious faces of Naya's clan members, she fell on her knees, her hands in a pleading namaskar. "The resistance needs you, air clan! We can't afford to lose you!"

"All our stories are connected, you stupid airheads!" Priya said angrily. She tried to get Mati to stand up, but my cousin stayed where she was, her head bowed in humility.

"The multiplicity of the multiverse must be protected!" Bunty said from their spot near the surgery door. "It's what Naya would want!"

Neel was looking furious, his fists balled at his sides. From the looks on his and Priya's faces, I could tell that neither of them was ready to apologize to the air clan. But then Mati looked desperately at me, and I realized what I had to do. I couldn't stop thinking of Naya in the operating room, maybe losing her wing, maybe even dying because of something stupid that I'd done. I felt tears stinging my eyes, and instead of trying to stop them, I let them fall in honor of my hurt friend. Naya's clanspeople were furious at us for good reason. I slid to my knees next to Mati.

"Please, friends! I love Naya too!" I choked out, my words coming from the purest, truest place of my heart. "I didn't understand before how humans and rakkhosh could be friends, how our stories could be so connected. But I do now! I do because of what Naya has taught me!"

I saw Neel's face soften at my words. He stayed on his feet, but his next words were measured and respectful. "Flying clans, we owe you our lives," he rhymed, adopting the speech pattern of his mother's people. "We need us all for the multiverse to survive!"

The air clan rakkhosh were still angry, but I could see

that Neel's words had an effect on them. "Son of our queen, think we should," said the black-toothed rakkhoshi. "If fighting this war is worth our blood."

"It's all we can ask," said Mati, rising slowly from the floor with Neel's help. "In the meantime, I thank you for risking your lives today. I thank you for standing by our dear Naya. And I thank you for showing us how much humans have to learn from rakkhosh."

My cousin moved as if to walk out of the room, but I stopped her, my hand on her arm. "Cousin, I just want to say—"

"What? That you were thoughtless?" Mati snapped. "That you risked all those lives without thinking it through, and now Naya's suffering for it?"

I bit my lip, tears swimming in my vision. "You're right," I choked out. "I would do anything to change places with her."

And I would. What I wouldn't give to have it be me in there on the operating table and not sweet, bubbly Naya. I felt Neel's warm hand on my shoulder but couldn't look up at him. I was so ashamed.

"It's my fault too," Neel said. "I was so busy trying to get to my mom I didn't even think about our escape route."

"Look, if there's anything that this fight against

singularity has taught me, it's that nobody can do this alone." Mati rubbed distractedly at her hip. I wondered again if she was in pain. "This war against the Anti-Chaos Committee isn't about being a cowboy—it's about all of us, with all our differences, still figuring out a way to work together. Don't you two numbskulls get that?"

I studied the ruby-red combat boots on my feet, wishing they could somehow help me turn back time.

"A symphony is not a symphony with only one kind of instrument!" said Tuni, trying to sound all wise and philo-sophical. "It takes a village to raise a nest of eggs! One wing cannot clap on its own!"

"Wait a minute, Tuni, you totally went along with the plan too," said Neel accusingly.

"In cases like these, it's exceedingly rude to have a good memory," Tuni sputtered.

"Just try to stay out of trouble, you two, all right?" Mati said. One of the PSS girls skated in with a big pile of notes for Mati to go over, and she quickly left the room.

As we waited to hear word of Naya's operation, Neel and I kind of wandered around the cave complex, checking out all the preparations for the next few pre-wedding days. Now that we had blown it, and Sesha knew that there was a human and rakkhosh resistance army of some sort out there, everyone had to be even more careful. The rakkhosh disguises, for instance, had to be perfect.

In one area of the cave complex, the fashion team was still trying wedding outfits on rakkhosh, clucking and cooing over outfits that didn't fit right, and also ones that did.

"I'm brilliant, if I say so myself!" announced the fashion designer Gyan Mukherjee.

"Such grace! Such vision!" agreed his assistants, their mouths full of pins as they tucked up a ginormous purple gown on a warty, three-eyed rakkhoshi.

"I wish there was something we could do," Neel burst out. "I hate all this waiting."

"We could help the fashion team." I gestured to Gyan Mukherjee's work space, covered in mountains of fabric and ribbons and things. There were at least ten rakkhoshi seamstresses sewing away on giant machines, a countless number of rakkhosh models milling around, and in the middle of it all, the fashion guru shouting meaningless orders. "Fix that top stitch! Steam those culottes! Tack those hems!"

"Nah, I'm good." Neel laughed. I laughed too. We kept walking.

In another area, a bunch of rakkhosh were practicing an over-the-top musical number for the sangeet, which was happening in two days. They fluttered their eyes and ground their hips and waved their arms in a typical Kingdom Beyollywood–style dance production, only, it looked seriously more scary, what with all the performers' warts and fangs and teeth and wings.

"We could practice a song-and-dance number for the sangeet," Neel said, pointing to the demonic dancers, who seemed now to be bumping into each other at every turn. The human choreographer looked about ready to pull out her hair with frustration.

"Step-ball-change, step-ball-change, kick, kick. Okay, close enough. Look left, look right, hip swivel, turn around, jazz hands! Get that finger out of your dance partner's nose!" she yelled.

"No thanks, no jazz hands for me," I said. "I'd rather face an army of supervillains again!"

Neel nodded in agreement. "But I could do without the fake beard this time!"

It would've all been funny, only I couldn't seem to concentrate on any of it. All I could think about was Naya, on the operating table. Naya, so happy to be rescuing us. Naya, risking her life for her friends without a second thought. It was a good few hours before we heard from the doctor that she had made it through the surgery.

"She's alive but I'm worried that she's not waking up."

Dr. Ahmed looked incredibly serious. "Our tests show there was a rare kind of poison in that monkey arrow—and the only antidote . . ." The doctor rifled through a copy of K. P. Das's *The Adventurer's Guide to Rakkhosh, Khokkosh, Bhoot, Petni, Doito, Danav, Daini, and Secret Codes.* ". . . is from a long-ago-extinct flower."

"What flower?" I grabbed on to that small hope. "What flower?"

"The juice of a blue champak flower is the only antidote to this kind of poison," the doctor said, shaking her head.

Naya's air clan friends next to me gnashed their teeth and hissed.

"What?" I looked around in confusion.

"The last-known blue champak tree grew on the grounds of the Ghatatkach Academy of Murder and Mayhem—the main rakkhosh school in Demon Land—but that last tree died back when my mom was a student there," Neel said. "I remember her telling me about it. It was their school flower or something—everyone was really upset."

"Unless we can find another antidote, we don't know if she'll make it," Dr. Ahmed said. Then she turned to go, her face back in the book. "Excuse me, I have a lot more research to do."

The news was such a horrible blow, I couldn't look at

Naya's other clan members in the face. The black-toothed rakkhoshi made an angry noise and turned away from me. Next to me, wordlessly, Neel squeezed my hand. I didn't have the heart to squeeze back.

As we walked away slowly from the clinic, I thought about Naya: the time she stowed away on the intergalactic auto rikshaw, the time she tried to give me a facial in outer space, the time she was captured alongside Ai-Ma because of me. And of course, this most recent time she'd saved my life.

I knew what we had to do, but I didn't have the courage to do it. "I guess we have to go find that tree," I said in a low voice to Neel. "To save Naya."

Neel didn't miss a beat. "We have to use the book Einstein-ji gave you."

We were in a deserted area of the PSS hideout, a narrow hallway by the dormitories. I leaned against the wall and heaved a sigh. "My last plan didn't go so well. That's how Naya got this hurt. Are you sure we should do this?"

"Kiran, listen, the Trojan horse plan may have been your idea, but I went along with it too," Neel said. His face suddenly had its old determination, like when I'd first met him last fall. "It's both our faults that Naya is in there, fighting for her life. We have no choice. We have to use the book. We have to save her."

"But to go back in time?" I pulled out the copy of *Thakurmar Jhuli* that Einstein had given me. "I don't know, Neel. Maybe I've gotten a little too sure of myself, a little too brave. Maybe we need to think this through."

"Look, Smartie-ji must have known something like this would happen. Why else would he have given us this book and made such a big deal about stories existing outside of *time*?" Neel asked, but I couldn't answer. I felt the weight of Naya's life squarely on my shoulders.

"Maybe Einstein was just being all metaphorical," I finally hedged.

"Don't be ridiculous!" Neel grabbed the book and flipped through it, "Here it is! A story called 'How the Demon Queen Chose Her Consort'!"

I started. "I've never heard that story."

Neel frowned, scanning quickly through the pages. "Weirdly, neither have I. But then again, this isn't just an ordinary book."

I peered over his shoulder at an illustration of someone who looked a lot like a crown-wearing young-looking Pinki standing before two men who had their backs to us. Behind her throne was a sign for Ghatatkach Academy of Murder and Mayhem—and just to the right of the throne was a tree with some bright blue flowers on it.

"Look, those must be the blue champak flowers the doctor was talking about. We've got to at least try, Kiran." Neel's voice was so low and urgent, it was almost a growl.

"Neel, we almost got killed on our last trip to Demon Land. The only reason we made it out alive was because of Ai-Ma," I reminded him.

"Well, we're a better team now," Neel said stubbornly. "And older. And more mature."

I didn't point out that neither of us could have gotten that much more mature in only four months. "But how does this time-traveling book work? Do we just ask it to take us back to your mom's school?"

"I'm not sure." Neel stared at the pages of the story. "I guess we could start reading it out loud and see what happens."

I bit my lip. I had learned my lesson, at too great a price, about making rash decisions after the fiasco of the Trojan horse. I didn't want to make the same mistake and hurt someone else again. "Neel, are you sure? Isn't a part of that butterfly effect that you're not supposed to mess around with time? What if we go back there and make things worse?"

"Einstein-ji gave us this book because he knew we'd need it!" Neel's voice was definitive, but I could tell he was worried too, because he was chewing on his nail. "We can't just let Naya die!"

That did it for me. He was right. I couldn't just let Naya die. I wouldn't just let Naya die.

"We can always join the rakkhosh dance team." I smiled weakly, remembered the huge, webby water rakkhosh who had tripped on a flying rakkhosh's wings earlier this afternoon and then proceeded to take about three fellow dancers out during a step-ball-change turn. The resulting demon pile was a disaster of talons, warty limbs, hair, teeth, and I don't know what else. It looked worse than a tractor-trailer pileup on the Jersey Turnpike.

"No thanks," Neel snorted as I recalled the image to him. "No step-ball-change for me."

"Then it's back to demon school we go?" I suggested. "For Naya?"

"For Naya." Neel's eyes locked with mine.

I looked away from him, feeling suddenly shy at his nearness. "What if it only takes the one of us who is doing the reading? We should probably read it together."

"That makes sense. And maybe just to be safe, maybe we should . . . uh . . . hold hands while we read." Neel's voice cracked in a funny way as he finished that sentence.

Without meeting his eyes, I held out my hand, hoping it wasn't too gross and sweaty for him to hold. He grasped it with his own warm one, interlacing his fingers with mine. I felt a zipping electricity where our skin touched, and my stomach gave a lurch.

"Okay, let's do this," I muttered. "One, two, three . . ."

Even as we started reading the first sentence of the story together, it was hard to stay focused. Neel's fingers kept a tight grip on mine, and he was sitting so close, I could feel the words of the story rumbling in his chest as he spoke them out loud.

"Nothing's happening," Neel whispered as we finished the first sentence.

"Keep reading. Stories don't work unless you keep reading, dive into them," I said.

And so we kept reading, our voices rising and falling together, the words rolling off both our tongues, the images and plot being built by both our voices. Not long after we'd finished the first paragraph, I felt it, the tugging at my belly. I looked at Neel, who was starting to look all smudgy—like a charcoal drawing being erased by someone's fingers. I saw his eyes widen as he looked at me, so I figured I must look the same.

"Here goes nothing," I said.

He nodded. "We're going to demon school."

CHAPTER 25

Romeo and Demon-ette

We landed with a thump on the rocky ground right below one of the many balconies jutting out from a majestic building of turrets, mosaics, and open porticos. I was at first really impressed by the architecture, until I realized most of the mosaics were images of bloody rakkhosh attacks— pictures of demons tearing people and animals apart in a bunch of gross and horrible ways. This was obviously the famed Ghatatkach Academy of Murder and Mayhem! It was twilight, and from the voices I heard just above us, I knew we weren't alone.

There was a light on in the balcony and two people up there, near the edge. Luckily, Neel and I had landed next to a broad tree with thick branches, so we were shielded from view. As I glanced over at him, I realized that he looked really different—with small horns peeking out of his dark hair, and fangs hanging below his lips, and even a little wart on his cheek. His eyes widened as he looked at me, and putting my hands to my face, I realized that I too had somehow been transformed by our magic time-traveling storybook into a rakkhosh! But I didn't have time to worry about how many warts I had on my face. Right now, we had to concentrate on not being found out. We both leaned hard against the tree, listening to the people in the balcony.

"Oh, my suave serpentine suitor! How patient you have been!" someone was saying. Neel put a hand over his mouth, like he was stopping himself from crying out. Wait a minute—the person talking was Pinki, his mother. I was sure of it!

"Oh, my demonic darling! You are more than worth waiting for!" This time it was my turn to clap a hand over my mouth. That voice—it couldn't be, could it? I snuck a quick look up at the balcony from around the tree. What was he doing here? Sesha!

Neel put his hand on my arm, like he thought I was stupid enough to leap out from behind the tree and confront my snake father. I shook my head. I loathed Sesha for all that he had done to us, but I wasn't that stupid. Plus, what exactly could I do to him from down on the ground when he was up in that balcony? But what in the world was he doing here in Demon Land? Neel and I eased ourselves out from behind the tree but were careful to stay well in the shadows so we could hear and see their conversation without any threat of being seen ourselves.

"Tonight is the night we have been waiting for, my darling! The night of the choosing ceremony! When I choose you as my consort and declare our love openly!" With the light behind her, and her thick dark hair pouring over her horns and shoulders, Pinki absolutely glowed.

"Everyone will know and we won't care, my sadistic sugarplum!" Sesha singsonged in his oily way. He was clean-shaven, younger, and his hair was shorter, but there was no mistaking his features. Maybe I was imagining it, but I could also hear a hint of the evil malice that would define his adult personality.

Neel shot me a questioning look, and I shook my head. What was happening here? It was uncomfortable enough hearing our parents' teenage selves talking about love—but with each other? I mean, yuck!

"I won the title of Demon Queen fair and square—after so many tests of intellect, bravery, and rodent disembowelment!" said Pinki, placing a long-clawed hand on Sesha's arm.

I mouthed, "Rodent disembowelment," at Neel, and he scowled, putting a finger to his lips.

"That you did, my clever, bloodthirsty, disemboweling minx!" Sesha tweaked her nose as he said this, earning another shocked look from Neel. I mean, the Pinki we knew would probably chop off the arm of anyone who dared to tweak her nose.

"And tonight's choosing ceremony will show everyone that I know how to chart the best course for our people's future!" young Pinki added breathlessly. "I'll show them that love is the answer to the riddles of the multiverse!"

"We will combine our powers and rule them all!" Sesha cooed. "Tonight, after you choose me at the ceremony and not that nincompoop Rontu, the human prince from the Kingdom Beyond!"

Yet again, Neel almost gasped. "Rontu is my dad!" he hissed. "She's choosing between Sesha and my dad!"

What? I'd understood from the conversation so far that there was some kind of choosing ceremony set up, where Pinki would have to choose a future husband. But it was shocking to hear that the choices were either my dad or Neel's!

"I can't believe my mother and Headmistress Surpanakha

want me to marry that buffoon of a human prince!" Pinki's voice was a little higher than I was used to, but it still had that same sarcastic confidence. "They say it's important for the future of demon-kind and humankind. I mean, blah blah blah! Who cares about that?"

"All that matters is our eternal love," Sesha drawled.

Neel looked like his eyes were going to pop out of his head. "Gross!" he mouthed at me. I was feeling just as horrified as he looked.

"Oh, Seshi!" Pinki tittered. "You're such a dreamboat!"

"I adore you, my sly sweetheart, my fanged femme fatale!" Sesha leaned to kiss her, and the two became a single silhouette against the light of the room. Neel made a disgusted face, and I felt like puking too. "Our love may be forbidden now, but it won't be after you choose me as your consort!"

"They say you just want me for my power!" Pinki scoffed. "I know you love me for myself!"

"Oh, I do! I do!" Sesha sounded way overconfident. "I adore you, my demented dumpling!"

Neel looked like he was about to burst. I felt like I was going to scream, or laugh, I wasn't sure which. Sesha and Pinki had been forbidden high school sweethearts? Like an evil Romeo and Juliet? And she actually trusted him? I was starting to wonder if Neel wasn't a little bit right about his mom being fooled by Sesha into marrying him.

"I'll see you at the ceremony," young Pinki was saying. "Don't be late, now. You're allowed to wander around Demon Land freely only for another few minutes. I had to work on the headmistress hard to get you special permission."

"I told you, as soon as you choose me, and we are officially engaged, the centuries-long trouble between our people will be over!" Sesha said smoothly. "The Kingdom of Serpents has decided that the rakkhosh will be given their own homeland, separate from the humans! The newly formed Demon Land and the Kingdom of Serpents will be allies now and forevermore! And we will reduce what's left of the Kingdom Beyond Seven Oceans and Thirteen Rivers to ashes!"

Neel and I exchanged shocked looks. Eek. That wasn't good.

"Not long now, my love!" Pinki said. "Among all the other graduating seniors at Ghatatkach Academy of Murder and Mayhem, I was chosen as Demon Queen. So it's my decision to choose my consort, and mine alone, no matter what Ai-Ma or the headmistress think about you."

"Oh, those old biddies are just jealous that you get to have me and they don't," said Sesha obnoxiously.

"Oh, I adore you, my slithering snaky suitor!" Pinki purred.

"I worship you, my ravishing rakkhosh-radish!" Sesha answered.

"Now go, silly snake boy. Let me get ready for the ceremony!"

"I'll see you there, you demonic darling!"

Our parents walked back into the room, away from the balcony. I whispered to Neel, "I can't believe it!"

"That was bonkers!" he hissed, pointing at the now-empty balcony. "They were in love? Your dad and my mom? Maybe she really is as evil as you said."

"I don't know. I was wondering if maybe that's why they're getting married now—because they were childhood sweethearts?" It sounded revolting even to my own ears.

"What happened back then—I mean, now—do you suppose?" Neel bit on a rakkhosh-length nail.

"Well, it didn't work out, obviously. She married your dad, not mine," I said. "I mean, otherwise, you wouldn't have been born. And the Kingdom Beyond would never have been!"

"I guess." Neel shrugged. "And then there was all that stuff about Demon Land being formed? But let's not worry about that now, let's find that champak tree and get out of here. We're here to save Naya, not worry about my mom and Sesha's past love lives!"

I looked at Neel a little more closely. "Um, Neel?"

"What?" He was standing up and dusting off his clothes.

"Look at your hands," I whispered. Oh, this was bad.

Neel looked down. The edges of his hands, like the edges of his body, were a little blurrier than they had been a minute ago. He looked up sharply at me. "What's happening to me?"

Just then, I saw a little blue insect fly by through the branches of the tree. I took in a sharp breath.

"The butterfly effect!" I whispered. "But not the way I thought."

"What do you mean?" Neel was looking panicky now. "Oh no. What's happening to me, Kiran? I feel so . . . wispy. Like I'm disappearing!"

"That's because you are! Oh my gosh—I thought if we came back in time, we'd mess up the future," I said. "But it looks like we're here just in time to *fix* the future! Neel, if we don't stop Pinki and Sesha from getting married, you'll never be born!"

"You mean I'm disappearing from existence?" Neel yelped, checking out his rapidly blurrifying form. "How do we fix it?"

"We've got to convince her not to choose Sesha, but your dad instead!" I bit my lip. Every second we talked, Neel was getting blurrier and blurrier! "I think I have an idea!"

I picked up a rock and hurled it at Pinki's balcony, hitting it with a little thunk. When nothing happened, I threw another rock, and then another.

"Stop!" Neel grabbed my arm with his own smudgy one. "What are you doing?"

I shook him off. "I'm trying to get her attention! She kicked Sesha out so that she could get ready! This might be our only chance to talk to her alone!"

Sure enough, almost as soon as I had finished saying the words, Pinki came out onto the balcony. Silhouetted by the light from behind her, she glowed like a horned and fanged angel.

"Who's there?" Neel's mom leaned out over the balcony even as we shrunk back more into the shadows. "Aakash, is that you, you air clan loser? Still upset I beat you out for the crown? Still whining you didn't become Demon King?"

"Listen to us—we're friends, my lady!" I said in a wheezy,

and I hoped demonic, tone. "Here to tell you Sesha's way shady!"

"How do you know about Sesha? Who are you?" Pinki demanded, leaning out even farther and squinting into the night.

"He wants you just for your power," Neel called out in a terrible fake voice. He waved his hands at me in silent panic as he tried to think of a rhyme for power. Finally, he finished, "Not because he thinks you're a flower!"

"Show your faces, you rakkhosh rubes! Or I'll mince you into little cubes!" Pinki snarled, growing into her full rakkhosh height and form.

I tried desperately to think of an explanation that would convince Pinki. "Rontu's soft, him you can control," I finally said. "But Sesha will dump you in a dark hole!"

Pinki's eyes scanned the darkness, panicky now. "Not true! Where are you?"

"Isn't it better to be independent?" Neel began, then, clapping a hand over his mouth, looked over at me. "What rhymes with independent?" he hissed.

"Transcendent? Attendant?" I volunteered in a whisper. "Why didn't you think it through first?"

"Than give birth to a bunch of snaky descendants?" Neel finally concluded.

"How dare you, Sonny Jim? I'm coming down there to rip you limb from limb!" screeched Pinki, turning away from the balcony.

"We better get out of here!" I tugged at Neel's arm. "Oh no, you're still not back to normal. Just look at yourself."

"Oh man! I'm better, but still kinda transparent," Neel said in a panicky voice. "There's still a chance I won't be born, isn't there?"

"Looks like it," I sighed. "We can't leave Demon Land just yet, not until we're sure your mom chooses your dad as her consort. Come on, we've got to get to the choosing ceremony before she comes out here and finds us!"

CHAPTER 26

The Gift Givers

"Hurry up!" I hissed at a blurry-edged Neel, who seemed to have trouble running with his blurry feet. "We've got to find out where this choosing ceremony is happening!"

"Probably where all those demon students are going, I'd guess," Neel said. The students, to my surprise, weren't walking toward the school, but away from it. We followed them, trying to get lost in the crowd just in case Pinki actually came after us.

The rakkhosh students all around us were pumped up—cheering, chanting, shouting about tonight being the night of the choosing. I saw that there were different sorts of rakkhosh all walking more or less together, and in front of each group were their clan banners. There were waves for water clan, flames for fire clan, wings for air clan, and a rocky mountain for land clan.

And all the rakkhosh students seemed to be dressed according to their house colors.

"Where's your shawl, you dirty ace?" a young guy with a warty nose asked Neel. "Headmistress catches you, she'll bite off your face!"

"Here!" A friendly-faced rakkhosh thrust two brown-and-green-colored shawls at us and we gratefully took them. We didn't have wings, or fiery breath, or webbed fingers, so I guessed we were land clan now.

"Hey, did you ever think about how much these rakkhosh clans are like that other story—with the magical students and their four school houses?" I whispered to Neel.

Neel looked annoyed. "Who's to say those witches and wizards didn't get the idea from us?"

Night had fallen as it always did in this dimension—fast like a curtain. The new darkness was already heavy with the smells of night-blooming flowers. In addition to the sound of rakkhosh students' chatter, all around us were the sounds of crickets and, somewhere in the distance, a running stream. The path from the school's main entrance was illuminated by rows of prodeep, teardrop-shaped oil lamps with burning wicks. I noticed with a shudder that each prodeep was held up by stakes designed to look like disembodied monster arms.

The lighted path ended in a beautiful outdoor grove. We entered the grove—which was made of four giant banyan trunks surrounding one central raised dais. The water, fire, air, and land clans each went to what looked like a designated tree. We settled ourselves on a thick banyan root with the rest of the land clan.

"Look!" Neel said. "There it is!"

I looked where he was pointing. On the central dais was an empty throne, I guess waiting for Pinki. Before the throne were two empty chairs—probably for her two potential consorts. And right next to the throne was the thing we had come all this way to find. The beautiful school tree with the fluttering, almost-alive-looking blue champak flowers.

"If only we could grab some and get out of here!" Neel said.

"Oh, sure, that'll be really easy to do right in the middle of these hundreds of rakkhosh!" I hissed. All the students looked powerful, and some were downright scary. "Anyway, we can't leave yet, not until we're sure your mom makes the right choice and you actually get born in the future!"

"Hey, wait a minute, check out the tree trunk," Neel whispered. I squinted at the champak tree and realized all its wood was etched with words.

"Did someone carve those?" I asked.

"I don't know," Neel whispered. "Shh, that must be the headmistress."

I wrapped my long shawl around my shoulders to protect myself from the buzzing mosquitos, and turned away from the tree to face the demoness climbing onto the platform. The headmistress of the Academy of Murder and Mayhem was a tall, formidable rakkhoshi, in a gorgeous silk sari shot with the colors of all the Ghatatkach clan houses. The shawl she had wrapped around her shoulders too was mixed with all the clan colors—brown and green for land clan, red and orange for fire clan, shades of dark blue for water clan, and light blue and white for air clan. The headmistress's dark hair piled at least three feet high above her broad forehead. She had fangs and long nails, but clear skin and an actually pretty face. Pretty if you ignored the fact that she had no nose.

"Her name's Surpanakha," whispered Neel. "My mother mentioned her. She became headmistress here after her nose got cut off in some kind of legendary battle. The students apparently used to make up funny names for her behind her back, like the Nosemeister and Smelly Smellopolis and stuff like that."

Huh, that nickname stuff sounded a lot like what Zuzu, Jovi, and I had been doing with Principal Chen. Back when I thought she really was Principal Chen, that is. Weird to think I had that in common with Neel's mom.

Headmistress Surpanakha stood stock-still, studying the rowdy students through the horn-rimmed glasses that somehow balanced on her noseless face. Then she cleared her throat and spoke.

"Students of Ghatatkach Academy. As you know, today is the day of the great choosing ceremony. When our newly elected Rakkhoshi Rani will become settled into her powers and select her consort for life!" She paused dramatically, waving her long-taloned hands in the air.

"Nose-illa is doing jazz hands," whispered Neel. "Maybe she's practicing for the wedding sangeet."

"Shh!" I poked him in the ribs, almost laughing out loud from nervousness.

I was surprised at how unfazed Neel was to be sitting here in this clearing full of hundreds of young, strong, drooling rakkhosh. I, on the other hand, was seriously fazed. Like, armpit-sweaty fazed.

There was a great wailing of shehnai, and the ulu-ulu call that marks auspicious occasions, and then there she was—Pinki. Up close to her now, and not yards below her balcony, I saw that she was dressed in elaborate wedding finery—a red sari embroidered with gold thread, golden rings attached by chains to the bangles on her arms, a nose ring attached by gilded chain to the ornaments in her hair, and heavy earrings. On her dark hair was a white shola pith tiara, like the little dolly I'd seen when I was looking for my moon mother. She was accompanied by several rakkhosh, and was led with great pomp to her throne to raucous cheers. Even the headmistress bowed as the new Demon Queen approached. Pinki smiled as she sat, breathing out a swath of fire and smoke as she did so.

"Look who else is with her!" Neel said, and I choked back a sob. Because right behind Pinki came Ai-Ma, looking just as wacky and gangly as she always had but a little younger, with more teeth and hair and substantially less drool. Her eyes glowed with such pride as she looked at her daughter that I felt like crying.

"Ai-Ma! Oh, it's Ai-Ma!" I didn't dare say it in anything louder than a whisper, but it was really hard not to go and throw myself into Neel's grandmother's warty arms. She might be a powerful rakkhoshi, but Ai-Ma had saved my life more than once, and she had actually died so that I might live. It felt so wonderful to see her again but bittersweet too, because I knew there was no way she would know who we were. The attendants led Ai-Ma to a smaller chair just behind Pinki's.

Then, with another call of the shehnai as well as a tabla drum roll, two more people were led out to the stage. Neel's dad, Rontu, and Sesha, both in splendid white wedding clothes—sparkling kurta and dhoti and even the pointy dunce-cap-like topor that bridegrooms wore in the Kingdom Beyond. But the moment they sat down, to my shock, there appeared around their chairs two giant, glowing cages, like they were giant, captured birds! The entire audience burst out in hoots and curses.

"What's up with that?" I wondered aloud. Neel's dad looked a lot like Lal, only softer, and was obviously terrified. He gave a little whimper from inside his cage.

"It's terrible to see him like this," Neel whispered. "I mean, I know he doesn't like the fact that I'm half rakkhosh, but I hate seeing him as a prisoner."

"It's so weird. I didn't realize that part of the choosing was locking up the potential bridegrooms!" I murmured.

As opposed to Neel's dad, Sesha looked like he thought

the cage was a joke. He grinned at Pinki through the bars, blowing her kisses and waving. For her part, I noticed, Pinki didn't look at him at all. Maybe our words to her were having some effect?

"Pinki of the fire clan has been elected our new Demon Queen due to her skill in the classroom and the combat yard, and of course due to all of your faith that she will fulfill the great cosmic duties of demon-kind," Surpanakha was saying. She peered around the clearing with her sharp eyes. On either side of her lounged two fierce-looking jackals on golden leashes that she held in her hand. Even as the animals feasted on some kind of bloody meat, their sharp eyes moved over the students just like their mistress's.

"Tonight, as has been our custom since the beginning of time, we have captured the princely sons from two neighboring kingdoms—from the Kingdom Beyond and the Kingdom of Serpents. One of these future rulers, Pinki will choose as her consort."

"She just said that they captured the two princes, but Sesha wants to be here!" I whispered to Neel.

"Obviously, Pinki and Sesha bent the rules because they were into each other!" Neel hissed back.

The headmistress went on, "Before our new queen makes her choice, she must swear to keep the balance of the multiverse. For the seeds of the multiverse's origins—the singularity—reside in our queen, and on her shoulders falls the responsibility of rakkhosh-kind: to keep in balance the light and the dark, birth and death, story and silence. On her shoulders falls the responsibility to keep the diversity of the multiverse ever expanding."

"Whoa," I whispered. It was all that stuff the scientists had been talking about. About the origins of the multiverse coming from something within black holes—aka rakkhosh. But that last bit, about rakkhosh-kind being responsible for keeping the multiverse expanding, that was the exact opposite of what Sesha was trying to do. I wondered if Neel could be right after all. Was Pinki not a part of the Anti-Chaos Committee but actually, somehow, Sesha's prisoner?

"To fulfill this great duty," Surpanakha went on, "our queen must gain the power of all four clans. She already has the power of her own fire clan, but tonight the other three clans will be sharing their power with her with offerings of symbolic gifts. I call first upon the air clan to make their offering."

"Look at the tree!" As the headmistress was speaking, my attention was captured by the blue champak tree to the side of Pinki's and Ai-Ma's chairs. The tree was full of bright blue champak flowers that seemed to be moving—almost as if the flowers were actually butterflies!

"Do you see what I see?" I hissed. Neel just made big eyes and nodded as one of the flowers-slash-butterflies took off from the tree and flew into the darkening sky.

"Wonder who's gonna be the gift giver for our clan?" singsonged a tall rakkhoshi sitting on the next root from us. She had on a necklace with her name, Harimati, in Bangla script, and giant jhumko earrings. She also had yellow eyes and fangs so sharp they looked like she'd stolen them from a saber-toothed tiger.

Harimati was nibbling from a banana-leaf plate piled high with what looked a lot like bat-ear fritters. "If it's not Gorgor-da, he'll be off on a killing rampage, won't he?"

I looked over at the rakkhosh she was pointing at, a muscle-bound fellow with three eyeballs and way too many rows of teeth. Gorgor-da caught me looking at him and made a threatening, knuckle-cracking-type gesture. I looked away quickly, gulping hard.

Harimati chuckled, shoving more fritters in her mouth even as she offered the plate to Neel and me. I shook my head no, but inexplicably, Neel picked up one of the fritters and tried it before gagging and spitting it out in his hand.

"Um, wow. That's got a bite to it," Neel muttered, and I saw that he was right. The half-eaten piece of food in Neel's hand did indeed have chomping teeth. Ick.

Harimati laughed. "That's what makes 'em so good, innit?" she said. It was weird how she was just accepting Neel's and my presence here even though she'd never seen us before in her life. Must be part of Einstein's storybook's magic.

In the meantime, the headmistress plucked one of the blue champak flowers from the tree. It fluttered in her hand as if it had wings. Then the wings turned into lips as, in a strangely breathy voice, it announced, "Gift giver for the air clan will be the flier Aakash!"

As soon as the champak flower said the name, it seemed to wither and die in Surpanakha's hand. She flicked off the wilted petals (or were they wings?) with a careless gesture.

"I think we know now why the blue champak tree died off," muttered Neel.

"Or maybe they didn't," I whispered, thinking of how many blue butterflies I'd been seeing in the Kingdom Beyond lately. "Maybe these flowers have been there all the time, but we just didn't know how to recognize them."

As his name was called, Aakash, a powerful and kind of scarily handsome rakkhosh, stood up from the air clan banyan and took a bow. The leaves and branches of the air clan's tree waved in what appeared to be a gusty storm. Aakash's giant insect-type wings spread out several feet when he extended them. His chest was bare under his light-blue-and-white house shawl, and I could see his muscles rippling as he waved to the crowds. I noticed that rakkhosh from a bunch of different clans seemed to give out long sighs all at the same time.

Aakash approached the throne and bowed. "For our queen, the air clan offers the power of flight."

Aakash made a little gesture, and where there had been nothing before, suddenly, there was a blue pulsating energy, like a little swirling storm, in Aakash's hands. The pulsing ball had, I noticed, tiny wings.

Pinki gave him a skeptical look. "Was it you calling to me today from the garden?"

"My queen?" Aakash looked confused, and I remembered Pinki had called out his name when Neel and I had tried to warn her about Sesha.

"Never mind." With a gracious incline of her head, Pinki took the winged storm from him. "Thank you, air clan, for sharing with me your power of flight," she said, promptly ruining the gracious effect with a huge burp.

The wild thing was, as soon as Pinki accepted the air

clan gift, there appeared on her arms the same tattoo-like swirling markings that were carved into the champak tree. Now that I saw them in the context of her wedding outfit, I recognized them for what they were: the mehendi designs that brides often had henna-ed upon their skin for their weddings. But there was something different about Pinki's mehendi; they almost appeared like they were . . .

"Stories!" Surpanakha intoned, holding up Pinki's arms to the crowd. "All the stories of the air clan and the creatures of flight are now the responsibility of our queen. They are etched into her very skin!"

Almost as soon as Surpanakha finished speaking, Pinki's mehendi disappeared, as if being sucked into her skin. Aakash, still bowing, backed away from the throne. Surpanakha waited for the applause to die down before reaching for the next magical champak flower. The gift giver for the water clan would be a sleek and strong rakkhoshi with a scaly crocodile tail named Kumi.

Kumi too approached the throne with a deep bow. Her hair dripped as if wet, and her tail swished as she walked. The rakkhoshi knelt before Pinki, then waved her hands and produced what looked like a giant teardrop. "From the water clan, we offer our new queen power over water in all her many forms."

Pinki graciously took the offered gift. "I thank you, water clan, for your gift." As before, as soon as she said these words, her skin was again covered by the swirling, beautiful mehendi designs, this time in the flowing shapes of waves and teardrops, rain and rivers.

"All the stories of the water clan and the creatures of the water are now etched into your skin," said Surpanakha. The headmistress then picked another of the blue champak-flowers-slash-butterflies.

"Our gift giver representing the land clan will be . . . Kiranmala!" shouted the small blue flower. The headmistress Surpanakha dropped the dying petals and wrinkled her brows. "I didn't know we had a student with that name," I heard her mutter.

It took me a minute to register what had just happened. "Don't be shy—that's you!" Harimati the rakkhoshi urged me forward, even as the rakkhosh she'd called Gorgor-da growled at me. "Never mind Gorgor-da, go give the Queen a land clan gift!"

"Wait, no—" Neel began, but Harimati cut him off.

"It's an honor! Get up there!" Before I could stop her, Harimati and another rakkhosh hoisted me up on their shoulders and carried me toward the stage!

Oh no, what was I going to do? I didn't have the ability

to conjure up a magical gift like Aakash or Kumi had done. But then I thought about the one magical gift I did have. Maybe this was meant to be, another part of Einstein-ji's book magic! And this might be my one last chance to convince Pinki not to choose Sesha!

I saw Neel dashing up behind us, a worried expression on his face, but as Harimati and the other rakkhosh put me down by the stage, I whispered reassuringly, "Don't worry, I got this."

"You better know what you're doing," said my still-blurry-edged friend.

"I do," I muttered. "Or at least I hope so!"

With trembling legs, I approached Pinki's throne and bowed low. She gave me a curious look, but nothing that told me she recognized me. Ai-Ma, on the other hand, kind of leaned forward and studied my face. "I feel like I know you from somewhere, little demon-ling," she murmured.

I pretended like I hadn't heard Ai-Ma, and turned my face up to Neel's mom. "Oh, Queen. The air clan has offered you flight, and the water clan control over water itself. What can the land clan offer you to compare?"

I heard titters from the water, fire, and air clans and growls of discontent from the land clan behind me.

"For our gift, we offer you these jewels, the Chintamoni and Poroshmoni Stones." I pulled out the pulsating white and yellow jewels from my backpack and held them out toward Pinki. "They are stars fallen to land from the heavens themselves. Powerful enough to give their owner wealth beyond compare, or even control over death!"

The entire clearing became still as everyone trained their attention on the pulsating, powerful stars-slash-stones. Pinki opened her lips as if to speak but was soon cut off.

"What a wonderful wedding gift!" Sesha's voice was smooth, but I could detect the eagerness within. "Perhaps I should keep them for you, my bride, for safekeeping."

The entire grove burst into laughter, and even Surpanakha chuckled. But I felt the triumph in my stomach. I knew that Sesha couldn't resist revealing his greed once he saw the stones. After all, they had driven him to almost kill me, Neel, and Neel's mom in the future.

Surpanakha called out, "You are in no position to make such an offer, Prince of Serpents. The gifts of the clans are for the Queen alone, not her consort. Besides, what makes you so sure she will choose you and not the prince of the Kingdom Beyond?"

"Oh, she will choose me," protested Sesha, and now I

could really hear the desperation in his voice. "And she wants to give those jewels to me, don't you, my dear darling Pinki?"

I could see Pinki's expression shift from flattered to confused to cautious. Sesha's words and actions alone might not have made her so suspicious, but in combination with the warning Neel and I had given her, she was clearly having some second thoughts.

"Don't tell me what I want or don't want. I am no weakling to be controlled by a husband," Pinki snapped. She grabbed the jewels from my open hands and stood up, holding the yellow and white stones above her head. As soon as she had taken the jewels, her skin was again covered by the elaborate mehendi stories. They glowed bright red before fading into her skin as the others had done before.

Pinki cleared her throat ferociously. "In fact, let me declare it now, loud and proud. As my headmistress and mother have chosen, my consort will be none other than Fatteshwar Orebaba, aka Rontu, Prince of the Kingdom Beyond Seven Oceans and Thirteen Rivers!"

With these words, the cage around Rontu vanished. With a triumphant look at Sesha, Pinki then handed Neel's dad both the magic jewels!

CHAPTER 27

The Choosing

The rakkhosh students cheered. Ai-Ma and Surpanakha beamed and looked pleased. Rontu, the future Raja of the Kingdom Beyond, looked stunned. "But . . . you're a rakkhoshi! I don't want to be married to you!" he blurted out.

Ai-Ma waved her hands before Neel's father. "True love will you see when you see your wife's face. No demon anymore, but with human replaced." And with those words, she snapped her fingers, and Rontu's expression changed entirely.

"Oh, I adore you, my queen, my love!" he burbled, grasping Pinki simperingly by the hand.

Pinki said nothing but looked disgusted at her new consort's rapid change of heart. She then turned to look at Sesha with tears in her eyes, like she couldn't believe what she had just done. Sesha, for his part, howled and snarled, rattling his cage with all his might.

"How dare you, you stupid demoness?" he yelled. "How dare you not choose me?"

"You want my power!" Pinki yelled. "Not me! It was never about me!"

"You'll regret this for the rest of your life!" shrieked Sesha. He turned, snarling, at the rakkhosh school gathered around him. "All of demon-kind will regret this. I will destroy your kind, if it's the last thing I do! No one will remember who you are! I will erase your stories from the multiverse!"

Sesha raged inside his magical cage, prompting a bunch of rakkhosh guards to hop onstage and surround him. Pinki moved aside, flanked by a dazed-looking but passive Rontu as well as a fierce-appearing Ai-Ma. Surpanakha shouted orders, and most of the students ran around in utter confusion.

In the chaos, I made my way off the stage and back to Neel, stopping to pick two champak flowers off the tree on the way. "Come on, I think our work here is done! Pinki's marrying your father, and she and Sesha hate each other— just the way things are supposed to be!"

"No, stop! Something's not right!" Neel sputtered.

"What? You're not blurry anymore, are you? What's the big deal?" I pointed to Neel's once-again-solid outlines.

"I may not be blurry anymore, but you are!" Neel said, his eyes wide in alarm.

"What the—" I sputtered, looking down at my now-blurry body. "What's happening?"

"The Queen has made her choice of consort!" Surpanakha boomed from the stage. "Now, to complete the ceremony, she must kill the other suitor competing for her hand!"

At first, I didn't get it, but Neel looked at me in horror. "Kiran! This is a disaster! We've made sure that my parents get married so that I can exist in the future. But now, if Pinki kills Sesha, that means you can't ever be born!"

Oh, blast. This was horrible. What were we going to do?

"My queen!" Neel called out, his voice desperate and urgent. "You can't kill the snake prince!"

"Why the heck not?" Pinki already had begun spitting hot fumes of fire at Sesha's cage, making him cower in the corner.

"Because . . . because . . . you're better than that?" Neel suggested.

The students all around us began to laugh, like Neel had made a splendid joke. Even the vicious-looking Gorgor-da slapped Neel heartily on the back. "That's a good one, kid!"

"Better than that!" scoffed Pinki, but I could tell, even if no one else could, that she was torn. "I'm not better than that. Why should I be better than that? What a thought!"

"You loved me once, Pinki," Sesha spat out. "But you got squeamish and turned your back on all that! We were a good pair, you and I! How could you want to dim your light, hitching yourself to someone who doesn't even see you for who you are?"

Even through his thick enchantment, Rontu, the future Raja of the Kingdom Beyond, seemed to understand that Sesha was insulting him. "Hey there, I'm not dimming anyone's light! I just want her to follow all the rules of my kingdom and be the picture of a good and docile wife to me, supporting me in all my dreams and having none of her own!"

This got the crowd laughing again. "As if!" chortled Surpanakha. "Oh, you poor demented little prince, your rakkhoshi wife is going to marry you and use you to rule your kingdom!"

Rontu blinked a little at these words, as if they were penetrating the magical fog around his brain. He looked what seemed like directly at Neel. "I hate rakkhosh," he pronounced.

"Husband-to-be, you are such a bore!" Pinki snarled. "Go to sleep now, and have a good snore!"

At a wave of her hands, Fatteshwar Orebaba, aka Rontu, Neel's father and the future Raja of the Kingdom Beyond, curled up next to the throne and went fast to sleep.

With that done, Pinki turned back to Sesha. "How dare you!" she snarled. "You pretended to love me only because you wanted my power!"

"Like you weren't doing the same thing!" he spat out through the glowing bars of the cage.

Pinki's expression faltered at these words, like she had loved Sesha for real, and thought he felt the same. Then a mask fell over her features again. "Of course I was, it was all a joke, and now it's over!"

Pinki jumped forward, reaching through the bars of the cage and putting her hands around his throat. Sesha gasped, and the crowd cheered. Sesha was strong, and powerful, but inside his magical cage, he could do nothing. The rakkhosh students all around me jeered and taunted him. Something in my chest constricted. I remembered Neel explaining how much rakkhosh hated snakes. I understood everyone's gut reactions pretty well, since I was having the same one too. The sight of Sesha's evil face made me want to claw his eyes out. He'd tried to kill me not once, but multiple times, when he wasn't trying to turn me into a snake, that is. He had tormented my moon mother and probably been the reason she was the vague, not-really-there-but-there presence she was in my life. He was the reason I'd been banished to New Jersey and never really known who I was for so many years. He'd tortured and later imprisoned Neel. He was evil. He was terrible. He was trying to destroy the multiverse and all our unique stories. I would think I would rejoice to see him looking so small and beaten and afraid.

Yet, with every squeeze of Pinki's hands, I felt myself growing weaker and more light-headed. No matter how much I hated Sesha, my fate was tied to his. Neel grabbed me by my elbows, holding me up. "Hold on, Kiran, don't disappear on me yet!" But with every passing second, I felt my essence growing fainter and fainter.

I tried as hard as I could to control my breathing. In and out, Kiran, I told myself. In and out. I couldn't control what was happening to me, but I had control over myself, and my reactions.

That's when I met Ai-Ma's eyes. And I saw the old rakkhoshi's eyes traveling over my fuzzy outline and then landing on Neel's worried face. She squinted at her grandson, like she couldn't quite believe what she was seeing, and then back at me. And in that second, I could see that something inside Neel's old grandma was beginning to recognize him.

Neel caught her glance too. "We need some help, Kiran, come on!" he said. Supporting my weight now entirely, he dragged me to his grandmother. "Ai-Ma, can you help us?"

"How do you know me, little desperate demon-ling?" she said, touching Neel's face in wonder. "Wait, why does this lollipop of a dung-beetle boy look so much like my daughter?"

"He's your grandson, Ai-Ma. Your grandson from the future," I wheezed, hoping that this version of past Ai-Ma was as loving as the one I would know in my own time.

"I can hardly believe it," she breathed, running her already-wrinkled hands over Neel's cheek.

"Will you help us, Ai-Ma?" Neel begged. "We can't let my mom kill Sesha or else Kiranmala will never be born. Look at how she's fading. We hate him too, but we can't let him die."

"Kiranmala, is it?" cackled the old woman. "The name of an adventuress, an underestimated heroine from a long-told tale."

"But will you help us, Ai-Ma? Please?" I breathed, holding on to the edge of her sari in supplication. Behind us,

Pinki seemed to be choking the life out of Sesha. I heard him sputter and choke as the crowd roared. My head spun, and I fell to my knees.

"Kiran!" Neel cried. "Ai-Ma! What should we do?"

"You must invoke the right of challenge kill," said Ai-Ma quickly.

"What?" I sputtered from my position on the ground.

But without explaining any more, Ai-Ma stood up, holding my fist in the air with her own. "Halt, my daughter! This young rasagolla of a demon-ling invokes the right of challenge kill!"

"What?" Pinki sputtered sharp blades of fire. Taking advantage of her confusion, Sesha somehow pushed Pinki's hands off his neck and took in some big shuddering breaths. I felt the strength entering my own body again as he did. "You invoke challenge kill? Based on what right?"

"Based on right of . . . relation," Ai-Ma said. "This young rakkhoshi has had, erm, loved ones harmed by Sesha's malice."

"What?" Sesha snarled. "I've never seen that hideous rakkhoshi wench before in my life!"

Of course Sesha wouldn't recognize me in my rakkhoshi form. I wondered if he would have recognized me in any form.

Ai-Ma wasn't wrong. He had harmed me and my loved ones—Ma, Baba, my moon mother, Neel, and, indirectly, Naya.

"Well, I've seen you before!" I snapped. "But I guess you've forgotten me!"

The rakkhosh students around us erupted in shrieks of mocking laughter. They yelled insults and taunted Sesha. "Water, air, land, and flames, the snake's gone and forgot his name!"

Sesha lost his cookies at that. He snarled at me, pointing with a shaking finger. "My name will never be forgotten! But yours will be—I will erase all of rakkhosh-kind from the multiverse's memory!" He frothed a little at the mouth. "Just you wait! No one will remember you; no one will tell your stories. You will become beasts from a long-ago and forgotten culture!"

That made my blood freeze. Sesha's plan for destroying the multiplicity of the multiverse had started this long ago?

"No, Sesha, it's your name that will be forgotten!" I said. To prove my point, and to buy myself some time, I pulled out my bow and arrow, aiming right at Sesha's head.

"Wait, I haven't granted you the right of challenge kill," Pinki protested. "What makes you think you have more right to kill than me?"

"Challenge kill is an ancient right among our kind, and if this rakkhoshi has the right of injury on her side, it cannot be denied." Surpanakha the headmistress stepped in between Pinki and me. "You say this serpent prince has harmed your loved ones, land demoness. If that is so, you must bind yourself to him and let fate decide if you have the right of vengeance upon him."

"Bind myself to him?" I asked, feeling weak again.

"Yes." Surpanakha waved her hand in front of Sesha's mouth and somehow magically extracted a fountain of poison from one of his teeth. This she caught in a little vial and handed to me. "Drink, young land clanswoman, and if you have the right of challenge kill, it will not harm you."

I heard Neel shouting a warning, but without knowing why, I knew I would be able to drink the serpent poison without being harmed. Giving Sesha an approximation of Neel's raised-eyebrow look, I lifted the vial, gave him a little "cheers," and then drank the venom in one gulp. For a minute, I felt queasy and dizzy, but then the feeling cleared up almost right away. Even those few sips of Sesha's venom made me feel sharper, stronger, and more powerful. I locked eyes with my serpent father, and I felt him begin to recognize me.

"Who are you?" he hissed.

I did not answer, because I heard Surpanakha asking me the question as if from far, far away. "What do you see, land clanswoman?"

What did I see? I strung an arrow in my magic bow again and peered down its shaft, my vision condensing to one sharp point, right in the center of Sesha's forehead. What did I see? I asked myself, my own voice thrumming through me like a song. What did I see? What did I see?

"I'll tell you what I see!" I heard Sesha shouting at me. "I see a monster made from hate!"

I hesitated, my bow arm quavering a bit. Then a shocked murmur rose from all the students, who were pointing at me and rising from their tree-side seats. The grove was buzzing with conversation, exclamations, and shouts, and even Surpanakha was looking at me with a seriously surprised expression.

My skin prickled with heat and power. I felt like myself, but a more beautiful version, a more powerful version, a more balanced and wiser version of me. Rather than killing me, I had survived Sesha's poison and it had made me stronger. I glowed with what felt like moonlight from the inside out. It was as if I was manifesting into my most pure and true self.

"What do you see?" Surpanakha had asked me.

What did I see when I looked at Sesha? I saw hatred. I saw cruelty. I saw pain. I saw greed and suffering, but longing too. An intense longing, like a hunger. A hunger to possess things, to rule things, to dominate things. These were Sesha's poison. These were the dark matter that had corrupted him. But even under all that poison, there was more there too. There was a desire to be more, do more, leave a mark on the multiverse. In these qualities, I saw myself. These were the parts of myself I had inherited from him. Parts of myself I could use for good or for evil. Ultimately, they were parts of myself I had to accept to truly know who I was.

Sesha was beside himself, frothing at the mouth even as he shouted at me. "You hate me, do you? Well, I hate you too! I hate you too! And you have no idea what future your hate will bring!"

As he snapped and hissed, banging against the bars of the magic cage like a demented animal, his words rang in my mind. *You have no idea what future your hate will bring.* Why did he say that? And where had I heard about hate bringing about some kind of future?

My arm trembled, so long had I held out my bow. I still had no idea how to save Sesha, but his words had triggered a memory. It had been the end of my moon mother's poem: Hate, not love, makes difference end. Hate, not love. That must be it. That must be how Sesha was making all these stories smush in the past, present, and future. That must be part of his plan to bring about the big crunch. To fan as much hate as possible in the multiverse. From petty rivalries to interspecies distrust to war, it was all a part of his plan. I thought of how Neel and I had been squabbling, and for that matter, Neel and Lal, me and Mati too. Was it all because of Sesha's hate?

Long ago, Einstein-ji had told me a riddle: Everything is connected to everything, but how? The answer, I had learned, was love. Love, and only love, would make the multiverse keep expanding. Love, and only love, would create more stories. Love, and only love, was the answer to how everything was connected to everything. So if love made stories, hate and fear killed them.

As I thought this, a single flower from the champak tree floated off, as if on a breeze, becoming a bright blue butterfly. The tiny insect landed delicately on the end of my arrow, as if trying to tell me something. And all at once, I saw. The butterflies were stories—each delicate and fragile on its own, easily crushed, easily discarded. But together, migrating in a beautiful, beating mass, the insects were mighty. "Use the butterfly effect," the scientists had told me. And I would.

"Butterflies, please, I need your help!" I called. "Your stories are in danger. You are in danger!"

They did not waste any time. A fluttering, rumbling, rustling sound made me look up. Layered thick along the banyan tree canopy were all the blue butterflies that had been flowers on the champak tree. The tree itself looked bare, dead. But the butterflies were layered so thick, their beating wings were like a living, breathing sky above our heads. As I looked up and saw them, so too did the rest of Ghatatkach Academy of Murder and Mayhem. The rakkhosh students snarled and whooped and tried to catch the delicate insects. The butterflies swooped down among the rakkhosh crowd, now changing a demon into a cartoon beagle, now changing a demoness into a glittering pony. The insects seemed to be playing with the rakkhosh, swooping down, landing on one, then flying away to land on another.

But the majority of the butterflies landed en masse on and inside Sesha's cage. They covered the cage, and him, so much I could hardly see him anymore. I lowered my weapon, mesmerized by the sight.

"What is this? Get off! Get off!" Sesha sputtered. But the butterflies were relentless, flapping in his eyes, his hair, his ears, his nose, his mouth. I caught a glimpse of him changing now into an evil king with a bad haircut, now into a beating eye hungry for power. Then, in the next moment, he was a riddling master criminal with question marks all over his clothes, and then he was a corrupt president who liked to wear white roses in his lapel. Sesha—who would become the terrible and hated King of Serpents—was becoming instead a series of other villains from other stories.

"He's losing his own uniqueness," said Neel. "The stories are mad that he's trying to destroy them."

"They've been around us all the time, all these stories," I wondered. "We just never recognized them."

"Sesha needs chaos as much as we do," Neel said. "He thinks the hate will save him, but it won't. It'll destroy who he is."

Finally, I lowered my weapon. "I'll tell you what I see, Headmistress." As I spoke these words to Surpanakha, I approached the magic cage. With a wave of my hands—a power I conjured from who knows where—I opened the door. It didn't matter, because Sesha was such a prisoner of the butterflies, he could barely move now.

I said, more to myself than anyone else, "I see my father,

who I can't love or hate. Who I can't even understand, really. But still, I can put him in my past. I can forgive him and move on. Because without his story, my story would never have begun. And for better or worse, we need all our stories. All of them, for the multiverse to go on."

It was as if the butterflies had been waiting for my words. They picked Sesha up as easily as if he were the tiny insect, and they the mighty prince. And like that, with him squirming and crying and carrying on, they carried him up out of the cage, along the length of the banyan tree clearing, and finally, out into the now-starry night.

The first to become unfrozen after this remarkable sight was Surpanakha, the demon headmistress.

"Who did you say you are, child?" she asked me, grabbing my chin with hard fingers. Her face was outraged, her fangs glistening and sharp. The place where her nose should have been began twitching, and she was drooling, as if despite not having a nose, she could smell me and my smell had suddenly changed from rakkhosh-kind to something far more edible and tempting.

I realized that just as the butterflies had revealed Sesha's true form as every evil father, every cruel king, every power-hungry wizard from every fairy tale I had ever read, they were revealing Neel's and my true forms as well.

"No more disguises," breathed Neel, pointing at my face.

"No more disguises," I confirmed, looking at his familiar one.

The rakkhosh students and faculty, who had been distracted by Sesha's flight with the butterflies, now started to react to Neel's and my real appearance.

"They're not rakkhosh!" someone shrieked. "Who are they? It was a trick! They let the prisoner go!"

The entire rakkhosh student body burst into confused shouts and exclamations. Now Pinki whirled on us too, claws out and fangs glowing. Neel wrestled Einstein-ji's book from my backpack and opened it at random. There, lo and behold, was a story I'd never noticed before. A story called "There's No Place Like Home."

"Don't ever marry that snaky scumbucket!" Neel said to Pinki in a rush. "Mother, no matter what, it's not worth it!"

"Mother?" shrieked Pinki. Horror, but also a strange sense of recognition, was etched on her face.

"Your Highness, hate, not love, makes difference end!" I shouted. "Sesha will try to marry you again in the future— but he won't have learned his lesson! He still wants to take your power!"

"Who are these students?" sputtered the headmistress. "Why do I not recognize them? Jackals!"

But even as Surpanakha and her jackal minions leaped toward us, Ai-Ma shot out a gangly arm—growing it in a flash into a long but strong hose-like barrier. The headmistress and animals bumped against it and fell backward with loud shrieks and howls.

"Good-bye, dear dung dumplings! Good luck, my beetle bums!" The old rakkhoshi waved with her other, normal-sized arm.

"Good-bye, Ai-Ma! Thank you!" I called.

"We love you!" yelled Neel. "Remember how much we love you!"

"Stop!" shrieked Pinki. "Who are you? How dare you?"

But we weren't stopping, and we did dare. Together, we started reading the words of the story that would take us home. Rushing through sentences, our voices tripping over the paragraphs and phrases, we read our way out of danger. Together, Neel and I read our way to safety. Together, Neel and I read our way out of the stories of our pasts, launching forward into a future story of our own making.

CHAPTER 28

A Council of Jazz Hands

Our first concern when we got back was getting the antidote to Naya. I didn't want to waste time running, so I borrowed a skateboard from one of the passing PSS girls and rushed the flowers I'd picked over to the hospital.

As we waited for Dr. Ahmed to send word on if the antidote worked, we went to tell Mati what had happened.

"You idiots!" my cousin yelled as soon as she heard about our adventures. "You could have been killed! Of all the callous, irresponsible stunts! Will you two never learn?"

Neel and I both looked sheepishly at the ground, not wanting to argue with her. She had a lot on her shoulders, I realized, and we hadn't been making it any easier for her.

It was Tuni, who had been with Mati when we found her, who defused the situation. "They may be idiots, but they brought back the antidote for Naya's poison," Tuni chirped. "Isn't that the most important thing?"

I shot the little yellow bird a grateful smile. He flew over and landed on my shoulder.

"We're still waiting to hear from Dr. Ahmed if it worked," Neel said in a soft voice.

"I'm sorry, I know you've been under a lot of strain," I added. "But since we've been gone, haven't things gotten better?"

"No!" Mati wailed. "If anything, since you two disappeared, the rate of story collapsing has gotten worse, not better! It's a nightmare! I don't even recognize my own homeland anymore!"

Neel and I exchanged horrified looks. We'd saved ourselves, hopefully saved Naya, but somehow, we'd made the fate of the multiverse *worse*? Was it because we'd filled Sesha with even more hate?

"What's been going on?" I asked.

"My mom and Sesha didn't call off their wedding?" Neel seemed stunned.

"No!" Mati said. "But while you two were gone, the royal wedding mehendi party got invaded by swarms of mythical creatures and story characters from the 2-D realm."

"Actually, according to this report in the *Seven Oceans*

Gazette," Bunty said as they strolled in, a pair of reading glasses propped on their broad nose and a newspaper in their mouth, "these strange guests called the henna 'nifty temporary tattoos,' thought the mehendi party food was too spicy, and insisted that Sesha change his name to Sam and wear a tuxedo instead of his sherwani. Ludicrous!"

"It's happening so fast now!" Tuni said. "It seems like all the people of the Kingdom Beyond and the Kingdom of Serpents and everywhere else in this dimension are starting to dress and talk and act like people from the 2-D realm."

"Worse, they're forgetting their language," said Mati, running a hand over her exhausted face. "Everyone is forgetting their stories."

As we walked around the resistance hideout with Bunty, Tuni, and Mati, evidence of the impending crunch was everywhere. Most of the PSS weren't even wearing saris anymore, but pink jumpsuits and jeggings and skorts. Even as we gazed at them things changed right in front of our eyes. In the corner where Gyan Mukherjee had been making his fashion masterpieces was suddenly a giant, rakkhosh-sized girl with curly blond ringlets, sitting on a tuffet and eating what I could only assume were curds and whey. There was also a very tiny boy in her hand who kept jumping over a candlestick.

The girl gave a startled yelp when she spontaneously arrived, and then proceeded to scream and cry, throwing a huge tantrum. The tiny-sized boy was oblivious and just kept on with his candlestick leaping. And although we were all expecting they would go back from where she came and return the fashion designer, hours went by and Miss Muffet and Jack were still there.

"Can't we get rid of them?" I asked Mati. Bunty began trying to reason with Muffet, to convince her to return to her own dimension, but the giant girl just lay down and stomped her arms and legs. "More curdsth! More whey!" she wailed. "And none of thath curry-flavor sthuff like lasth time! It's too spithy!" As for Jack, he was so small it wasn't even possible to understand anything he said. Tuni flew him up on top of one of the sewing machines for safekeeping and let him keep on with his obsessive jumping over the machine's bobbin.

My cousin shook her head sadly. "I'm scared, Kiran. I don't know who's going to be next. Did you know there's a beanstalk growing in the middle of the unisex bathrooms? I mean, will I change too? I don't want to forget my heritage; I don't want to forget who I am. I don't want to vanish into somebody else's story."

I grabbed Mati's hand and held on. "I won't let you

forget who you are, my sister," I promised, remembering that in Bengali there was no real word for cousin. All cousins and even friends were our brothers and sisters; all adults were some version of aunties and uncles.

Mati smiled and squeezed my hand. "I'm sorry we fought, Sis."

I wrapped my arms around her and gave her a big hug, feeling my heart expand to the size of the growing universe. I realized how small and tight everything in my chest had felt when we were fighting. "I am too."

Together, we decided to call an all-hands-on-deck planning meeting for that afternoon.

"A council of war," Mati had started to say, but I'd put my hand over her lips.

"No, a meeting of friends and allies," I'd corrected her. "No war, no hate. There's enough strength in our love and friendship."

We sent a message via Tiktiki One and called back Lal, Buddhu, and Bhootoom to the resistance hideout. Soon, we were all there: Lal, Neel, Mati, Tuni, Bunty, Buddhu, Bhootoom, and those of the PSS who hadn't forgotten who they were yet.

Right before the meeting, we got some wonderful news. We heard from Dr. Ahmed that the poison antidote had worked! This made our little band of friends cheer and shout. With the doctor's permission, we all went to visit Naya.

My rakkhoshi friend was weak but awake. She would need a few weeks to recover her wing power, but the doctor felt confident that she would.

"You went back to the past for me?" Naya asked, grasping our hands in gratitude.

"I'm so sorry, Naya. I'm so sorry you got hurt. I'm so sorry for not thinking things through and risking your life." I laid my head down on her bed, letting her stroke my hair. "Thank you for saving me."

"Silly. That's what friends are for, isn't it? To save each other?" Naya said. "You taught me that."

Naya was saved, but unfortunately, everyone else in the multiverse was not. Right after we visited the hospital wing, tragedy struck our little group. The formerly tough rakkhoshi Priya suddenly dubbed herself Princess Petunia Pants and started screaming at the sight of the other rakkhoshis.

"Who are they? What is this? Where am I?" she screamed, pulling at her nonexistent hair. We knew then that she was a goner. Another victim of story smushing. Another sign that Sesha was winning and the big crunch was on its way.

Abandoning her camo pants and sari cape for a tutu, crown, and wand she got from who knows where, Priya was even starting to look like a bald version of the cutie-pie Princess Pretty Pants™ doll. Which was, as you can imagine, way disturbing. We left Priya-slash-Princess-Petunia with tiny Jack and the giant Miss Muffet, as well as Sir Gobbet, who was now convinced he was the short, moustachioed sultan from a popular 2-D cartoon about a boy and a flying carpet.

"A whole new world!" he warbled really loud in a super off-key way.

We were so few in numbers that we needed all of our brainpower now, so we even got the doctor's permission to hold our planning meeting in Naya's hospital room. Mati opened our meeting with a summary of all that had happened, and then called on Neel and me to report on our experiences in the past, at Ghatatkach Academy.

"We got a glimpse as to why Sesha wants to marry my mom—he obviously wants to use her power to kill the diversity of the multiverse, what he calls chaos, and make all our stories collapse into one," said Neel. "And we know now that my mom, as the Rakkhoshi Queen, holds the multiple stories of the universe somehow inside of her, that she's at least partially responsible for keeping the stories of the universe expanding. But we haven't a clue as to why my mom's agreed to the marriage."

I shot Neel a curious look, and he shrugged. "What?" he said. "We don't. I mean, there are multiple theories, but we don't have enough, um, data, to know which of them is right."

"I don't know about that, Neel," I said. I saw him look warily at me, so I rushed to continue. "Going into the past, Neel and I learned that even if Sesha was using her, Pinki really loved him, at least back when they were young." I turned to Neel. "I'm sorry I was so quick to judge your mom. I was wrong."

He smiled gratefully at me, and again, I felt my heart do that expanding trick.

"What we need is some help," Mati said. "Oh, look, he's here."

"Ask and you shall receive!" a voice called. It was Einstein-ji!

Naya smiled up from her hospital bed. "I'm so glad you received our gecko-gram, Your Smartness!"

I realized Tiktiki One was once again sitting on Naya's shoulder, swiveling his eyeballs and rolling and unrolling his tongue.

"Two correctly delivered messages in one day! Good job!" I congratulated the little lizard.

"I told you the technology worked," Naya said with a proud, if tired, smile.

Neel looked wonderingly up at the scientist. I realized his presence was fainter than it usually was, kind of see-through and transparent. Also, all around him, there were little chirping star babies. "Are you using Essence-Tyme, and calling in from Maya Pahar, Smartie-ji?" he asked the scientist.

"We are starting to feel ze beginnings of ze big crunch even here!" said Albert Einstein. "Star babies are refusing to sing! Ze nebula is starting to look more and more like a multilevel parking lot, and ze wells of dark energy are drying up. No more rakkhosh babies being born!"

"No more wells, no more babies!" Naya gasped. "My people—are we to die off, then?"

"If Sesha and ze Anti-Chaos Committee of intercultural villains have their way, we will all die off, even ze serpents of the Kingdom Beyond," said Einstein-ji. "Ze only ones left after we collapse into ze singularity will be those who have most intergalactic power. Sadly, power has always determined whose stories are told and whose stories are allowed to be remembered."

Then, just as abruptly as Einstein-ji had appeared, his Essence-Tyme signal cut out and he was gone.

"I guess we're on our own," Mati whispered.

I reached out and grabbed her hand. "We have each other."

"So what can we do?" asked Lal.

Neel raised a surprised eyebrow in his direction. "We? You tired of being Raja already?"

Lal blushed a little. "Brother, I take our responsibilities seriously. But I also know that they are ours together. Not mine alone."

"All for one and one for all!" said Buddhu, running up between Lal and Neel and embracing his two brothers.

"Bhootoom and I humbly accept your generous offer to be co-Rajas!"

Neel and Lal exchanged an amused look and laughed, but they didn't contradict the monkey prince.

"So what's our next move?" I wondered out loud.

"If only we had some way to ascertain if the Rakkhoshi Rani received her son's missive," mused Bunty.

Of course! Neel's letter to his mother that had been hidden in the tottho presents! Had she gotten it, and more importantly, had she answered?

"From what our spies were able to tell us, we think she got it," Mati said. "But I'm sorry, we haven't intercepted any notes from her."

"She was my first storyteller," Neel said in such a soft voice, I wasn't sure anyone else heard him. "And she's sworn to protect the diversity of the multiverse's stories. I just don't think she would help destroy them."

"I think you're right, Neel," I said honestly. "There has to be something else going on." That's when something clicked in my head. "Wait a minute, last night, when Neel and I were away, was the big mehendi ceremony, right?"

"Don't tell me you're sad you missed getting henna on your hands while you were attending demon school?" squawked Tuni.

Instead of answering the bird, I scooched over to Naya's hospital bed. "Naya, do you have your phone on you?"

"Pfft, what kind of a question is that?" my friend said, pulling her cell out of a pocket in her gown. "I had wing surgery, not a personality transplant!"

"Look up if Twinkle Chakraborty or Suman Rahaman, or anyone, really, made a video diary of the mehendi ceremony. Anything that would give me a closer look of Pinki's hands and feet," I demanded.

"Arré Pinki, is it?" Buddhu drawled, chuckling. "If you're brave enough to call my stepmother that, hats off to you, yaar!" The monkey collapsed in giggles, and Bhootoom the owl hooted his laughter too.

Despite everyone else looking confused, Neel seemed to catch my drift. "You think she might have sent me a message in her mehendi design?"

"If she couldn't send something more openly, it would make sense," I said. "I mean, you saw how at her choosing ceremony all those stories got marked and soaked into her skin."

"Mehendi isn't actually traditional to the Kingdom Beyond Seven Oceans and Thirteen Rivers," sniffed Bunty. "Here, alta, or the outline of the palms and feet in red, is far more common. Mehendi has been imported from other regions in the dimension. If you'd like, I can explain the history of this cultural transmigration . . ."

"No, I'm good right now!" I assured the tiger as I watched Naya scroll through her search results. "Maybe later!"

Bunty sniffed. "Fine, fine, don't know your own history."

But I did know my history. In fact, I'd just traveled through it. I also knew that it was okay—wonderful even— that stories and practices sometimes traveled from place to place, influencing each other and even creating new stories. That was okeydokey by me. The more stories the better, in fact. The dangerous thing was when we tried to shut some stories down, silence them, smush them into more domi- nant stories.

"Did you find anything?" I asked Naya.

"No video feed. I guess Ms. Twinkle and Sooms were really banned from reporting on any more wedding events," said Naya. "But I did find this picture, taken by none other than your brother, Naga, apparently."

It was a weird image. Seven separate lens exposures combined into one big image. But the seven separate pic- tures actually let me see the mehendi on Pinki's arms and hands from multiple different angles. I could tell there were words there, but the more I magnified Naya's phone, the blurrier the images got.

"Hey, Bhootoom, can I borrow this for a minute?" I asked. When the owl prince hooted his approval, I carefully took his monocle and looked at the phone through the magnifying lens of it.

What I saw took my breath away. A very clear message was written into the decorations on the Demon Queen's right arm:

Stories keep the multiverse growing.

And on her left arm, over and over, in the shape of flowers, birds, dancing peacocks, the words: *Save the Stories. Save the Stories. Save the Stories.*

"I knew it," whispered Neel.

"No, you thought she was a prisoner," I said slowly. "But Pinki's no prisoner. She's marrying Sesha because she thinks she can stop him! She must think it's her responsibility as the Demon Queen to stop the Anti-Chaos Committee from destroying the multiverse's stories!"

"She's on our side?" said Lal wonderingly.

"Stranger things have happened," said Naya pertly.

We all watched as Lal sheepishly walked over to Naya's bedside. "I'm truly sorry I said those, erm, unkind things about you earlier."

Gentle Naya's eyes got a little shiny, and I noticed Mati's did too. "That's okay, Your Princeliness," Naya said in a muffled voice. "But I appreciate the apology."

Neel seemed too occupied with his mom to even register Lal and Naya's interaction. "My mom is marrying Sesha so that she can stop him!" he exclaimed. "She wants to save the multiverse!"

"But she's obviously not doing a very good job of it," said Mati. "I mean, look at what's going on!"

She pointed at Buddhu and Bhootoom, who were gathered at Bunty's feet, singing some kind of a song about a lion king.

"If she's going to keep the multiverse's stories expanding, Pinki can't do it alone." I thought back to Mati scolding Neel and me because we were trying to go off and do things on our own, instead of relying on the connections and strength of our family and friends. "She may not realize it, but Pinki needs our help!"

CHAPTER 29

The Big Musical Number at the End

The sangeet is tonight," Mati said, her eyes dancing with a suspiciously merry expression. "And we do have a musical number planned for it."

"No. No. No. No!" Neel said, his hands out. "I've already told Kiran, no step-ball-change or jazz hands for me."

"You have to do it, Neel!" I insisted. "It's a part of the plan!"

And that's how Neel and I found ourselves being measured for last-minute costumes by Miss Muffet and Jack, who had most surprisingly taken over the role of fashion designer Gyan Mukherjee. All of tiny Jack's candle jumping made him both nimble and quick with a needle and thread. And as Miss Muffet explained, designing over-the-top sparkly and shiny sangeet costumes was a lot more interesting than designing tuffets. "My creathivity was being blocketh," she explained while chomping on some spicy curds and curried whey.

And that's also how Neel and I found ourselves maniacally rehearsing the end of the grand song-and-dance number that the demon dance troupe had already been practicing for days.

A lot of the rakkhosh dancers were jealous of us being allowed to jump in at the last minute—and the fact that we were getting prime center stage placement.

"We've been rehearsing for a long time!" a fire rakkhosh complained to Mati. "It's not fair."

Mati explained about the whole end of the multiverse being prevented but the dancers weren't happy until she promised they could have an extra curtain call and extra time to bow and wave to the audience at the end.

When it came time for the sangeet, Neel and I were exhausted but ready. He was wearing horribly showy sherwani-pajamas and a turban encrusted with multicolor pom-poms. I was in a bright red sari embedded with holiday lights that went on and off at random intervals. It was so hideous but at least it was red, so I could wear my ruby-red combat boots underneath. Both of us had a ridiculous amount of makeup and fake noses to disguise our features.

Plus, I had on a giant bouffant wig, and Neel was wearing fake glasses with no lenses.

"Ready?" I asked him, my heart racing from nervousness even as my limbs were aching from all the last-minute practice.

Instead of answering, Neel just flashed his jazz hands.

I was sure we were going to get caught in the extensive security for sangeet performers. But because of Mati's coaching, we actually made it through. "Don't look suspicious, and look them straight in the eye," she had told us. "Also, blather about silly things like the weather, and the latest cricket scores, and how much you like their clothes."

"Beautiful weather you're wearing!" I'd nervously said to the first guards. "Also, have you heard? Cricket is a thing people play with a bat!"

They had given me strange looks but let us go through.

The sangeet performances were all taking place at an outdoor stage in a huge amphitheater that had been set up next to the palace complex. I paced nervously backstage, sure we were going to get caught, sure something was going to go wrong. This was a risky thing we were doing, and since my fight with Neel and of course Naya's near death, I was pretty sensitive about jumping to conclusions, or putting my friends in danger. I was learning by experience about humility—to believe in myself but also not let my overconfidence swell my head.

"Take a breath, and look up," Neel whispered. He took my hand in his and pointed at the bright moon, high and dazzling in the sky. "She's watching over us."

I looked up and let out a sigh. "I'm glad she's here," I said, squeezing Neel's hand in gratitude.

In the dark backstage, standing so very close to him, I felt something skip in my chest. Neel's hand reached out and touched my cheek super softly. "Thank you for doing this with me. Thank you for saving me—so many times. Thank you, Kiran, for everything."

I thought about how badly I had wanted his thanks just a few days ago. Now it felt so totally unnecessary. "You're welcome," I whispered. "But as my baba always says, no thank-yous among family."

Neel chuckled, low and soft. "My mom always said that too."

"But thanks all the same," I said. "To you too. For all the stuff."

I felt rather than saw Neel nod, and I don't know why, but I felt so cracked and open all of a sudden, I almost cried. I could feel everything—the light, the dark, the stories, the stardust that made up each of us.

But then I was stopped from crying by the awful, fateful words of the sangeet announcer, a dude in a headset and horrible purple velvet suit who waved maniacally in our faces: "You're on!"

Our mostly rakkhosh secret-resistance-group song-and-dance number started out okay. Everyone step-ball-changed and hip-swiveled in the right order and in the right directions. There was silly eyelash-batting followed by arms-in-the-air-dancing followed by a lot of really literal acting out the words. Like "my heart" (touch my heart) "beats" (flutter my hand on my chest) "for" (hold up four fingers) "you" (make like a sheep and baah on the ground). Get it? Because a female sheep is a "ewe"—which sounds the same as "you." Anyway, you get the idea.

It was at the second set of step-ball-changes and jazz hands that everything that could go wrong did go wrong. One rakkhosh tripped, knocking off a nearby rakkhoshi's wig, and then the two dancers were pushing and punching and biting each other as the lyrics of the song were dripping on about how much love was like a shyly blooming flower. Even as they fought, the two dancers kept trying to smile at the audience. "You're in my spotlight!" "No, you're in my spotlight!" "You're blocking me!" they shrieked. And soon other dancers who also felt their spotlights were being blocked got into the fight too, and there were claws scratching and fists flying and all mayhem breaking out even as most of the dancers kept on going, fake smiles on their faces, pretending like nothing was wrong.

The audience started booing long before we were meant to be done—there were still two more sappy verses left about souls and eyes and hearts and lips and ladybugs and who knows what else. "Neel, I think the performance is going downhill fast!" I whispered.

When a fire rakkhosh set his partner's costume ablaze, it was clear the time had come. "We'd better get going with our plan now!" Neel shouted, waving for the spotlight to move away from the fighting rakkhosh dancers and onto us.

As soon as the giant spotlight hit me, I froze in place, terrified. It hadn't occurred to me when I was just one of many dancers, but now I could feel Sesha's presence out there in the audience. His eyes were on me, and I could practically feel them burning my skin. I hoped my disguise was holding—I had a lot of makeup on, not to mention the giant bouffant of a wig. I got so nervous, I couldn't remember the choreography from this part of the song, so I started doing all the stupid dances I could think of: the running man, the moonwalk, the dad party dance of a side-to-side foot shuffle and butt wiggle. In short, I looked like a total fool. "Neel, come on!" I hissed out of the side of my mouth.

There was a rise in the music, a heartfelt warbling of notes, and with that Neel kind of kangaroo-hopped to center stage and gave a big, silly ballerina twirl. As he twirled, he tossed me a copy of *Thakurmar Jhuli*, not Einstein-ji's magical time-traveling copy, but a regular old copy of the folktale book that a grandma or dad or aunty might read to their kids.

As the music changed, Neel kept dancing to the middle of the stage. Here it came, my part. It was now or never. Copying a move from a 2-D movie I'd seen a long time ago with Zuzu, I shouted, "Nobody puts our stories in a corner!" and ran at Neel, the book still in my hands.

I jumped and he caught me, holding me up by the waist with his strong rakkhosh arms and twirling me around. I flew, arms extended, the book held out from my hands like a glittering beacon in the dark. The other dancing rakkhosh gathered all around us, pulling out their copies of the book too. At my signal, we all opened our books and started simultaneously reading whatever story each of us had stumbled onto.

I don't know how or why, but the moment I began to

read, my voice rising and falling in story, clashing and meshing with all the other voices reading their stories at the same time, I felt something magical happen. We storytellers began to glow, as if there was a power beaming out of us. The kids in the sangeet audience—children of villagers and lords, servants and ministers—ran forward toward the stage, to hear our stories better. They giggled and shouted at the funny voices some of the storytellers were putting on, chiming in at the familiar parts, begging for more when someone's story ended.

I heard a gasp from the audience and shouts of alarm. And then I heard it, clear as a bell, Sesha's horrible voice from the darkness of the audience.

"Stop reading! Stop laughing! Stop telling those dratted Kingdom Beyond stories!"

As we had planned, he shot out green bolts of power at me from the audience. Just as they were about to reach me, I tossed down to Neel my regular copy of the book and he tossed me Einstein-ji's magical one. Where Sesha's power hit the powerful volume, the light already coming off it expanded and grew. Neel carefully put me down, but I held the magical book up over my head, like I'd once seen a boy in a movie hold a boom box playing love songs for his girlfriend. Only I was playing a different sort of love song. A love song for our stories, our lives, and the continued life of the multiverse.

Shockingly, the magical book now glowing in my hand wasn't just absorbing Sesha's bolts; it was shooting them back out at him too. I heard where the little zings and zips of power whizzed through the audience, finding their target only in him.

"What are you doing? Stop that!" Sesha growled. And now I could see him. He had run up right in front of the stage, from where he blasted me again with his bolts of power. His handsome face was screwed up with anger, his eyes flashing with venom. Right behind him, dressed in a brilliant lehenga choli and dripping with diamonds, was Pinki, Neel's mother. She froze at the sight of us onstage, obviously recognizing us both.

"You? Here?" she whispered.

"I read your mehendi, Mother," Neel said, throwing off his disguise. "You don't have to marry this clown to protect the multiverse's stories! You don't have to protect them alone! We are on your side! We will do it together!"

"I remember you!" Sesha looked from his bride-to-be to Neel and back again. Then he looked at me. His voice was wild with fury. "You were at the choosing, when I was captured by those monsters at Ghatatkach Academy! You called me father then! That day has haunted me for all my life—but no more!"

"You were there!" exclaimed Pinki almost at the same time. "You were both there on that day—and it was you who convinced me not to marry Sesha!"

I realized that by going back in time, Neel and I had changed our present. Both of our parents remembered seeing us when they were young people. "And we're here now to give you the same message!" Neel shouted. "You shouldn't have married him them, and you shouldn't marry him now!"

"Haven't you learned your lesson?" I said, glaring at Sesha. "If you bring about the big crunch, not just our story lines will end, yours will too! But listen—everybody can change! Why not rewrite the ending to your story? You don't have to be a villain! You can choose a different ending! You can choose to tell a different tale!"

"Don't tell me what to do, you impudent imp!" Sesha snarled. He increased the power of his green bolts so that now my arms ached from the stress of holding up the glowing-book-slash-weapon-slash-shield. "You are the part of my story I will change! You have always been the problem, the nagging sore, the out-of-place character! But not for much longer!"

"Yesss! Kill her, Father!" It was Naga, that seven-headed pain in the rear end, right behind dear old Daddy, as per usual. "End her story! Close the book on her! Burn her library *down*!"

"Nah, man, I don't think so!" Neel leaped from the stage directly onto Naga's heads. He slashed and fought with the seven-headed snake, leaving me alone with my past.

"Die, Daughter! Die, you chaos curse!" Sesha snarled. "I will not have this confusion, these many stories! I will rule one universe united in singularity! I will erase you at last from the pages of the multiverse!"

I kept deflecting Sesha's evil blasts with Einstein-ji's book, but I was getting tired. The glowing volume grew so hot I almost wanted to drop it. The book was buzzing and humming, searing my hands with heat.

"Ahh!" I cried out in pain, almost crushed by the power of the stories in my hands. Neel looked back, and that was his downfall. As he turned to look at me, one of Naga's giant fangs caught him through the shoulder.

"No!" I screamed.

Hanging there from Naga's fang, Neel started to shake.

His skin became crisscrossed with venom. His eyes started to roll to the back of his head, and I knew I was losing him.

"My son!" Pinki shrieked, leaping on Naga with all her terrible power. She flung the seven-headed snake to one side, cradling Neel's form in her arms. Then she turned on Sesha with such a terrible cry, he stopped shooting out his green lightning at me. I fell to my knees, the book still in my hands.

"You're almost my wife—you can't fight me," said Sesha, but he could say no more, because with a multiverse-shaking move, Pinki opened her mouth and screamed. With Neel still lifeless in her arms, the Demon Queen's jaw became unhinged from her face and the darkness of all of outer space came shooting out. I saw planets, moons, and comets, and then, awfully, the Victrola funnel shape of a black hole. The black hole reached out to swallow Sesha, like a formless cosmic rakkhosh, now creating life, now ending it. And then, not with a bang, but with the tiniest of whimpering, popping sounds, Sesha was gone.

"Father!" Naga cried, writhing around in agony. But the seven-headed serpent had never been as stupid as our father had made him think he was. When he realized Sesha's fate, he quickly slithered down the audience aisle and away into the night.

As soon as Sesha disappeared into the void of the black hole, Pinki laid Neel tenderly on the stage. The sangeet audience all gathered around now, clucking their tongues, oohing and aahing as if this were a part of the show. Neel shuddered and gasped, the lines of venom slowly disappearing from his face. But still his eyes were closed.

"He's not waking up!" I cried.

Pinki screamed again, her cries generating new universes that sprung out of her open lips. As if aware of the galaxies spinning out of Pinki's mouth, the magical book leaped out of my hands to expand and grow into the shape of a small star in the cosmos that Pinki had created. I heard every story in the book, every story in the room, every story in the multiverse, being told in a rising babble of voices. The words manifested themselves in the air, in all sorts of languages and images and metaphors spinning around and around one another, finally coming together in a fireworks display of star collision. The light was so bright, I had to shield my eyes from it. The audience, as well as the rakkhosh dancers behind me, began yelling and howling, protecting their eyes and ears from the brilliance too.

When Neel began to stir, Pinki sobbed in relief.

"I think he's going to be okay!" I breathed.

Finally, with a huge inhale, Pinki swallowed it all once

again. The planets. The galaxies. The magical storybook turned star. The black hole containing Sesha. All of it. And then she let out the most giant burp I have ever heard.

"Impressive, my gaseously gifted daughter!" said a wibbly-wobbly voice so familiar and dear I almost screamed with joy.

It was Ai-Ma, with her gangly limbs and three-toothed grin and galumphing walk and all her love and all her stories and all her wisdom. It was her. Neel's grandmother—who was monster, goddess, crone, ancestress, teacher, and friend. It was her, but also not her. She was so transparent, we could see all of outer space through her form. She was so huge, her feet were like ships, her arms were like highways, and her head touched the sky.

"Mother!" cried Pinki. "The stories brought you back!"

"Not in the way you are thinking, my silly demon-drop of an evil daughter," Ai-Ma cooed, holding her see-through hands above Pinki's head in a blessing. "No, my silly-billy chitty-boo of a booger blossom! I am gone from this plane, but as long as you are all alive, my story is not ended."

"You gave your life in that undersea detention center to save me, but I wish I could save you!" Pinki had tears streaming down her face, and I felt my own heart breaking at her sorrow. How could I have been so wrong about her?

Some villains, like Sesha, choose not to change, but some, like Pinki, do.

"You already have saved me," Ai-Ma called as she vanished more and more into the ether. Where her body had been was the gold and platinum stardust we had experienced down in the underwater hotel. The glittery rain fell all over us, and when it hit Neel's face, he finally opened his eyes.

"Ai-Ma?" he said, his eyes uncertainly straining toward the spot where the dear rakkhoshi had just been.

"Live in joy, my toadstool baby bats! Sing your varied stories, my dung-covered lily pads!" Ai-Ma's disembodied voice crooned from the darkness. "And tell of me, and how much I loved you, to all who want to hear!"

And so we would. To tell her story was to tell our own. We would tell it, and add to it, and let it nourish us forever.

Even though the wedding was called off, the second sangeet was a huge success. The groom wasn't present, but the entire Kingdom Beyond decided to have a giant song-and-dance performance in the royal palace square. The Raja had returned from exile and was now gathered on the dais to watch the performances with his four sons: Lal and Neel, Buddhu and Bhootoom. To the other side of the dais sat Mati, Naya, and a lot of the PSS crew.

As a surprise, Neel sent Bunty as well as the pakkhiraj horses Snowy and Raat to go get my parents, Jovi, and Zuzu from the right version of New Jersey and bring them to the festivities. Ma arrived in her second-best sari—since she'd brought her wedding sari for me to wear. She'd also dressed the real Jovi and Zuzu in full lehenga choli and Indian jewelry. Baba was elegant in his pajama-panjabi.

"How's the store?" I asked Ma as she helped me pleat and pin my outfit.

"The store? Oh, it's wonderful, my little piece of the moon, my princess, my darling," Ma replied. "We will have to all go back soon to help your father with the inventory." I was relieved to see her hair was in its usual impeccable bouffant bun. She waggled her eyebrows at me. "Now, you tell me about that handsome Neelkamal!"

When I saw Baba, he gave me a huge bear hug and wiped away his own tears on my hair. Finally, he let me go enough to look weepily at me. "You're looking tired, darling. Have you been eating enough fiber? Are your bowels regular?"

In the past, I would have been furious at my parents for being so embarrassingly loving, so ridiculously themselves all the time. But I'd learned to appreciate all their strangenesses. They might be weirdos, but they were my weirdos, after all.

With Jovi and Zuzu, it was a little bit harder. "I had to explain to Jovi about everything, who you are, where you're from," said Zuzu, pulling me aside. The bright blue lehenga choli Ma had put her in beautifully complemented her hair and eyes. "She's confused; she's not even sure why she's here. Are you guys even friends?"

"Well, she's on the fencing team with you, isn't she?" I grinned, taking my friends' hands. "I'll explain later, but I'm really glad you're both here."

"I am too. These outfits are tremendous!" Jovi spun around, her green skirts spreading dramatically wide. "And everyone here seems awesome!" she said, giving Priya a little wave. It must have been a good wave, because the rakkhoshi Priya, who had been super embarrassed about her whole Princess Petunia episode, actually smiled and waved back.

The sangeet was amazing. No one wore disguises, so the rakkhosh clanspeople danced in their full fangs and tusks, twirling their wings and tentacles to their hearts' abandon. Singing and dancing weren't the only thing on the performance roster, though. Some of the PSS girls did a skateboarding show, setting up a half-pipe, and proceeding to drop, whirl, and fly for the roaring crowds.

The last performer at the sangeet was quite a surprise. It

was Neel's mom, the Demon Queen, decked out in her elaborate wedding finery. Her red silk sari was heavily embroidered with gold, her sparkling nose ring connected by a gold chain to the shining butterfly clips in her dark hair, her ears and neck dripping with jewels that sparkled like the stars.

"I needed a place to wear this, right?" she explained with a snap of her teeth and a righteous belch. "But before I go onstage, Kiranmala, find me an antacid, won't you?"

The humans in attendance were a little nervous at first, but Pinki's song-and-dance number was a huge hit. There were strobe lights, images projected behind her, and a huge entourage of backup dancers in elaborate costumes.

"Everything is connected to everything," she sang.

"But how?" sang her backup dancers, doing super-coordinated twirls and jiggles.

"By the love of those who came before!" crooned Ai-Ma in our hearts.

"But how?"

"By the love of family," sang Ma and Baba.

"But how?"

"By the love of community," said our extended friends and family.

"But how? But how? But how?" asked the backup

dancers, swirling and leaping, sashaying and flossing, step-ball-changing and doing all the jazz hands.

"By love," I told Neel, smiling.

"By love," he agreed. All around us, I noticed, were the blue butterflies, dancing as if to their own magic rhythms.

And as the festivities continued, long into the night, we felt the multistoried multiverse pulsing and swirling all around us, in an ever-expanding cosmic dance. Because there was love, there would be more stories, and a multiverse that kept growing and thriving. Love and stories, stories and love, these were the stars that lit our way forward.

Author's Note

The Chaos Curse (Kiranmala and the Kingdom Beyond Book 3) is an original story that, like the first two books in this series (*The Serpent's Secret* and *Game of Stars*), draws from many traditional Bengali folktales and children's stories. These are stories beloved in West Bengal (India), Bangladesh, and throughout the Bengali diaspora. I've used many of these stories as a basis for inspiration while writing the books in the series, and as a way to tell my own story as an immigrant daughter.

Thakurmar Jhuli and Rakkhosh Stories

Folktales involving rakkhosh are very popular through-out all of South Asia. The word is sometimes spelled "rakshasa" in other parts of the region, but in this book, it is spelled like the word sounds in Bengali. Folktales are of course an oral tradition, passed on verbally from one generation to the next, with each teller adding spice and nuance to their own version. In 1907, Dakshinaranjan Mitra Majumdar collected, wrote down, and published some classic Bengali folktales in a book called *Thakurmar Jhuli* (Grandmother's satchel). This collection, which involves separate stories about the Princess Kiranmala, the brothers Neelkamal and Lalkamal, and the monkey and owl princes Buddhu and Bhootoom, is also full of tales involving rakkhosh and khokkosh, as well as stories about the Kingdom of Serpents. The giant birds Bangoma and Bangomee make an appearance in the story of Neelkamal and Lalkamal, as do pakkhiraj horses. The Demon Queen appears in the original Neelkamal and Lalkamal story, as does the lovably goofy rakkhosh grandmother, Ai-Ma. Lalkamal and Neelkamal never meet Kiranmala in their original stories, but brave Kiranmala does have two brothers named Arun and Barun whose lives she must save. A version of the Serpent King appears in this collection as well, although not exactly as he appears in this book. Of course, a magical version of *Thakurmar Jhuli* plays a role in *The Chaos Curse*, as it is the time-traveling and otherwise protective object given by Albert Einstein-ji to Neel and Kiran.

Although this book didn't help me actually time travel when I was younger, the stories in it were magical to me and as such, I wanted to honor the collection in this way.

The rakkhosh figures Surpanakha and Ghatatkach in *The Chaos Curse* are not from *Thakurmar Jhuli*, but from Hindu epics. Surpanakha is the sister of Ravana, the main antagonist of *the Ramayana*. She's attracted to the hero Ram, but when she approaches him, she is rebuffed by him. When she then tries the same tactics with his younger brother Laxshman, she is again rejected. Humiliated by the two heroic brothers, the demoness goes to attack Ram's wife, Sita, but has her nose cut off by Laxshman instead. She runs to her brother Ravana to report this shameful event, and sets off the events of the epic, including Ravana's kidnapping of Sita. I always thought that *the Ramayana* treated Surpanakha pretty unfairly, so I made her the headmistress of the rakkhosh academy in this book. Ghatatkach (after whom the made-up demon of the Academy of Murder and Mayhem is named) is a rakkhosh from another epic, *the Mahabharata*. The son of the second heroic Pandav brother Bhim and the rakkhoshi Hidimbi, enormously strong Ghatatkach fought alongside his father and Pandav uncles in the great war upon which the epic is based. Even though he was raised by his rakkhoshi mother, he was enormously loyal to his father and family and was an almost undefeatable warrior, so it made sense to me that he would have a rakkhosh school named after him!

Thakurmar Jhuli stories are still immensely popular in West Bengal and Bangladesh, and have inspired translations, films, television cartoons, comic books, and more. Rakkhosh are very popular as well—the demons everyone loves to hate—and appear not just in folk stories but also Hindu mythology. Images of bloodthirsty, long-fanged rakkhosh can be seen everywhere—even on the backs of colorful Indian auto rikshaws, as a warning to other drivers not to tailgate or drive too fast!

Tuntuni and Other Animal Friends

The wisecracking bird Tuntuni is a favorite, and recurrent, character of Bengali children's folktales. Upendrakishore Ray Chowdhury (also known as Upendrakishore Ray), collected a number of these stories starring the clever tailor bird Tuntuni in a 1910 book called *Tuntunir Boi (The Tailor Bird's Book)*.

Bengal tigers are of course an important animal of the region. I'm particularly fascinated by the swimming and human-eating tigers of the Sundarbans, who have smartly adapted to their mangrove-swamp environment (tigers in other places don't know how to swim). Tiktikis, or geckos, are almost ubiquitous in Bengali homes, stickily clambering up walls and keeping mosquitoes and other pests at bay. As a child, I was super afraid of them, and still kind of have a love-hate relationship with the slimy lizards.

Bengali Nursery Rhymes and Poems

The story about an old woman who escapes a hungry fox by hiding in a rolling gourd is a popular Bengali folktale. The image of the doll wedding party accompanied by dancing insects, horses, and elephants is from several popular Bengali children's poems.

Global Myths, Folktales, Novels, Movies, and Stories

Since *The Chaos Curse* is about the collapsing of the world's stories into each other, there are many direct and indirect references to some of my favorite Euro-American stories, including J. R. R. Tolkien's *The Lord of the Rings*, Lewis Carroll's *Alice's Adventures in Wonderland*, L. Frank Baum's *The Wonderful Wizard of Oz*, Roald Dahl's *Charlie and the Chocolate Factory*, J. K. Rowling's Harry

Potter series, Philip Pullman's *The Golden Compass*, Rob Reiner's film version of William Goldman's *The Princess Bride*, and even A. A. Milne's *Winnie-the-Pooh*.

There are also references to both Greek and Norse myths in this book. Greek myths are primarily referenced in the form of Kiran's Gorgon principal, Stheno (a snaky-haired sister of Medusa who didn't have her propensity for turning people to stone) and the story of the Trojan horse, which was originally the way that the Greek army was able to sneak into Troy during the Trojan War. I drew from Norse myths to come up with the handsome dragon boy Ned Hogar, or Nidhoggr. Nidhoggr is of course the mythological dragon (sometimes considered a snake) who guards the base of Yggdrasil, the Norse tree of life that connects the various cosmic planes of existence. In this novel, Yggdrasil becomes transformed into a tree in the heart of Parsippany, New Jersey, which is clearly not true to the original tale in the least!

Weddings

Like other South Asian weddings, Bengali weddings are usually grand, multiday affairs. Guests are invited by elaborate, hand-delivered wedding cards, although not usually with as mean-spirited messages as Sesha and

Pinki's card! I have included or referenced several pre-wedding events in this book, including engagement ceremonies, where the marrying couple usually asks elders for their blessings, and the gaye halud ("turmeric on the body") ceremony, where everyone traditionally dresses in yellow and the groom and bride are (separately) purified with turmeric paste. In Bengali weddings, this is also the time that the two sides of the family often exchange gifts in the form of elaborately decorated "tottho"—trays of everything from fancy clothes to makeup to food that travel from one house to another. Bengali weddings don't traditionally have a mehendi ceremony, where the bride has her hands and feet decorated with swirling henna designs, or a sangeet, where song-and-dance numbers are performed by and for guests, but these North Indian traditions have been adopted by many Bengali couples these days and so I include them here (although Bunty the tiger does comment on them not being traditional practices). Bengali brides usually wear red silk saris embroidered with silver or gold thread, gold jewelry, shola pith tiaras, and have their faces decorated with sandalwood paste designs. Bengali grooms usually wear white dhotis (cloth wrapped and folded around the waist) and kurtas (tops) along with shola pith topor, a pointed white hat, on their heads. The doll bridal party that Kiran sees during her search for her moon mother is dressed in these traditional ways, and the bride is riding in a palki, or small house-like palanquin carried by two or four bearers.

Astronomy

Like in *The Serpent's Secret* and *Game of Stars*, there are many references to astronomy in this book, most notably the idea of string or membrane theory, that there may exist many universes in parallel to one another that are simply not aware of the other universes' existences. This to me seemed very much in keeping with the immigrant experience—the idea that immigrant communities are universe-straddlers! In this novel, I also played with the idea of the big bang, or the beginning of the ever-expanding universe, and the potential of a big crunch, or the eventual collapsing of the universe as we know it. I connected this idea of an expanding universe to the need for many types of stories, and linked Sesha's plan to collapse down diversity and smush stories together to the notion of the collapsing of the universe. I also was intrigued by the idea of a gravitational singularity in the center of a black hole, which contains a huge mass in an infinitely small space and where the known laws of physics cease to operate. The dragon boy Ned Hogar/Nidhoggr also refers to a theory called Laplace's demon, an all-seeing entity which to me seemed like a very ominous and scary monster—which also fit with Sesha! Albert Einstein makes another appearance in this book and Stephen Hawking is also mentioned, but these characters have nothing to do with the real scientists—they are merely fictional imaginings of space scientists I admire!

Like in the previous two books in this series, rakkhosh in *The Chaos Curse* are the manifestation of black holes. Even though this pairing of folktales and cosmology may seem strange, I did so to tear down the stereotype that cultural stories are somehow unconnected to science. In fact, like in every culture, traditional Bengali stories are often infused with stories about the stars and planets. That said, please don't take anything in this book as scientific fact, but rather use the story to inspire some more research about astronomy, astronomers and physicists, the big bang, singularities, and string theory!

Pink-Sari Skateboarders

The Pink-Sari Skateboarders of this book, and *Game of Stars*, were inspired by at least two groups of Indian women that to me exemplify female power. The first is the Gulabi Gang—a group of modern-day pink-sari-clad women activists in Northern India who, armed with bamboo sticks, go after domestic abusers and other men committing violence against women in their rural communities. The second group is the young women involved in India's slowly emerging skateboard and surfing scene, some of whom are featured in the movie and organization *Girl Skate India*.

Nonbinary Gender Identity

Like Bunty the tiger, who goes by "they" or "them" pronouns in English, there are many ways that people in South Asia express nonbinary gender identity. The hijra community, considered a non-male, non-female third gender in South Asia, is one such group. Koti and meti are other terms sometimes used in different parts of South Asia to express nonbinary gender identity. The Supreme Court of India has in fact stated that recognition of third gender groups "is not a medical or social issue, but a human rights issue." This is not to say that there isn't discrimination faced by nonbinary people in South Asia, but to point out the important history of nonbinary gender in South Asia, and also to honor the activism of these groups in making space and combating prejudice.

Other Random References

As in the previous two books of this series, jokes and riddles are a big part of *The Chaos Curse*. Variations of the riddle about three doors and three keys can be seen in many places. I learned my love of logical puzzles from my own father, Sujan, who adapted and translated many Western puzzles into Bengali, including his Bengali children's book, *Dhadhapurir Golok Dhadha* (The Labyrinth Riddle of Riddle Land).

"O Amar Chander Alo" is a popular song written by Bengali Nobel Laureate Rabindranath Tagore, while Bauls are a traditional group of nomadic singers whose music is an important part of Bengali culture. In fact, many of Tagore's songs were influenced by Baul tunes, and my own childhood visits to my paternal grandmother's home in Santiniketan, West Bengal, the location of Tagore's Visva-Bharati University, were often marked by visits by mystical Baul singers and truly transcendental Baul performances.

As an immigrant daughter whose connection to her own past was mediated by limited visits but unlimited stories, I am particularly drawn to the idea of love and stories being the forces at the heart of everything. I often worry about dominant stories taking over and silencing stories from more marginalized communities, but have faith that the community of diverse authors, editors, publishers, and readers, as well as groups like We Need Diverse Books, will keep our many-storied multiverse expanding and growing.

Acknowledgments

It takes a village to bring a book into the world, and I am so grateful to all the members of my story village. As always I'm indebted to my superstar agent, Brent Taylor, and his colleague Uwe Stender, for believing in me and my stories. I'm also beyond lucky to work with Abby McAden, editor extraordinaire, and her brilliantly brilliant assistant, Talia Seidenfeld.

I'm delighted that all three of the Kiranmala books can be judged by their covers! And this is entirely because of the beautiful work of artist Vivienne To and genius art director Elizabeth Parisi. Heartiest of thank-yous to Melissa Schirmer, my production editor, Jackie Hornberger, my copy editor, and to the rest of #TeamKiranmala at Scholastic, including Ellie Berger, David Levithan, Rachel Feld, Lizette Serrano, Michael Strouse, Emily Heddleson, Danielle Yadao, Tracy van Straaten, Lauren Donovan, and Elisabeth Ferrari! Thank you to the team from Scholastic Book Clubs as well as that force of nature, Robin Hoffman, and the team from Scholastic Book Fairs for getting this series into the hands of so many readers. Thank you to Donalyn Miller, John Schumacher, and all the other wonderful reading champions around the country who are out there doing the good work!

Thank you to my writerly siblings Sheela Chari, Veera Hiranandani, Heather Tomlinson, Olugbemisola Rhuday-Perkovich, and all those author friends I've made on this wonderful journey. Thank you to Debanuj DasGupta, as well as Autumn and Kristin Reynolds for their valuable insight into the character of Bunty the tiger. Thank you to my We Need Diverse Books, KidLit Writers of Color, and Desi Writers families, as well as my dear friends Kari, Kerri, and Jovi for being always there and always supportive. Thank you to my narrative medicine/health humanities colleagues and students at Columbia and around the country. Thank you to my extended family in India and this country, as well as my wonderful Bengali immigrant community of aunties, uncles, and friends.

Thank you to the teachers, librarians, booksellers, and readers who have read, enjoyed, and shared Kiranmala's adventures. It's still such a dream that I get to share my stories with you.

To my superstar cheerleader parents, Sujan and Shamita, my husband, Boris, and my darlings Kirin, Sunaya, and Khushi, eternal gratitude. As the Rakkhoshi Rani says, it's all about love and stories, stories and love.